Raymond Flynn's ~~Underthorpe novels:~~

Also by Raymond Flynn

Seascape with Body
A Public Body
A Fine Body of Men

About the author

Raymond Flynn spent twenty-six years with the Nottinghamshire Constabulary. Starting as a uniformed constable, he later moved to the CID and then served for twelve years as the detective inspector in charge of the Fraud Squad in Nottingham, where he still lives.

He turned to writing after taking medical retirement. He was a finalist in the 1992 Ian St James Short Story competition and won the Gooding Prize for short stories in 1994.

Busy Body

Raymond Flynn

NEW ENGLISH LIBRARY
Hodder and Stoughton

First published in Great Britain in 1998 by Hodder and Stoughton
A division of Hodder Headline PLC
First published in paperback in 1998 by Hodder and Stoughton
A New English Library Paperback

10 9 8 7 6 5 4 3 2 1

ISBN 0 340 67217 X

Printed and bound in Great Britain by
Clays Ltd, St Ives plc

Hodder and Stoughton
A division of Hodder Headline PLC
338 Euston Road
London NW1 3BH

For Joseph

1

It sounded like a fire bell, the last trump and the call to arms combined, and I was out of bed and halfway across the room before I recognised it for what it was: that blasted telephone again, the volume turned up high. Pitch black outside; definitely the middle of the night.

However often I try to minimise the noise, however frequently, however forcefully, I try to point out to my wife that her diligence with a duster is likely to earn her a long, unhappy widowhood, she still manages to polish me into a potential heart attack two or three times a month. Anybody would think that a sound moderator on a phone was an unheard-of technological refinement in this neck of the woods. Nineteen years' police service, and I still achieve maximum lift-off with about half a pint of adrenalin pumping around in my system by the second ring.

It's not even as if she ever wakes up herself. The most she ever manages is a luxurious feminine grunt as she gathers up the whole of the duvet and ensures my attention to duty by leaving me pyjama'd and shivering in the dark.

'Hello,' I said.

'DCI Graham?' asked a wary voice at the other end of the line. Wary was definitely appropriate. I'd found the switch to my bedside light; it was twenty minutes to four.

'Yes; who's that?'

'Inspector Rodway, sir.' Oh God; my newish detective inspector. The guardian of law and decency over heaven knows how many square miles of mud and fen, and stationed on an insignificant bump on the ground next to an estuary, a good twenty miles away. Please, please let this be something we could deal with over the wire.

'Sorry to disturb you, sir.' Two sirs in ten seconds. That probably meant that he wasn't sorry at all. Ripping a senior officer out of bed in the middle of the night used to count for twenty-five canteen chuckle-points when I was a junior plod. Fifty if there was a frost on the ground.

'I wouldn't have,' he assured me, 'but it's a suspected arson. One of Blatt's battery houses has been burnt down.'

'Battery as in hens?'

'Yessir.'

'You woke me up,' I said slowly, 'at three-forty a.m. precisely, because somebody's torched a hen-coop? Believe me, Derek, this had better be good.'

'It's a big battery house, boss.' The voice acquired something of a defensive whine.

'How big?'

'About fifty metres long.'

'Lots of roast chicken, eh?' Just to show that I too could be callous and macho, whatever the state of the clock.

'No, boss. It had just been cleaned out. It was empty at the time.'

'OK.'

'It's just that it's worth about thirty or forty thousand quid, give or take. And Blatt . . .'

'Sir Jeremy Blatt?'

'Yes, boss, he—'

'Used to be a county councillor,' I finished. 'Closely associated, if not friendly with, the Chief. You'd better give me some directions, then, hadn't you? Or do I just follow the glow in the night sky?'

Cheap, very cheap; but you can't expect even your most caring, sharing senior officer to empathise much with his staff when he's dragged out of his pit on the dim and dusky side of 4 a.m. Besides, it was February, the central heating didn't come on until seven, and there was an especially hard frost. A steal at fifty points; a hundred as soon as all those sniggering wooden-tops got around to revising the rules.

'Are you awake?' I said to Angela, using one of the most irritating phrases known to man.

'No.'

'I've got to go out.'

'Take care; don't wake the baby.' Was that an expression of general concern for my welfare, plus a gentle reminder; or all part of a specific instruction relating entirely to seven-month-old Laura, sleeping in the next room? Opting for the personally flattering interpretation, I kissed Angie on the forehead and struggled into my clothes.

'Take your sheepskin,' she muttered. 'I think there's a bit of a frost.' Very perceptive, but I've already covered that.

As for the sheepskin, it had been a Christmas present from Angie; expensive, and I'd suggested it too. The trouble is, I'm now having second thoughts. Would you, I keep asking myself, fancy being arrested by a man in a coat like that? Besides, I was going to the scene of an arson; floaters from a dead chicken house were unlikely to enhance the so far immaculate pile. I selected an ancient gor-blimey cap, a thick scarf and my old, heavily lined Barbour instead.

Angela peered at me through reluctant, screwed-up eyes. 'You look like a rat-catcher. Or a criminal,' she said.

I was outside, starting the engine of my elderly Volvo, against the background cacophony of imprisoned terrier dog, before I got the cream of the joke. This was Saturday morning; I was not on call. This was supposed to be my weekend off; Headquarters cover had been arranged.

Derek Rodway, I promised, this one had better be really, *really* good.

The notice was encouraging:

DAISY DEW FARM EGGS LTD
A Division Of The Daisy Dew Group
Lowbarrack Farm

But that was only the beginning of my troubles; there was an open gate, a cattle grid and a concreted strip masquerading as a road winding around the side of a wood, but that was about all. No immediate sign of my destination, let alone a fire.

The concrete strip soon deteriorated into a narrow semi-metalled track gouged with ruts which wandered excitingly from verge to soggy verge. The Fire Brigade, I hazarded, had recently passed this way. I slowed down to something less than ten miles an hour, and concentrated on keeping my wheels out of the ploughed-up mud, listening to the occasional music of tailpipe against stone. The firemen had probably deployed some imaginative language on the subject of their current call. Apart from a vague glow in the distance it was very, very dark.

Eventually, I saw the lights and four squat shapes like low-slung aircraft hangars picked out in the distance, with a smaller building which I took to be a packing shed set close by. A cottage of some sort, well lit up, stood about a hundred and fifty yards away. Vehicles, lights, voices, an all-pervasive stink of steam and burning, but no remaining fire.

Fifty yards from the poultry units a proper road reasserted itself, and I pulled into a big concrete yard. Sodium lights surrounded the buildings, and the Fire Brigade, vehicle doors swinging, radios blaring and vehicle spotlights trained on the blackened hulk of a half-demolished hangar, were still merrily squirting their hoses on a fire that to my untrained eye appeared to be well and truly out.

I stopped well clear of the two appliances, thanked heavens for foresight, opened the driver's door and swung my legs out before changing my shoes for a pair of green wellies. Cap, Barbour, green wellies; and why not? These days, I flatter myself, I've definitely joined the rural élite. Two whole divisions to supervise; call-outs in the middle of the night. In any case, the centre of the yard was inches deep in water; enthusiasts had been at work.

Derek Rodway, shortish, stoutish, overcoated, with ruined shoes and soaking trouser bottoms, appeared as if by magic accompanied by two detective constables. They all gazed enviously at the wellies; they didn't seem all that chuffed. So much more satisfactory when the chiefs have to suffer the same discomforts as the Indians on the ground.

'Sorry to drag you out,' muttered Rodway insincerely, 'but it's arson all right.'

'How do they know?' I choked back the immediate query that came to mind. Why hadn't the control room checked the duty rota? Why hadn't he called out the listed victim instead of me?

'Paraffin,' he said succinctly. 'Whole place reeks of it; the station officer reckons they probably climbed on to the roof and poured it through the ventilators; then they threw down the tins.' He looked at me squarely; that, he was implying, is what they call a clue. I was not alone in resenting being roused in the middle of the night.

'Seems a bit extreme; climbing up on the roof, I mean,' I added hastily.

'They've been locking the doors lately,' one of the anonymous detective constables said. 'Animal rights.'

'Trouble?'

4

'Bit of graffiti, that's all.' Rodway was dismissive. 'Painted a slogan or two a couple of weeks ago. Nothing heavy.'

'Reported?'

'Yeah, to the local rural man. He's around, somewhere. I called Scenes of Crime as well, but the Fire Brigade say there's nothing much anybody can do till it's daylight. They're bringing in a fire investigation team of their own.'

If I get out of bed, *everybody* gets out of bed. The Derek Rodway philosophy at work.

'You didn't fetch the Chief Constable out, by any chance?'

'Eh?' The two DCs grinned; their detective inspector was obviously a man on whom irony was a waste of time.

'Nothing much to go on,' Rodway hastened on. 'The manager reckons he heard the sound of an engine just after two. Motorbike, he thought. The dog barked, but it was a fairish way off and he didn't go out. He woke up again half an hour later, looked out of the window and saw flames bursting through the roof.'

'What did he do?'

'Called the Brigade, and shot out to turn off the ventilation systems in the other battery houses in case a hundred and fifty thousand chickens choked to death in the smoke.'

'How many?'

'That's what I thought, but he reckons it's true. Standing room only in those ruddy huts; enough to put you off your bit of bacon and two fried, innit?'

I looked at the blackened hulk of the half-collapsed building, at the gaping hole replacing roughly forty per cent of the roof, and made the obvious remark. 'Insulated wooden walls with a corrugated roof,' I said, surprised. 'It's a wonder there's anything left. Says something for the Toytown Fire Brigade, does that.'

'Don't let their station officer hear you, boss,' murmured one of the DCs. 'The farm manager's already made a funny about the local fire service. We've witnessed one serious sense of humour failure tonight.'

'This, er, manager: he's taking it well, then, I assume?'

'Paul Kinsley? I wouldn't say that.' Rodway looked sour. 'It wasn't so much a joke, more a nasty remark about the time it took 'em to get here.'

'From the state of the building, I'd say they'd done pretty well.'

'Not them, not us, according to Kinsley. We should have prevented it in the first place, and the firemen should have been psychic and had an appliance ready at the end of the road in case of emergency; that's his line.'

'One of those.'

'Yep, one of those.' For the first time Rodway allowed himself a bit of a grin. 'Personally, I think he's shit-scared he's going to lose his job, once the Chief Chicken finds out.'

'Blatt? He can hardly blame his manager for the ways of nutters with paraffin cans, surely?'

'You've never met Sir Jeremy, huh? In comparison with him, the late Robert Maxwell was a pussycat. boss. And just to make things perfect, Lowbarrack is the apple of the old bastard's eye. This is where he started out, thirty-odd years ago.'

'The beginning of the empire, eh? In that case you'd think he'd have built a proper road to the place, and replaced these old buildings with something modern by now.'

'His manager says he likes to come and look at it,' said Derek Rodway. 'Likes it just as it is – was. Apart from that, he never spends a quid without kissing the coin goodbye. He's about as willing to put his hand in his pockets as a Glaswegian with amputated arms.'

One of the detective constables choked; the other gazed dreamily over my head, searching, apparently, for non-existent stars. Silence fell. Their immediate superior looked puzzled; a close observer could almost have seen the wheels turning. Then he caught on.

'Oh yeah, sorry. Graham's a Scottish name, innit?' He did his best to look repentant. 'Always thought of you as English, myself,' he added generously. 'Right, well; present company excepted, boss.'

The assembled peasantry shuffled in an anticipatory sort of way. Worthwhile, after all, all this cold and misery and fire stink; all this night and wet. Their faces brightened: any moment now.

'I think I'll go and have a word with that rural constable,' I said equably. Two eager faces fell.

Time to lumber off, splash through the deeper puddles and give those nice watertight wellingtons an airing. Whatever my ethnic shortcomings, I, at least. was weatherproof, waterproof and warm.

2

They call it a harbour, although it's four miles inland. In reality Aylfleet possesses a single concrete dock, an ageing ferry terminal, three or four grain silos and a couple of cranes. The basin is just wide enough for a smallish cargo ship to swing round to enable it to pass between the mud banks on either side of the river and so back to the sea. Constant dredging keeps the passage open and Aylfleet limps along, making some sort of living as an East Coast port.

The continental ferry service, such as it is, grubs for a living in competition with smarter, better-financed outfits to both the north and south. If it wasn't for the low-grade commercial traffic passing through the port, the whole place would curl up and die.

Not that the locals see it that way, of course. They are the citizens of an ancient, proud, dynamic working town. They have *seamen* in their pubs, for heaven's sake! Do not on any account confuse them with that louche gang of Johnny-come-latelies with their sandcastles, amusement arcades and fat, half-naked tourists a few miles up the coast. Aylfleet hates Eddathorpe, and Eddathorpe hates Aylfleet. As Superintendent Teddy Baring would say, a great gap is set between them and us. Fond of the occasional biblical outburst is the Eddathorpe boss.

Unfortunate, then, that police reorganisation has resulted in this mutual exclusivity being spoiled. Eddathorpe and its surrounding area make up a complete division of the force. Aylfleet, roughly two-thirds of its size, but with better communications and surrounded by a massive hinterland of agriculturally rich reclaimed fen, makes another. As the detective chief inspector for the whole area, I've been left to wander uneasily between the two. Nobody at Headquarters had taken this into account when the powers that be reorganised the DCI's job description into an ersatz detective superintendent's post. All the kicks and only a few of the halfpence; that was me.

The moment I got promoted Teddy's piratical instincts came into play. He promptly appropriated Robert Graham as an extra Eddathorpe body, his very own DCI. On the other side of the estuary, Superintendent Dorothea Spinks, whose elevation to the rank Teddy contemplated with an incredulity approaching total disbelief, didn't see matters in quite the same light. A DCI, she figured, would nicely make up for perceived deficiencies in her own CID personnel. As the meat in their political sandwich, I was currently being alternately chewed and buttered up by both sides.

Ten o'clock on the Saturday morning, and it was still my weekend off.

'Sorry,' said Thea sweetly, 'to drag you in; but it's partly your own fault. You should have told that idiot Rodway to get stuffed, the moment he tried to get you out of bed.' That's Thea, about as subtle as a Chieftain tank, but she knew all about the mix-up with the duty rota, of course.

An odd diminutive, Thea; a kind of tribute to her personality, I suppose. Nobody, to my knowledge, has ever dared call her 'Dotty'. Few, according to canteen gossip, would care to mess her about.

I smiled my accommodating Foreign Office smile; then I gave her both barrels, straight between the eyes. The way I saw it, if I rolled over now, I'd be rolling over for ever more.

'Derek Rodway,' I said, doing my best to coat the pill, 'is a good DI. Not, I admit, the most diplomatic man who ever lived, but he's well capable of investigating a malicious fire. I'll give it a couple of hours, make sure everything's running smoothly, and then I'm going home.'

'Mr Graham; Bob . . .' She was changing tactics in midstream already. 'As divisional commander, I have the final say on the deployment of resources in my division.'

'Miss Spinks' – time for a gentle counter-prod – 'ma'am. You are the divisional commander, as you so rightly say, and I wouldn't deny your right for a moment. I am not, however, a divisional resource. I am answerable directly to the head of CID.'

Awaiting the reaction, I watched her face. Big, bold, handsome once, and on the wrong side of fifty, she started by trying to stare me down. Then she placed both elbows on the table, leant forward and scowled, giving me a view of what it was like to be a six-foot female, cross and fourteen stone. Throwing the hammer for the former Soviet Union, that was the style.

'Is this,' she said, 'Teddy Baring's doing? The Eddathorpe way?'

'No, ma'am; it's likely that Superintendent Baring and I are also going to have to come to an understanding.'

'He used to be your immediate boss, but times and circumstances change, eh?'

'I've now got two divisions to cover; I've got two competent inspectors, Paula Baily at Eddathorpe and Derek here. I intend to do my job, but there are only so many hours in a day.'

'You intend to tell that to Teddy?'

'Given a similar opportunity, yes.'

'Good grief!' As suddenly as the thunderclouds had rolled over, the sun came out. 'I hope you're going to sell tickets to that one: may I be there to see!'

'Mr Baring,' I said hypocritically, 'can be a very reasonable man.'

'So could Attila the Hun,' she replied. And what's all this about senior management presenting a united front? 'No, sorry; forget I said that.'

I could save that up for future reference. In the meantime, I ought to deploy a spot of tact. She was either genuinely open to persuasion, or awaiting a battle on ground of her own choosing.

'You'd like me to sort out this egg man, Paul Kinsley?'

'Derek Rodway seems to think there's some sort of undercurrent there.'

'Kinsley's worried; he thinks he might lose his job.'

'Exactly. Blatt's been chewing up the phone already this morning, or haven't you heard?' She waited for my reaction and, getting none, she added, 'Do you know Jeremy Blatt at all, come to that?'

'No.'

'Lucky you. Lost his seat, you know,' she said with unconcealed satisfaction, 'at the last county council elections. He's now the chairman of what he calls the Conservative shadow opposition group, whatever that's supposed to mean.'

'I'd heard that much,' I said cautiously, unwilling to take sides too soon. The shadow anything group sounded ominous. A gang of self-selected busybodies, probably, all whistling in the wind.

'Did you also hear about his knighthood?'

'No, ma'am.' Scandal was in the air.

'We-ll, I'm not repeating this just out of malice, you understand.'

'Of course not.' Mere malice? Perish the thought!

'Just to give you some idea of what he's like.'

'Yes.'

'Our Jeremy,' she said, 'got his knighthood in the birthday honours last year, at the same time as the Chief. Anyway, Jeremy being Jeremy, and wanting to suck up to anybody in authority, he invited him out to lunch on the big day. It was a very long lunch.'

She paused significantly. Point taken. One new knight, at least, had got well and truly smashed.

'While they were out together his wife telephoned our switchboard and asked where her husband and the Chief Constable were having lunch. This young girl in our control room took the call and said, "Sorry, Mrs Blatt, I don't know. I'll find out and get him to give you a ring."

'About an hour later, Jeremy telephones the control room inspector and starts bawling and swearing down the phone. When he eventually manages to disentangle the message, poor feller, he discovers that Mrs Blatt is not Mrs Blatt, any more. She's Lady Blatt, and don't you lot forget it!'

'And the Chief?'

'Relations,' said Thea dreamily, 'have not been quite the same since.'

It did, I silently agreed, tend to put our little professional disagreements into perspective. And Thea sounded as though she was biding her time, awaiting a suitable opportunity for well and truly blighting the life of one Jeremy Blatt, Kt. I was a lucky, lucky man, I decided. Backbiting Eddathorpe as well as feud-infested Aylfleet, both on the same CID patch.

Paul Kinsley; not what you would call a happy man. He'd come off his high horse, nevertheless.

'Sorry,' he muttered to Derek Rodway, 'about last night. Bit of a shock.'

'That's OK.'

No need to apologise to me; we'd scarcely exchanged more than a couple of dozen words at the scene. He'd been scooting in and out of the remaining battery houses like a demented fox the night before, and I'd had no intention of following him around. Not with the overpowering stench of ammonia and chicken shit emanating from the three remaining sheds.

Come to think of it, there was something slightly foxy about the man sat in front of us at Aylfleet nick. Somewhere between thirty-five and forty, brushed-back sandy hair. Not furtive, not bad-looking in an anorexic sort of way. But nervous, very nervous: incapable of keeping still.

'Are we going to be long?'

'I hope not, Mr Kinsley. A few questions, then we can take a statement, OK?' A spot of reassurance; no need to get his back up right from the start. A good job he'd started with the apology, all the same; what did he expect, a witness statement drafted via telepathy, no time wasted, no trouble for him?

'It's definitely arson, I suppose?'

'Definitely. Surely you could smell the paraffin yourself?' I glanced across at Derek Rodway, who lifted his eyes heavenwards in exasperation, and gave an infinitesimal shrug. A variant on his original opinion; we've got a right one here.

'Yeah; just wondered, that's all.' Kinsley's shoulders slumped. He paused for a moment, and added, 'Much less trouble all round; an accident, I mean.'

'What sort of trouble, Mr Kinsley?'

'Oh, you know . . . problems with people asking questions; the boss.'

A vein well worth mining straight away; the man was wriggling on the end of some sort of hook. Short of an instant burst of '*Please, sir, I done it myself 'cos I'm a nutter!*' I didn't know what to expect.

'There's something worrying you, isn't there?'

Derek Rodway stared at me as if I'd spontaneously produced a particularly nasty smell. He immediately followed on with his CID special; the hating do-gooders and social workers look. It was all he needed. a compassionate, soft-hearted DCI.

I stocked that one up for future reference too. Left to himself, he might prefer the bright light and the rubber hose to the softly-softly technique. Metaphorically speaking, of course.

'I got into trouble, you know; reporting the graffiti and stuff.'

'Why was that?'

'I got the blame when the Ministry inspectors came round. He said it was all that nosey copper's fault; he'd gone and dropped us in the mire.'

'Sir Jeremy Blatt,' I hazarded, 'said that about the rural constable, PC Marshall, because he thought he'd reported something to the Ministry of Agriculture inspectors, right?'

'Not Blatt, the divisional manager, David Lang. He said I'd probably

11

get the sack if the old bast . . . Sir Jeremy ever found out.'

'*Blatt is a mean, cruel bastard. Blatt is breaking the law! Prosecute, prosecute, persecute Blatt!*' I was quoting verbatim from the messages painted on the sides of the sheds and recorded in the rural constable's pocket-book a fortnight before.

'Yeah,' he murmured, scarcely above a whisper. 'That's right.'

'And now you're worried in case you, er, drop the business in the mire again?'

He nodded reluctantly.

'Constable Marshall didn't report you; he put it down to malice. Animal libbers, OK?'

'Yeah, OK.'

'But there was more to it than that, eh? Tell me about it. If the men from the Ministry have already done their worst, you can't do any damage to your employers now.'

'Yeah.' A man with a one-word vocabulary; either that or the record had stuck. I gave him time to gather his thoughts.

'We-ll,' he said at last, 'there's these EU regulations, see.' Derek Rodway deliberately stared out of the window; I could feel myself beginning to disengage. Thank you, and goodnight. This we did not wish to know.

He took our silence for encouragement and ploughed doggedly on. 'We used to have four battery houses.'

Yes, we knew that: one of them burnt down. History, not news.

'No; you don't understand. The remaining sheds are aviaries – percheries – now, we've changed over.' Very good; they'd changed the image. Rat-catchers, as Angie would say, are now rodent operatives; dustmen are refuse recycling executives. So what?

'There's different sorts of eggs.' Nothing there to rivet us to the spot, either. Maybe they were producing them square.

'Battery eggs, barn, deep-litter and so on; get it?'

Got it, for what it was worth.

'The EU made regulations for the minimum size of cages.' Well, they would, wouldn't they. 'If there's four or more birds in a cage, each hen has got to have four hundred and fifty square centimetres of floor space, and they've got to be a minimum height. Ours were old cages, too small, and we had up to last year to change. Otherwise we were breaking the law.'

'OK.' I could see it all: sirens, flashing blue lights. An armed response team. *Come out with your hands up, you chicken squeezers!* Probably.

'We were in the process of changing the policy,' he said grandly. 'We'd got rid of the cages in three of the sheds and changed them to percheries to produce barn eggs. The public are turning against battery eggs.'

'So' – Derek wasn't exactly dim – 'your company didn't have to go to the expense of buying new cages, and the public probably pay more for these barn eggs, right?'

'Sort of, yes.'

'Those hens are still stuffed in like sardines,' he commented rudely. 'Go on.'

'We'd not changed the fourth shed; we were waiting for harvest. It only happened the other day, so we haven't had time to refurbish yet.'

'What harvest?'

'When the hens come to the end of their laying lives they're harvested and sent to slaughter.'

'You mean we eat those manky, stinking old boilers?' Derek Rodway was failing to preserve the objectivity demanded of a police officer. Having had a few lungfuls of the Daisy Dew operation, I was beginning to feel the same.

'No, you don't eat 'em.' Kinsley's voice was reluctant. 'They're too tough. They're made into soups, puree, that sort of thing.'

'Baby food.' Laura, aged seven months. I was appalled.

'Lots of them go for pet food, too,' he offered. He'd somehow got the impression that he'd lost the sympathy of the meeting somewhere along the line.

'Anyway, your bosses didn't get rid of the old cages, therefore they were breaking the law. Somebody found out and spread the message all over the sheds. You got done by the Min. of Ag. before you emptied the last one; then that same somebody came back and torched it. Right?'

This question-and-answer stuff could go on for ever; it was nitty-gritty time. We'd not even got round to starting a statement, and I'd meant what I'd said. Two hours, top whack, and I was going home.

'We-ll . . .'

'There's more?'

'There were these other problems. I might as well tell you, you're going to find out anyway.'

13

'Too right.' Derek sounded as if he knew the whereabouts of the thumbscrews and a working rack.

'The hens go into the batteries at eighteen weeks.'

'Yeah.' It might be a subject of endless fascination for Paul Kinsley; apart from inducing a certain distant disgust, it bored the pants off me.

'People usually keep 'em a year, then production falls off and they get rid.' He watched our faces carefully, saw he wasn't getting through and hurried on. 'In our case, Sir Jeremy ordered us to, er, continue production.'

'How?'

'Turn the lights out, reduce the feed for a fortnight; force moulting. Then they start again. Anyway, we had this youth working for us—'

'It's illegal, this method of yours?' Derek was short-circuiting now. Amazing what these ignorant coppers pick up from time to time.

'Yes.'

'Let me guess; your little mate spilled the beans to the Ministry men when they called?'

'Yes.'

'What's his name?'

'Kevin Cooke.'

The good news at last. I knew a Kevin Cooke: Kinsley couldn't have mentioned a nicer lad. Once he made his acquaintance, the judge was probably going to like him too. Kevin was a lad who believed in following up other people's advertising slogans; especially the one about coming home to a real fire. The nice thing about a comparatively small community from a copper's point of view: the same old faces, the same old suspects, time after time.

'He got the sack and that gives us another suspect for the fire?' Derek had the bit well and truly between his teeth.

Correction; this gave us our one and only suspect, so far.

'More or less. Sack, resign; telling Sir Jeremy to stuff his job. You tell me.'

'And are MAFF going to prosecute the directors as well as you, as a result of all this?'

'Probably.'

'So much for the Chief Chicken,' said Derek Rodway with blatant self-satisfaction. 'Egg all over his face.'

Nevertheless, it was two hours and twenty minutes before the statement

14

was finished and I finally got away. But we'd quite exhausted the subject of ex-employees and their enthusiasm for motorbikes before I left Aylfleet nick.

It was not, however, the end of the weekend's entertainment; not quite. Lunch-time, and he did the absolutely unforgivable; he rang me at home. If I ever discover the name of the weak-willed idiot who gave Jeremy Blatt my ex-directory number, he'll be sorry. I can promise him that.

'Are you in charge?' blared an angry, hectoring voice.

'In charge of what?'

'Don't you get smart with me, sonny. It could cost you your job.'

'Who's speaking, please?'

'Sir Jeremy Blatt!' He'd forgotten to turn on his recording of the fanfare by the State Trumpeters, but I got his general drift. I was supposed to be incredibly impressed.

'I am not,' I said politely, 'running the investigation into the arson at your premises, Sir Jeremy. It's a local matter.'

'Don't give me that: Thea told me you were in charge.'

'Superintendent Spinks? Well, I'm the area DCI, but the investigation is being run by Detective Inspector—'

'Passing the buck, are you? You idle, toffee-nosed bastard, we'll see about that!'

Crash! Silence; then a soothing, nerve-enhancing dialling tone, courtesy of BT. I know you mean well, I quite like the adverts and I sympathise with your motives, fellers, but despite the cosy image you're promoting, it's *not* always good to talk.

3

'It's not that I've got anything against Paula,' said George.

'You've worked with her long enough.'

George Caunt, Eddathorpe's bulky detective sergeant, lounged inelegantly against my office window-sill, adopted his earnest expression and ran one hand through his thick, iron-grey hair.

This had, I realised, been coming for some time. George and Paula had always got along; as colleagues, as detective sergeants, that is. Paula at Retton and George in the seaside town. Joy, risky jokes and the occasional tingle of sexual frisson had been unconfined.

Detective Inspector Paula Baily directly supervising her senior by twenty years was a different cageful of stoats. Male chauvinism didn't rule any more; probably never had, OK? It wasn't that she was overbearing. Paula had been the soul of tact; consulting, conferring with George, taking care not to tread on his toes. Could that be part of the problem?

'Look,' muttered George, 'I've always liked her, I'm glad she's got on. I've nothing to complain about 'cos I never took my inspector's exams, but we're always under each other's feet. And she's so careful when I'm around; she's so bloody *nice*.'

'So you want a transfer. Don't you think that's just a bit extreme?'

'It's not exactly a transfer, is it? She's the Eddathorpe DI; her old job at Retton hasn't been filled, so why can't we have the detective inspector at Eddathorpe, and a substantive sergeant at Retton, four miles down the road?'

'And the new detective sergeant, whenever he's appointed, comes here?'

'Exactly. Then you've got a proper supervisory officer at both stations, and you can cut out Retton's acting rank.'

'George,' I said warningly, 'I rate Paula, and however we juggle it, she's still your immediate boss whether you work from Retton or work from here.'

'I haven't got a problem with that. But she's new, she needs to find her feet; she doesn't need an old feller like me lumbering around. If she gets a new sergeant here, she's in charge right from the start.'

'And you can go a few miles down the road and declare UDI, is that it?'

'No, boss. But I do get to breathe a bit easier..'

'Eddathorpe's bigger than Retton,' I said cunningly, 'so in some senses, this is the senior sergeant's post.'

'Seniority,' said George, 'goes with a spot of autonomy. It's difficult, boss, teaching an old dog new tricks.'

I could do it; no problem at all. Sure, I'd consult Teddy Baring, the divisional commander, but he'd say it was up to me to decide where I was going to deploy my staff.

Retton, under the control of a detective constable acting as the DS, left Paula scuttling between the two stations to keep an eye on whatever was going on. George was a safe pair of hands . . . On the other hand I could be setting up the conditions for a feud; George with a semi-independent fief, and Paula feeling slighted because she thought I was criticising her ability to deal with the male menopause. Oh hell.

'George,' I said, 'how long have you been stationed at Eddathorpe?' Not that I didn't know perfectly well.

'Eighteen years.' Mentally, I measured that against my fifteen months. Would I become as downright sneaky as one of its average isolated, tourist-twisting seaside citizens in the due course of time?

'Almost as long as I've been on the job, right? And practically not a sparrow falls unless either you or Sarah gets to know about it, eh?'

Mrs George was, as he hardly ever tired of telling me, related to half the town. The National Crime Intelligence Bureau was a pale, semi-competent shadow in comparison with the network of hard information, gossip, innuendo and downright misrepresentation tapped by Sarah Caunt.

'We – I, that is – know a lot about Retton. I wouldn't let you down.'

I sighed. 'I'll think about it,' I said.

'OK.' It's far worse when he turns casual; enough to make senior officers worry. He's very devious is George.

'I suppose you know about Kevin Cooke?'

Knowing about Kevin Cooke was something I did fairly well. Kevin, my up-and-coming arsonist. He'd attempted to set a house on fire less than a year before. The fact that the house in question had been a murder scene had piled complication on top of complication in an already difficult enquiry. Kevin, now on probation, motorcycle owner and ex-employee of Daisy Dew. A youth with career ambitions as a Ministry of Agriculture grass, and currently appearing, I hoped, in the Aylfleet police station cells. What else did I need to know?

'He denies the arson,' said George.

'He would.'

'Derek Rodway says he's got an alibi.'

'Go on.'

'He says he was in bed with his bird at the time of the fire. In fact he says he was in bed with her all night. And Inspector Rodway's checked.'

'What am I supposed to do, award him a sexual endurance trophy or something?' I'm not inclined to be pleasant when our one and only viable suspect gets flushed down the pan. As soon as I'd heard his name from Kinsley, I'd had these very satisfying thoughts about putting Young Lochinvar away for a couple of years.

If Kevin was out it was back to plan B: why, for example, was Daisy Dew insured to the tune of sixty thousand pounds (including fittings) for what this ignorant copper could only describe as a big wooden hut?

George suppressed a self-satisfied grin. Irritating; I didn't see that he'd much to grin about. He was supposed to have a long memory for insults, and George had been well and truly insulted by Kevin Cooke. Something to do with a spot of graffiti scrawled on a police car, and the misspelling of the old and honourable name of Caunt.

'Kevin says he wants to talk to you.'

'Oh yes?'

'Says he'll pop up and see you sometime.'

'How nice.' More bad news; he was not only denying it, he'd obviously got police bail. Besides, I didn't care for George's sly turn of phrase. I was not suffering from an identity crisis, and he seemed to be implying some sort of connection between me and the late Mae West.

'Derek Rodway thinks that Kevin thinks you might hand over some informant's money.'

'Pigs might fly,' I muttered ungraciously. And what the hell was Rodway doing in any case? He was supposed to lean on the little toe-rag and suck him dry. Information; the price of freedom, that was the usual form.

George departed; I brooded. Criminals one, policemen nil, and I wasn't pleased. Kevin had apparently run rings round an experienced DI. It was, however, possible, I reluctantly concluded, that he was turning out to be quite a versatile lad.

'We've got a hijack, boss!' Paula burst in like a fragrant cyclone, struggling to extract her blond hair from under her winter coat; glittering, animated, rarin' to go.

It's not that I'm getting old and crotchety. I do not yet need a post-prandial snooze to set me up for the rest of the day, but I do not go in for giddy enthusiasm and people rushing around crying, *'Where's my hat!'*

'What sort of hijack, and where?' Damn all this eagerness, as Wellington used to say. Paula looked at me with a tinge of pity; poor old man. I'm slightly less than six years older than the new Eddathorpe DI.

'You aren't going to believe this,' she said, trying to maintain the momentum. Want to bet?

'Somebody's nicked a lorry-load of frozen chickens, boss. The driver only stopped at Forster's Tranny for a cuppa and a wad. Came out twenty minutes later and his lorry had gone.'

'That,' I said severely, 'is not exactly a hijack, is it? You know – stocking masks, sawn-off shotguns, drivers beaten up?'

'No-oo . . .' She sounded truly deflated. 'What would you call it, then?'

'Joyriding,' I suggested crushingly. 'Taking a motor vehicle without owner's consent.'

'A great lumbering mobile freezer, full of frozen poultry?' She was, I had to admit, on safer ground here. And this was the point where I experienced a growing sense of unease.

'Daisy Dew?' I said.

'Daisy Dew,' she confirmed, 'Poultry Division. Straight from the Farm to Your Home!'

'Or your friendly metropolitan fence, as the case may be,' I murmured sourly, getting to my feet, reaching for my coat at as steady, as unexcited a pace as I could manage. Exhibit the highly experienced air, the unflappable manner to the junior ranks.

Then in the distance, but trundling ever closer, I saw this great big ball of manure rolling in my direction. Graffiti, treachery, arson and now theft. Scarcely coincidental, not just your average run of industrial bad luck. It sounded as though somebody was definitely out to put the skids under Daisy Dew and its principal director, Sir Jeremy Blatt. Telephones would be ringing, wires would be melting at divisional, or even force, level, even as I thought. To hell with the stoic image – time to get out of here!

We almost made it to the door, and a man of lesser public spirit and moral fibre would have ignored the shrill of the phone. Then again, there's not a lot of future in trying to ignore the boss.

'On your way out, Bob?' Teddy Baring, and it was more of a command than an enquiry.

'Yessir.' No need for either of us to ask where.

'I've just had a telephone call from the man Blatt.' And no need whatsoever to enquire further into the Blatt ancestry, present attitudes or future prospects from Superintendent Edward Baring's point of view.

'He's heard, then?'

'I think you can safely say that he's heard.' Teddy, I could almost have sworn, was amused. 'He says he'll meet you at the scene; personally.'

'I'll look forward to it, sir.'

'He also says that most of his employees are liars, or thieves, or both, and this was undoubtedly an inside job. He feels you can get the driver to confess to being part of a conspiracy, and he hints that a bit of strongarm stuff wouldn't come amiss.'

'He gives us his permission, huh?'

'Quite.'

'Anything else I ought to know?'

'Yes,' said Teddy. 'I'm sure I don't really need to say this, Bob, but don't think you have to take any bullshit from a man like that.'

There was a click on the line, and I was left staring incredulously at the handset. There's a first for everything, I suppose, but our highly ethical, religiously motivated boss never, *never* swears. It was a bit like discovering the Pope spaced out in a pew at St Peter's, sniffing a line of coke.

It wasn't just a form of words, I *was* looking forward to it. Not only did I fancy a rematch myself, but anybody who had that sort of effect on Teddy after a single phone call must be pretty special. I'd always thought that it would take somebody with the public relations skills of Torquemada to entirely piss him off.

We assembled what was for us an impressive display of CID strength. Then I entertained Paula with details of the life and times of our self-made millionaire throughout the journey to Forster's Café.

4

'All dressed up and nowhere to go!' The traffic man was talking to George, but his voice was just loud enough to carry to where I was sitting opposite a couple of lorry drivers, each man giving his jumbo all-day breakfast the attention it deserved.

Stealing frozen food lorries was one thing. Letting eggs, bacon, sausage, beans, mushrooms, tomatoes, fritters and double fried bread, not forgetting the toast and tea, get cold was quite another. I asked the questions; they concentrated on their overloaded troughs. Not that they were being deliberately unhelpful, but I expended a fair amount of energy evading the sight of their debris-packed mouths every time they spoke.

I shifted in my screwed-down green plastic seat, glanced over my shoulder and awarded the traffic man the glare. He did, however, have a point. The cavalry had turned out; one detective chief inspector, one detective inspector, one detective sergeant and two DCs, and all for what? The Chief Chicken, aka Sir Jeremy Blatt, had been and gone a long time before we came riding over the hill. Nobody left to impress with our massive response.

He had, according to our gloating uniformed source, turned up at Forster's transport pull-in ten minutes before our arrival, stepped out of his chauffeur-driven white Roller, sacked his lorry driver for what he'd called industrial misconduct, and buggered off, pausing only to shrivel the lurking constabulary with a quick round of applause. Not what Teddy had predicted, after all.

Paula was almost tempted to like his style. 'Expect the unexpected,' she'd said. Not the sort of remark to console the newly unemployed lorry

23

driver much. His name was Frank Pollard and he'd got a wife and three kids.

'A feller's entitled to his cuppa tea, isn't he? Right!'

Not, apparently, within twenty minutes of loading up, following the official canteen lunch. Not when you let somebody half-inch seven hundred and twenty-eight cases of frozen chicken, not to mention a Daisy Dew refrigerated lorry, from under your very eyes. Not, above all, when you're an employee of dynamic Jeremy Blatt, the well-known country gentleman and self-made millionaire.

'And if he's a gent, I'm a baboon's arsehole,' offered one of my witnesses through a gargantuan mouthful of fried egg.

I bowed to his expert opinion; he was, after all, a front-row spectator to the confrontation between Pollard and Blatt. In common with the rest of the café's customers, however, he hadn't got much information about the thieves.

'Couple of youngsters hanging about on the carpark,' said my second informant, 'when I came in. Motorcyclists, I think.'

'Specially as they were both toting 'elmets,' nodded his mate. 'Gives you a bit of a clue, dunnit? To them being bikers, I mean.' Nothing, absolutely nothing, like hammering the point home.

'So, the Daisy Dew lorry was here when you arrived?'

'Yeah, we were following each other, and the bikers had just pulled in.'

'You saw their bike?'

'There was a bike. They weren't too far away; I suppose it was theirs.'

'Red,' said the victim of sarcasm. 'It were definitely red.'

'And they were standing four or five yards away,' added his companion, not to be outdone. 'Arguing.'

'Or maybe having a chat.'

'Arguing, I'd say.'

'Anyway, they never came in.'

'Probably only stopped to go to the bog.'

'Or nick the poor bastard's rig.' Somebody, I suspected, had been sharpening his big bold truckie image by watching Road movies and picking up the slang.

'One,' said the fried egg man helpfully, 'steals the lorry, and his mate rides off on the bike. Clean as a whistle.'

'You saw all this?'

''Course not. Just telling you how it's done.'

'Clever bleeder; bet he coulda worked that one out for hisself.'

'This bike,' I said hastily, 'you say it was red? What about the make?'

'Big, flashy; that's all I can say. I hate sodding motorbikes an' the bastards who ride 'em. Loada clowns!'

'That's right; forever cutting you up.' Common ground at last; I had considerable difficulty in getting them back to the subject in hand. I hoped that Paula, talking to the shocked and sullen ex-driver, was having better luck.

'What about a description?'

'I told you; both young. One was older than the other, though.' I chewed on the stunning brilliance of that particular remark.

'Yes?'

'The one wearing black leathers was in his early twenties maybe. Tallish; broadish; ruddy face.'

'Anything else?'

'Them leathers must have set him back a bit. And the boots. Oh, yeah, the helmet he was carrying was one of those smoky-visored things: black with a lightning flash.'

'Fascist,' muttered the other.

'What?'

'Y'know: lightning flash, like the SS.'

'He was wearing some sort of Nazi gear?'

'Nope, just saying about the lightning flash, that's all.' Verbal diarrhoea and total bloody irrelevance; thank you very much.

'What about the other one?'

'Bit younger, I'da thought. Yes; younger. Definitely.'

'Padded anorak; washed-out jeans. Still had his helmet on; same sort.'

'Might not have been younger; just littler, I'd say. And the anorak was sort of red.'

'Burgundy.'

'Darkish red.'

'OK.' Bitter experience suggested that conversations like this could go on for hours. Taking consensus descriptions; not the wisest way, but there was absolutely no possibility of separating Tweedledum and Tweedledee from each other, or their chloresterol-loaded stodge. Besides, they could well be describing a pair of bikers innocently astride their machine, and fifty or sixty miles away by now.

25

'Did you notice anything else, inside the café for example – people leaving before the Daisy Dew bloke?'

'Sure; fair amount of to-ing and fro-ing while we was waiting for our grub. Thought they were growing the spuds for our fries.'

'Well?'

'Well what? They was all proper drivers s'far as I know.'

'But we didn't count 'em in; and we didn't count 'em out. OK?'

Another humorist; ha, ha, bloody ha. I knew where I'd very much like to deposit my squadron of Harrier jump-jets, given half a chance.

George, accompanied by the traffic man, came over to the table.

'He went looking for his lorry,' moaned the uniform, aggrieved. 'I told him we'd circulate it, and that we'd got cars in the area looking.'

'Blatt?'

'Yeah, boss. He's a nutter, if you ask me. Swearing like a trooper, and yelling at his chauffeur to get a move on before he missed the thieving bastards. He hadn't got a hope.'

I stared warningly at him; the lorry drivers were agog.

'Like James Bond,' said my original informant with a grin. 'Chasing the baddies in a Rolls-Royce; d'ya reckon he's got a bird with legs all the way up?'

'That was an Aston Martin.'

'With legs?'

'And big tits too, if you like.'

I glanced at my pocket-book. Names and addresses recorded; one from the Wirral, the other from Greater Manchester. I'd had enough of my self-appointed comics; time to leave 'em to their fry-up and their one-track minds.

Pollard, I discovered, hadn't been a lot of help. No, he hadn't been followed; not as far as he knew, that is. No, he'd never noticed two men in motorcycle gear hanging around outside the café. Why should he? Who'd be stupid enough to heist five gross of cases of frozen chicken, anyway? Why not steal a high-value load while they were about it, huh?

How many? How much? Oh, six chickens to the case; ranging between five-forty and eight pounds seventy the case, according to size. He was due to make drops at Nottingham, Derby, Hanley and Stoke on Trent. Supermarkets, mostly; some smaller shops.

Could he have a lift back to the factory so he could collect his

26

belongings and his car? And if he was out of a job, why should he make a statement on behalf of that old scumbag and his business, anyway? Personally, he hoped Blatt died of cancer, and his whole effing business burned down in the middle of the night.

I treated Sir Jeremy to a long, hard, silent cuss. It's hard enough to sort out your witnesses anyway, without some cheap imitation of John Pierpont Morgan rushing along and turning them sour.

I looked significantly at Paula, and she scooped up loudmouthed Patrick Goodall and his mate.

'Why don't you take Mr Pollard back to Daisy Dew,' she murmured, 'so he can get his car. He can follow you to Eddathorpe. We can make a start on his statement when I come back.'

Which, roughly translated, meant something along the lines of, '*Be reasonable with him, Pat, be nice; but keep an eye on him, and don't, unless you want to go and draw a blue uniform and a big hat, let him out of your sight.*'

Now there's your average copper; nasty-minded, and making a grab for the obvious solution every time. No stolen lorry; no hard suspects; no clues. So when in doubt, talk to the immediate victim and see if you can cast him in a starring role in the hoary old play about the insider job. Where else could we start?

Even so, I was still reluctant to go along entirely with the wit, wisdom and criminal conspiracy theories of our absent, ever so slightly crackpot entrepreneur.

Kevin Cooke tried to lounge; tried to make himself look at home. Not easy when you're parked on one of our metal-framed interview room chairs, the ones with the flat plywood seats. He was not an honoured guest; he was not coming upstairs to sample the comforts of one of the fake leather executive chairs in my office.

'He's a real sod, that Rodway; know that? He had me down in their manky old cells ever since Sunday afternoon.'

'A lost weekend,' I countered. I was not in the most sympathetic of moods. It's a bugger when your chief suspect comes snivelling round looking for a handout from a very much depleted informant's fund within weeks of the end of the financial year.

'Thought I'd drop in and give you the SP on the old pig. Don't mind talking to you.' A switch, I hoped, from Derek Rodway to Sir Jeremy

Blatt. Kevin, I noticed, was as cocky as ever; and somebody else had been picking up a few bits of TV Metroslang along the way.

'Oh, yes?' Enthusiasm was out. Kevin the arsonist; Kevin of the rigid finger, an ever-ready digit for display to passing cops. I was not in business to forgive and forget, but I didn't crush him; let him chatter for a while. Then jump on him from a very great height, if there was nothing in it for us. In the meantime, I smiled encouragingly; didn't pretend not to know the name of the pig he had in mind.

'What's it worth?' He really did have the instincts of the most promising kind of grass.

'About two minutes of my very valuable time.'

'Aw, come on, Mr Graham, don't be like that. I know things about him you wouldn't believe.'

'Not a lot of point in telling me in that case, is there?'

'F'r instance' – he leaned forward confidentially – 'I might even know who burnt down his battery house, and why.'

I waited; he deflated. 'Probably.'

'It wasn't you?' I managed to inject a whole world of cynical disbelief into three little words.

'No it wasn't, an' I'd be daft to try that, what with the probation order and all. Unlawful dismissal, that's me. I'm gonna sue the pants off him and get damages instead.'

'From what I heard, you quit of your own accord. After you'd put the bubble in to the Ministry men over the illegal cages for stock.'

'Yeah; being a good citizen.' Somehow, somewhere, he'd lost a tooth; it added a positively sinister element to what was meant to be his open, confiding grin. 'Hurt my feelings, he did, using obscene language an' that. Grounds for constructive dismissal, I reckon.'

'How long did you work for Daisy Dew, Kevin?'

'Five months.'

'Well, before you start counting your money, go down and have a few words with Citizens Advice.'

'What for?'

'I think they'll have bad news; you have to work for a company for two years before you can make a claim. Besides, telling your ex-employer to stuff his job isn't all that likely to help.'

'It's a bastard, innit? They're always out to screw the working man!' Chrome leather jacket, torn jeans, hair like an unmade bed, and sounding off like a mixture of Arthur Scargill and John Stuart Mill. I was almost charmed.

'Of course,' I said, striving for the right minimal-interest note, 'we might run to a tenner from the informant's fund, if you do know anything worthwhile.'

'A tenner? I'm not crazy; we're talking major crime!'

'That's what I said the time you nicked off school and started a fire in a house, less than twelve months ago.'

'I was just a kid then. Anyway, that poultry unit's worth thousands of pounds.'

They never cease to amaze you, however often they come. What the hell did he think a detached, five bedroom des. res., three bathrooms, two *en suite*, was worth? Fortunately, a born incompetent, he'd only managed a spot of smoke damage to one room downstairs. The Fire Brigade, axes, water, trailing hoses and big boots on expensive carpets, had done a far better job than Kev.

He lapsed into silence. Discouraged, I thought.

'Well,' I said, 'maybe a bit more, once we've checked. But this isn't the National Lottery, son.'

Very true, but the insurers might be persuaded to distribute largesse to a genuine informant, once we'd got a conviction. No need, however, to excite the little toe-rag unduly at this early stage.

'Tell me,' I said, 'where have you been all afternoon?'

'Coming back from Aylfleet on the bus.'

'What time did Mr Rodway let you go?'

'Around twelve.'

'And what time was the bus?'

'Quarter past two.'

'What did you do before that?'

'Had a bite to eat; looked around the town. What is all this?'

I smiled quietly; Kevin could hardly have been involved in the great frozen chicken mystery, not unless he'd mastered the art of being in two places at once. But questions get asked, not answered, around here.

'Still got the motorbike?' I remembered seeing it, months before, wheelless, and propped up in his front yard at home.

'Yeah, but they don't let you ride it around in Aylfleet nick.'

'What colour is it?'

'Same as last time; blue.'

'Not your favourite colour; not like a fire engine, huh?' No need to pull them up for cheek; thick or not, they still recognise a good old-fashioned threat.

'Look, Mr Graham . . .' That was better. 'It was nothing to do with me. My probation officer says—'

'OK. Who do you reckon did it, then?'

'Dunno for sure, mind you, but I think it was that New Age lot. The men, anyway. Maybe the women themselves; more likely the men, though. It's not a woman's sorta job.'

Convoluted, even for him. But I'd no intention of embarking on a seminar covering gender as a determining factor in the psychology of crime. Besides, I'd no idea what he was on about. What New Age lot?

'They only gave 'em two ninety-two an hour.'

'Well, that explains everything. Thanks, Kevin; makes my job so much easier, does that.'

'Sorry; but it was slave labour, wannit? They had these gals scrubbing out stinking sheds at two ninety-two an hour. Would you scrub chicken shit for two—'

'It's not much,' I admitted. Personally, I couldn't imagine doing anything – well, practically anything – for two pounds ninety-two an hour.

'Not much? Have you been inside one of them sheds after they've cleared the poultry out? Poison gas, mate. Poison gas!'

Interested, yes; but I was definitely not his mate. He took my point and hurried on. 'They put them birds in cages, about five or six to a cage at eighteen weeks. Then they leave 'em to lay; cages stacked six deep with automatic feeding, and eggs and gunge removed by conveyor. Get the picture? Right?'

'I have heard.' Kevin the crusader; fancy that.

'Well, once the gang comes over and pulls out the birds, they get women to clean it out ready for the next lot.'

'Or in this case,' I said wisely, 'they cleaned up ready to change from battery to perchery production.'

'Yeah, well, that's probably worse, if you ask me.'

'Stick to the point, Kevin. This isn't the RSPCA.'

'OK; they employ these women on a really shitten job at next to nothing. There were rows about the rates and the conditions. They wanted proper toilets and a place to wash; then the old bastard strung 'em along and waited until they'd nearly finished before he sacked 'em 'cos they were casuals, and he got somebody else to finish the job. Oh yeah, and they had trouble collecting their money as well.'

I could see him now: General Secretary of the TUC.

'You seem to have missed your vocation, old son.'

'Eh?'

'Vocation, Kevin. It means—'

'I know what vocation means; I've got A-levels, mister.'

Memory stirred; not such a thicko, and serve me right. He'd been suspended from school during his final term. Only allowed in to take his exams. *Two* cases of arson; one at his former school. And now he was an ex-shoveller of chicken turds; a bit of a waste to say the least.

On the other hand . . . Resentment, followed by revenge. New Agers; pseudo indignation; we could still be on the right track.

'Sorry, Kevin.'

'Huh!' And it still served me right. An expression of disgust directed at patronising DCIs. Not exactly difficult to unscramble the thinking, either. Somehow, Daisy Dew had managed to recruit a female cleaning crew at next to nothing an hour. New Age travellers had feelings, followed causes. Animal rights?

'These New Agers; got any names?'

'First names, that's all. Lisa, Donna, Peggy; I forget the rest.'

'Never mind, they'll have wages records at Lowbarrack, eh?'

'They'll have addresses, too.' The grin was back. 'Buckingham Palace and the Houses of Parliament, most like. They're probably down in the books as self-employed poultry consultants, if they're down at all. Funny,' he added, 'I didn't have you down as daft.'

'Tax fiddle?'

'Tax fiddle, National Insurance fiddle; you play the tune, Mr Graham, and that mean old bugger'll hum along.'

'Do you know where these people live?'

'Not sure; not exactly, anyway. I think they're wintering somewhere along the estuary, Aylfleet way.'

Wintering was right; if they were somewhere down by the estuary at this time of year they might as well be in Siberia. I had a vision of broken-down buses, a few vans, tents perhaps; dirty bundled-up people; piles of rubbish; kids coughing and spluttering, and everybody with a streaming nose.

31

'Kevin,' I said, 'this is much against my better judgment. And I'll get it back, one way or another, if you're stringing me along.' He examined the five-pound note without enthusiasm.

'What about the ten?'

'That, and a bit more if you're right.'

'A *lot* more; you just won't believe—'

The phone rang; saved by the bell. 'Yes,' I said impatiently, 'so you said. Excuse me.'

'This,' rasped a familiar voice, 'is Sir Jeremy Blatt.' The man must be welded to a handset with a megaphone attached. Kevin sat back and winked.

'Good afternoon, sir.' Polite, but flat. This time, at least, it was still in working hours. 'I had hoped to meet you earlier.'

'I was doing your bloody job for you, instead.' Hectoring yet again. 'D'you know where I am now?'

'No.' I confined myself to one or two unspoken hopes.

'I am on my mobile, next to a blasted *sewage farm*! And I've found the stolen lorry myself. What do you think of that?'

'I'm pleased, sir. Is the load intact?'

A few seconds of silence. Strength, I gathered, was being mustered at the other end of the line. 'Oh, yes; yes, you could say that all right. Half of it's been tipped into a slurry pit, and the other half's covered with green paint. *Get your arse over here and see for yourself!*'

A click, a crackle, and I was left with a purring handset once again. The almost inevitable end, I realised, to any conversation with Sir Jeremy Blatt.

Kevin gave me a look of studied calm, sucking air through the gap in his teeth. He must have heard both ends of the conversation, and to do him credit he remained totally unimpressed.

I glared back, three priorities in mind. Get rid of him, pronto; find his former employer's mobile number, and ring the silly old sod back; what sewage farm, and precisely where?

'Makes a lovely lot of noise, does Uncle Jerry,' observed my visitor appreciatively. 'If I can teach him not to piss on the furniture, would you like to take 'im 'ome as a pet?'

5

I stood in front of the wardrobe mirror and tied my new bow tie. The prelude, I suppose, to one of life's little milestones, an event; but to tell the truth I was not altogether looking forward to this.

Behind me I could see Angie reflected in the glass; nose in the air, doing her best to look snooty and remote.

'May I,' she said, 'assist you with your waistcoat, milord?'

I gave her a sharp, disdainful, hopefully aristocratic glance. 'Yes, Graham, you may; but please try to call a mess vest by its proper name in future.'

Abandoning her role as valet to the nobility, she applied her knuckles to the small of my back; it hurt.

'This monkey suit cost us two hundred and sixty notes, my lad,' she muttered grimly, 'so don't push your luck.'

I shrugged my way into the slate-blue mess vest and silk-faced jacket, the epaulettes embroidered with three Bath stars and the silver Force blazon shining on the lapels. I admired the well-fitting mess overalls with their blatant double stripe. Somebody had sent us up-market; turned us into cavalry rather than infantry with one masterstroke of design. Sadly, perhaps, he'd decided against the spurs.

I preened: mess dress, chief inspectors for the use of. Whoever would have thought it? Not so long ago I would have worn my ageing dinner jacket, looked down my nose at the constabulary peacocks, and sneered.

Angie peered maliciously at my shoulders. 'Those Bath stars are upside down,' she said.

Discomforted, I craned and sidled sideways for a better look; her father had been an army officer at some stage, so she should know. I could

33

hardly tell, but there appeared to be one almost indistinguishable blob at the top; two below. They were OK.

'Liar!'

'Amazing what the lower classes get to find out these days,' she smirked. 'But then again, I suppose you're still wearing your underpants instead of your shirt tails on top.'

'You pinched that from the *Sunday Telegraph*,' I said accusingly, clocking the source straight away. 'Snobbery with violence.'

She grinned. 'I don't want you to shame me, what with the guest of honour being a knight and all.'

There it was in a nutshell; either the Mess Committee was going crackers, or somebody was after a retirement job. A convivial night out; a band, dinner, port and cigars. All enhanced, or more probably blighted, depending on your point of view, by the presence of Sir Jeremy Blatt.

Personally, I'd just have soon gone drinking with Gerry Adams as Jerry Blatt. Well, no, not exactly, but it was a close run thing. The Chief Chicken and I had not entirely hit it off.

He had, I admit, some cause for complaint. He was entitled to express a degree of disappointment, even disapproval, perhaps. Stolen company lorry driven through sewage farm fence, a few dozen cases of chicken unloaded and dropped in the poo, and the rest, together with the inside walls of his vehicle, smeared with a particularly nauseous shade of green paint. I wouldn't have fancied my Sunday dinner much either, once the packaging had been garnished with several gallons of sewage or decorated in a carefully chosen shade of vomit green.

Unfortunate, too, that he'd discovered the disaster himself. Where were the Traffic boys? Why couldn't the coppers find something as big as a brightly painted refrigerated truck? Something I'd wanted to know myself. Dusk on a freezing February afternoon, and I bet most of 'em had sloped off for a comforting cup of tea. Not that I'd have said anything of the sort to bawling, shouting, raving Jerry Blatt.

We'd done our best; a total negative at the sewage farm. No staff around at the time. Two distinct sets of tyre impressions in the mud at the side of the country lane; a motorbike and some sort of medium-sized van.

Derek Rodway's team had visited the travellers' camp and conducted a slightly illegal search. Denials of involvement; lots of old vans, but no paint and negative results. The same results from Paula: Pollard had proclaimed his innocence for hours on end. He'd spent an unhappy evening with her, had still been making his witness statement at half past ten that night.

Since then, two separate divisional CIDs had persecuted every likely suspect in sight: employees, ex-employees, animal libbers and animal rights activists, *et al*. Nothing; nobody knew a thing, and Jeremy must have spent a fortune bawling out policemen down the phone. The Chief, the Assistant Chief (Operations), Peter Fairfield, the head of CID, Teddy, Thea, me . . . We all knew about eggs, we all knew about chickens and now we all hated his guts.

Our Mess Night, adorned by Jeremy, was unlikely to live in song and story as a great night out. Never mind, hints had been dropped: it would be *appreciated* if the remote rural bumpkins, Baily, Rodway and Graham, would attend, smile bravely in the face of adversity and applaud the after-dinner performance of our honoured guest.

Angie eyed me critically, 'And when are wives going to be allowed to participate in all this glory?' she asked.

No way round it; I hesitated, nevertheless. 'Ladies Night; the, er, summer ball.'

I studiously avoided her eye; painful memories, no doubt. Almost two years now; the annual Ladies Night in my former force. The glitter, the excitement, Robert Graham's flying fists. The night I'd decked her superintendent boyfriend and ended up getting legally separated, immediately prior to being ingloriously transferred.

After that we'd spent something like six months apart, and when we'd eventually come back together it was against all the odds. Now, despite all the current badinage and fun, we both found ourselves carefully keeping off one or two patches of emotional grass: little Laura's exact paternity for one thing, Ladies Nights or summer balls for another.

Neither of us said much while I pocketed handkerchief, wallet, keys and change. Not a huge shadow lying between us, I hoped, but it was there all the same. I tried giving myself the usual mental kick; why should a few words matter? I never felt like that about Laura herself; never wished her unborn. All the same, I could feel Angie's eyes on the back of my neck when I went into the baby's room to say goodnight.

Was she wondering? About me playing the perfect father; putting on a bit of a show? You can be as well intentioned, as loving and sentimental as you like, but you find it never absolutely unscrambles; not for either of you, deep inside your heads. It hadn't been a mistake, patching it up, but there's no such thing as invisible mending. There are occasions when you can rub your hand over the damaged part of your life and feel the rough edges of the darn.

She grabbed me fiercely when the taxi came, Teddy Baring and Paula waving to her from the back.

'Now you just behave yourself,' she said. The glitter of Paula's engagement ring was a guarantee in one direction, but it did occur to me to wonder exactly what else she had in mind.

We joined the line-up and shook the hand of Dorothea Spinks, who, with a very new, faintly pink male inspector in tow as her Vice, was President of the Mess for the evening. Bosomy, in a slate-blue brocade evening gown, and wearing the presidential jewel, she looked like a substantial warship with a smallish tug in attendance. No sign yet of the Chief Chicken and the guests of the honoured guest.

Teddy, Paula, Derek Rodway and I formed a tight little Aylfleet – Eddathorpe coterie at the bar, gossiped, and waited on events while the room gradually filled. Mess dress, mostly: unlike the army, where even ancient generals content themselves with dinner jackets, retired policemen tend to cling to their fine feathers and their badges of rank. The occasional discreet letter 'R' for retired on a shoulder strap was the only evidence a predatory traffic officer would find, should he be unfortunate enough to breathalyse an old fogey instead of the genuine article, later on. I can never work out whether this is evidence of snobbery, a misplaced enthusiasm for the job, or a laudable ambition to get their money's worth once they've bought the kit.

Paula fixed a cold and sardonic eye on the eagerly jostling group surrounding the chairman of the Police Committee and two of our three Assistant Chiefs. The Chief Constable and the Operations ACC had apparently decided to deny themselves the pleasure of an evening with Sir Jeremy, but the young and ambitious, with a leavening of the old-and-still-hopeful, were practically slopping their drinks in their eagerness to impress the rest. It looked a bit like a mixture between a lesson in etiquette at the court of King Arthur, and a brisk bargaining session in a North African souk.

'Interesting,' Paula said.

'Your first time here?' Derek Rodway gave her a lopsided grin.

36

''Course it is; you've not been promoted long. The cattle market: you'll get used to it in due course.'

Impassively, Teddy sucked gently at his tomato and Worcester sauce. He let his cold, grey, slightly protrudent eyes rest on Rodway for a moment. Hard to tell whether he disapproved of the sentiment, or whether he was simply deploying a spot of senior officer's subtlety and tact. A message to the troops: shut up, if you're overheard you won't do yourself any good.

A bit of a stir at the door: the ceremonial arrival of Sir Jeremy Blatt, accompanied by his dose of moral support, and all three dressed in white tuxedos, red ties and matching cummerbunds.

'Taraaa!' said Paula.

'It's a flock of white Wyandottes,' enunciated Teddy clearly to grins and chuckles in the immediate vicinity of the bar. His face didn't even twitch; another message. Don't do as I do, only do as I say; I'm past caring about promotion myself. Teddy, I gathered, was a snob.

I had, however, to admit it: the white dinner jackets were a mistake, notably in the case of Jeremy Blatt. Short and squat with bushy white eyebrows, his jacket generously cut for length as well as breadth, he bore a passing resemblance to a red-and-white pool ball with legs. Just one thing, bless him; he made me feel a lot better about my own fancy dress.

Dutifully, Thea led her charges over to the ruck and introduced Blatt and his companions to the Assistant Chiefs. There was a brief orgy of flesh-pressing, the exchange of amiabilities, then, to my horror, having left Jeremy in the hands of the top-tablers, she advanced on us with the lesser fry.

'This,' she announced, 'is Superintendent Baring; Teddy, meet David Lang and Simon Weatherby, two of Sir Jeremy's managers. I'll leave you to introduce our colleagues; you're all seated together tonight.'

'*General* manager, Eggs,' muttered Lang.

'*Director*, Frozen Products,' said Weatherby aggressively. Frozen was right; I knew him. We'd already had more than one uncomfortable professional chat on the subjects of lorry-lifting followed by criminal damage: he'd taken both as a personal affront.

Thea smiled at Teddy and flapped one vague hand in the direction of the small queue developing at the door during her absence. 'Excuse me,' she said, 'I'm sure you'll have a lot in common,' and retreated.

A quick introduction to Teddy; the minions of Blatt quickly foisted on a personal adversary and a smart departure. It was, I immediately realised, one of Thea's better-organised dirty tricks.

'Should be a good night,' offered Lang, shaking hands. Teddy did the honours; from the expression on his face he was probably already plotting his counter-measures against Dorothea Spinks.

'Have you caught those bastards yet?' Weatherby, oblivious to the social niceties, barely glanced at Derek Rodway and Paula, and gave me the direct benefit of his twenty-four-carat scowl.

'We're working on it.'

'Not hard enough!' He sniffed. Another short, broad-shouldered man, twenty years younger than the Chief Chicken, still working on the paunch, and obviously determined to follow in the footsteps of his suave, socially superior boss.

Teddy stepped in with the offer of drinks. Just as well; short of violence I couldn't for the life of me think of an adequate reply. Perhaps Angie was psychic; warning me about good behaviour well in advance.

The conversation stalled while Teddy bought the drinks and handed them round with the air of a Borgia expecting instantaneous good news. Oblivious to our thoughts and hopes, Weatherby downed his double Scotch in one. Paula silently sipped, Teddy looked down his nose. Only Derek Rodway and David Lang looked happy, seemed prepared to let the good times roll, while on the other side of the room, I could see Sir Jeremy wrapping himself around a spectacular series of brandies with the merest promise of ginger, at constabulary expense.

The music started; uneasily, we lesser fry joined the shuffling queue from anteroom to mess. The canteen had been transformed into a suitable vehicle for gracious living. The tables, set with constabulary-crested mats, shone with polish; the cutlery gleamed, flowers, and gifts of silver from retiring officers graced the tables. Lots of ice buckets, I was pleased to see, presaged adequate supplies of anaesthetic to dull the virtual certainty of after-dinner pain.

The folding doors to the snooker room had been thrown back and the band, consisting of policemen, special constables, and, it was rumoured, anybody else they could grab who didn't actually have previous convictions, could be seen tootling away at the 'Roast Beef of Old England', next door.

Teddy, the forward thinker, was the only one of us who'd bothered looking at a seating plan in advance. He led us unhesitatingly towards a table set for ten. Unfortunately, in our enforced role as friends of Sir Jeremy's friends, we found ourselves with an unobstructed, even intimate, view of the table reserved for the President, the High Command and the Chief Guest. Definitely in the front line.

'I think,' whispered Paula, amidst a flurry of introductions to the other people on our table, 'his employees have been put here on purpose – he wants to make sure they laugh at his jokes and clap.'

'Correction,' said Derek Rodway softly. 'Thea's done it on purpose to show how much she likes and admires your boss!'

'Me?' I have this tendency towards unjustified egotism from time to time.

He shook his head, eyes flickering towards Superintendent Edward Baring, busy with Weatherby, Lang, two strange superintendents and their businessman guests. Conscience struck; time to help him out. No reason to leave him isolated, doing all the hard work as an officer and a gent.

'Ladies and gentlemen,' piped the baby inspector with the Vice-President's badge, 'please be upstanding to greet your President and distinguished guests!'

We already were; standing that is, but he meant well. The band struck up again, and the assembly awarded the advancing procession a slow, rhythmic clap. A traditional greeting, apparently. Mean, if you ask me, giving the cabaret the bird even before it's had a chance to show you how well it can perform.

'Heard about you,' whispered one of the strange superintendents as the procession advanced. 'You'll enjoy this; your best friend's here tonight!'

'My best friend?'

'Ron Hacker. Didn't you know?' He nodded in the direction of the immaculately dressed elder statesman of the constabulary advancing towards us immediately behind Thea and her chief guest. Grey hair sweeping back in wings on either side of his brow; smooth, well-fed face; clipped military moustache. The face that had launched a thousand professional disasters; Detective Superintendent Ronald Hacker (retired). A man I'd hoped never to set eyes on again.

'Ruddy Silver,' I muttered to nobody in particular, employing the nickname he'd acquired throughout the Force. 'My cup definitely runneth over. What a night!'

Teddy, the usual source of biblical quotations, looked at me sharply. He obviously suspected me of taking the mick; that was before he followed the direction of my gaze.

'Good heavens,' he said mildly. An exercise in Christian forbearance, if ever I heard one. Teddy and Ron Hacker went back a long way; all the way back to an occasion when, among thirty other duff suspects in a murder enquiry, Hacker had arrested Teddy's son. Charity was certainly being exercised on an impressive, not to say superhuman, scale.

Lang, tall, slightly stooping, a gloomy man with spaniel-brown eyes, sensed a scandal, and leaned across the table towards me. 'Why Silver?' he queried. 'He's joining our firm.'

'Oh, just a nickname,' I said airily. 'You know policemen: anything for a bit of fun.'

'Dear God.' Derek Rodway, as usual, the epitome of tact. He was about to say more, but Teddy awarded him the Glare; for blasphemy, I think. Paula, practical as ever, and following the old coppers' code – if we don't hang together, we'll all hang separately – dug Derek surreptitiously in the ribs. Not the sort of thing to share with outsiders; he promptly shut up.

Ron Hacker, back in the mists of time, had been a greedy, selfish, tuft-hunting DC, nicknamed the Lone Ranger by some disgruntled plod. Later, when his talents became more widely appreciated, somebody else had renamed him Silver; they'd discovered that his intelligence and abilities were more in line with the masked crime-fighter's horse. Not something to be bandied about among civvies; an in-joke with a meaning strictly confined to the members of the club.

The band stopped playing; silence fell. I was saved from any further comment by the President intoning grace, but as soon as the usual shuffling of feet and scraping of chairs was safely over, Lang returned to the attack.

'What's this ex-policeman like?' he asked.

'What's he going to do at Dairy Dew?' I countered.

'Head of security.'

Derek Rodway opened his mouth, but Teddy was in there like a flash. 'He should get along with Sir Jeremy extremely well.' Not a flicker of an eyelash; not a twitch of the lips. You have to hand it to our superintendent; at least three police officers stared at him in rapt admiration. You can see exactly why Teddy got on.

The smoked salmon and Muscadet, followed by beef Wellington and lots of Côte du Roussillon, went down very well. Even Weatherby eased off, although he did tend to dwell on burning hen-coops and paint-sprayed vans.

'Insufficient evidence,' he said abruptly through a mouthful of potato. 'Is that it?'

I continued eating, contenting myself with a vague, interrogative, 'Hm?'

'Insufficient evidence to lock that little bastard away for a couple of years. Sir Jeremy should never have employed him in the first place: soft.'

'Oh, come on,' Lang chipped in from across the table, 'blood's thicker than water, you know.'

'We are,' I said, surprised into taking part in the conversation, 'talking about Kevin Cooke?'

'Who else?' Weatherby snapped impatiently, giving me the sort of look he reserved for the retarded child.

'So, what's all this blood being thicker than water bit?'

'Kevin Cooke is Sir Jeremy's first wife's nephew,' said Lang helpfully. 'Didn't you know?'

'Not exactly Sherlock Holmes, are you?' Weatherby drained two-thirds of a glass of red wine and promptly reached for the bottle for a refill.

'Oh, Uncle Jerry, you mean? Of course I knew.' I'd known all right; Kevin himself had told me, but I had not believed. I thought Kevin had been deploying his version of irony, using 'Uncle Jerry' in a spirit similar to the way I sometimes called Joe, my homicidal Lakeland terrier, 'Uncle Joe', Stalin for short.

'He's only a nephew by marriage, then? Not a blood relation.' Not too bad for a spur-of-the-moment recovery; anything to put Simon Weatherby down.

A few yards away his boss was busy disposing of another bottle of red wine with even greater efficiency and speed. Thea was staring at him, trying desperately to keep some sort of conversation going, and, from the expression on her face, obviously wishing she was elsewhere. On his other side, one of the ACCs was in earnest conversation with Ronald Hacker, his back half turned to the principal guest. Things, I decided, were getting pretty desperate all round.

'Jane Peters,' said Lang, with the air of Lyon King-of-arms explaining

41

a tricky genealogical point, 'married Bernard Cooke; Sylvia Peters used to be married to Jeremy Blatt.'

'Pair of tarts,' said Weatherby loudly, drawing several sets of curious eyes from the tables around. 'Still, all's well that ends well; he's got a new one now.'

'New tart?' murmured Lang, grinning subversively. That Roussillon was pretty potent stuff.

'New wife,' hissed Weatherby sibilantly, switching from foghorn to steam valve. As an attempt at discretion, it did not succeed. Teddy glanced despairingly at Paula: he looked as though he'd swallowed a frog. Derek Rodway was the only one of us to look entirely happy; they were apparently singing his song.

'Got a son, hasn't he?' he asked. 'You know, with his ex?'

'That depends,' said Lang, and winked. 'Personally, I'd have found meself another milkman, long before.'

'One son.' The Blatt loyalist sounded indignant. 'Jeremy junior; he's buggered off. A bit of a bad lot.'

'Blood will out!' David Lang, I suspected, could soon be looking for another job. 'The Peters woman, I mean.' There are occasions when explanations only make matters worse.

Derek looked thoroughly pleased with himself; I thought I could see why. Kevin Cooke, the disgruntled nephew, was about to get a second interrogatory whirl. And what about the dissident son? Oh, Absalom! as Teddy might say.

I took a slurp or two myself, chatted with Paula, and thought about Kev. I recalled arresting him last time at the terrace house near the site of the old Eddathorpe gas-works. I remembered his mum; the attitude of the neighbours; the succession of men. Not the kind of family that gets tapped upon the shoulder with a sword by HM; belted with broken bottles in dark alleys, more like.

The meal ended; the port circulated in the proper direction, we drank the Loyal Toast. Some made a dash for the loo and others lit cigars. Derek and I both stumped up for a couple of rounds of drinks: if you can't love 'em, get 'em sozzled, that was the general idea.

Eventually, with a faint but noticeable lack of enthusiasm, Thea rose to her feet. Catching her mood, I conducted a quick straw poll of the top table. The two ACCs looked apprehensive; the chairman of the Police Committee was studying his fingernails; only Ronald Hacker, Esquire, looked totally at ease. He, at least, after a spot of successful toadying, had secured a new job.

Even to the uncritical eye, our prominent industrialist, after-dinner speaker and raconteur looked pretty smashed. After the shortest of short introductions, our distinguished guest made a gallant effort and struggled, red-faced and beaming, to his feet.

Co-operation, he informed us indistinctly, was the name of the game. Co-operation between the wealth-producers, like himself, and the public shector. We were part of the public shector, did we know that? We helped to consume the wealth he produched, but not to worry, because we did a very good job. Sometimes.

No, sorry; mostly, that is. Not all the time. He was a tolerant, not to say phi-philosophical man, and he was prepared to be flexible. He did not expect miracles; he was sure the good ole public felt that way about it, too. Flexibility should also be the w-watchword among the guardians of law and order, but they had to produche results. Industry, the public at large, he himchelf, demanded reschults . . .

And that's where I switched off, until, that is, he started on the homosexual jokes. The one about the gorilla, the snake and the duck, closely followed by the one about the abbot who, regrettably, dishcovered that his entire community of monks was queer.

Personally, being a crude, unregenerate copper, I don't really care about political correctness all that much. I hardly ever remember 'em, but I'm not even especially against gay jokes. OK, I admit it: his tales were ancient, his diction was blurred, he swayed, he leered. There was, however, a specialist pleasure to be derived from watching the Young Turks from the Personnel Department getting more and more embarrassed as he went along.

Equal opportunity policies crashed around their ears; industrial tribunals loomed, and threatening glares winged their way towards any lower-ranking bigots who laughed. Fascinated, I watched one or two senior administrators sliding lower and lower in their seats, and looking around anxiously to see if anybody had been stupid enough to invite a member of the press.

'Did you hear the one' – Jeremy took another fortifying gulp of brandy and ginger ale, thoughtfully supplied by his ex-constabulary friend – 'about the two lesbians sitting in the bath? "Where's the soap?" says one. "Yes," replies the other, "I've noticed that myself." Haw! Haw!'

Teddy Baring looked puzzled. Simon Weatherby guffawed loudly and patted him on the back. 'Y'know,' he said helpfully, '*wears the soap*. W-E-A-R-S, as in erodes, geddit?'

'Thank you.' For once, Teddy was apparently bereft of anything else to say.

By this time, Thea, scarlet, presidential jewel swinging across her substantial bosom, was half out of her seat, struggling to support the bulk of our honoured guest. Even Hacker, purveyor of spirits to the gentry, looked uneasy. Possibly, just possibly, he'd been over-generous with his supplies.

I was an eye-witness; I was watching; I was there. It was only later that rumour added malicious lustre to the tale. Thea did not, I am absolutely certain, drag him down. He collapsed into his seat entirely of his own accord. Nor did he scream with pain as he fell; there was no question of our lady superintendent applying a hammerlock to his left arm.

It was on the whole, however, value for money. Memorable, even. A better-than-expected night in the senior officers' mess.

6

———◆———

'It's a double whammy,' said George. I sighed gently down the phone; he has a tendency to say these things from time to time. I think he does it to preserve his illusions; if he's still in touch with the language, he's still young.

'Fascinating; go on.'

'His wife rang first: her husband hasn't been home all night. Now they've called in a three nines from the factory. The office has been trashed and there's blood on the floor.'

I grimaced over the top of the handset to Angela. 'Trouble,' I muttered, covering the mouthpiece. 'I've got to go. Jeremy Blatt's gone missing and his offices have been screwed.'

'An extra ten minutes won't matter,' she said calmly. 'You're not entirely at their beck and call; finish your bacon and drink your tea.' She stared at me challengingly; *Never mind the police force; if I get up just after seven o'clock to cook breakfast, the least you can do is sit still and eat it, my lad!*

'OK.' A useful remark, delivered simultaneously to Angela and to George. 'What have we done so far?'

'Paula's gone straight to the factory with Pat Goodall; Derek Rodway's on his way to see Mrs . . . Lady Blatt, and I,' he added a trifle bitterly, 'have been left to hold the fort.'

It figured. Trippe Hall, Blatt residence and Victorian monstrosity, was well and truly in Aylfleet Division; the Daisy Dew factory was just inside the boundaries of Eddathorpe, and set in the flat, desolate countryside on the far side of the Retton Road. And Detective Constable Pat Goodall was obviously Retton Section CID's early morning man.

The location of the factory, I thought gloomily, was just our luck. The way the divisional boundaries twisted and turned, another three-quarters of a mile and the burglary, or whatever it was, would have been somebody else's problem. Heigh-ho! Another day, another dollar. Or, putting it in its proper police context, another dawn, another load of grief.

'Who discovered all this?' I asked.

'At the factory? A man called Weatherby; in charge of frozen food, or something. He usually turns up early anyway, and when Lady Blatt rang to tell him she was worried about her husband being out all night, he volunteered to take a look.

'No sign of Blatt, but when he unlocked the offices he discovered the damage and dialled three nines. He says he's waiting for you.'

'In that case,' I said vengefully, 'he's going to have a long wait!'

I not only ate the bacon, I demolished the tomatoes, and the fried bread; the chef looked moderately pleased. I made the usual donation of bacon fat, rind and over-crisp crusts to Joe, the starving, miserable, unwalked animal lurking beneath the breakfast table. There are Hollywood actors earning millions whose performances pale beside what a Lakeland terrier can do for the price of a snack.

He went crazy when I collected my car keys. Rank definitely has its privileges; I occasionally take him around with me, a hangover from our enforced bachelor days when I didn't like leaving him alone for eight or ten hours at a time. But not today; it hardly sounded like a suitable occasion for a visit by the eccentric chief inspector, accompanied by his bloody-minded dog. Angie held him under one arm while quivering, indignant, swearing under his breath, he watched me depart.

I'd never visited the main Daisy Dew building before. Call me a coward if you like, but I prefer not to dwell on the minutiae by which I achieve my Sunday lunch. I'm sure it's all very clinical and hygienic, but the word 'factory' when applied to premises largely devoted to the mass execution of poultry might put me off my grub. I am an omnivore; I intend to stay that way, so the less I know about the killing, scalding, plucking, dressing and freezing end of the Blatt operation, the better.

The premises stood alone, set back from the road and surrounded by a high wire fence. Access was by a counter-weighted barrier guarded by a brick-and-glass hut bearing a big red and white sign, NO UNAUTHORISED ENTRY. ALL VISITORS REPORT HERE.

The factory itself, with a two-storey brick office block partly concealing two grey, sectional structures behind, was metal-windowed, bleak. The whole effect was shabby, leaning towards the sinister; like something set up in the middle of nowhere for unguessable purposes by the Ministry of Defence.

I joined a short queue of vehicles, elderly cars mostly, with the occasional motorcycle, and a gaggle of pedal cyclists waiting patiently at the gate. Eventually, the security man, elderly, uniformed, the giveaway blue-and-white medal ribbon on his tunic, got me to sign a numbered carbonated strip, tore off the top copy, and slid it into a plastic identity label which I clipped to my breast pocket. Authorised visitors were tagged; employees wore plastic cards with photographs dangling from their lapels.

'Security seems to be tight.'

He gave me a crooked, knowing grin. 'Seems,' he said, 'is exactly right. It's amazing what these buggers can get away with round here.'

'Lots of leakages?'

The crooked grin was supplemented by a vestigial wink. 'Let's put it this way, sir; we've got a random search policy for employees' cars, but I reckon this lot practically live on frozen chicken and packets of veg.'

'Ah, well.' I prepared to move off. 'Nice to meet an ex-member of the cloth.'

'Thank you, sir.' He drew himself up, pleased. Then, with a snap in his voice, 'If I wasn't drawing a decent pension, I couldn't afford to be doing this tuppence-ha'penny job!'

'That bad, eh?'

He shrugged. 'Not a lot of employment, is there? So the old bastard's got everybody by the balls. Still, you know what they say: pay peanuts and you get monkeys, an' that's a fact!'

All the way up the drive I reflected on the implications of Blatt's industrial relations policy as revealed to Teddy, and the trust and loyalty he so obviously inspired among his staff.

Clumsy, hurried, superficial; but trashed was right. Downstairs wasn't too bad; an emergency exit had been forced, leaving splinter marks on the edges of the double doors, and an overturned stationery trolley had been wedged into the gap. Three or four computer VDUs had been thrown on to the floor, and the plugs had been fitted into every single washbowl in the lavatories and the taps turned on, leaving many of the floor tiles curled, soggy, or completely adrift. The intruder or intruders, whoever they were, had also smashed the control box inside the lift, but it wasn't much of a hardship to climb two flights of stairs.

Up on the first floor the chairman's office had borne the brunt; somebody appeared to have taken a case-opener or something similar to Blatt's rosewood desk and the pretentious panelled walls. Two filing cabinets had been smashed open; a bank of small closed-circuit television screens had been reduced to a chaos of glass shards, distorted metal and wire, and the entire contents of the cleaner's cupboard had been sprayed, squirted or spilled all over the room.

Worst news last: a six-inch-diameter pool of coagulated blood occupied a prominent position beside Sir Jeremy Blatt's leather-covered executive chair. A strange, dark, sinister shining; a thin film of dust had already dulled it in parts. There were occasional spots and stains on the carpet towards the centre of the room. Nothing spectacular; nothing else.

'Big Brother,' said Pat Goodall callously, indicating the closed-circuit TV, 'is no longer watching you, boss.' For once, he kept his voice down; Simon Weatherby was mourning and moaning about the damage with Paula in the next room.

'Big Brother?'

'Blatt. He keeps an eye on the chain gang from here,' explained my uncrushed DC. 'Literally. If you want to watch chickens being hooked to an endless chain and electrocuted, or women chopping heads off and ripping out their guts, then this was definitely your place.

'Or,' he added, 'if you wanted to see innocent carrots getting the mechanical chop, you could switch over to the vegetable unit across the yard.'

Detective Constable Goodall, humanitarian; an entirely unexpected side to the character of my youngest, brashest DC. Either that, or he was harbouring a grudge. Somewhere, somehow, I figured, the local boy had probably already had some kind of run-in with the absent Jeremy Blatt.

'Which screen,' I said flatly, making an unwarranted assumption straight away, 'shows me who got belted over the head in here, and what happened to him after that?'

'Sorry, boss.' He didn't sound it. 'Just putting you in the picture, that's all.' Inadvertent, that one, from the expression on his face. But with previous experience of the wit and wisdom of Patrick Goodall, I couldn't be absolutely sure.

Weatherby, accompanied by Paula, entered the room. Another one, from the look of him, with a very bad dose of the early morning blues. He grunted something that might have been a greeting. I knew exactly how he felt.

'You were here first this morning, I understand?'

'That's right. Came a bit early. I'd already heard he was missing; had a phone call from Lady Blatt. Saw the damage, then I panicked a bit; didn't see the blood at first.'

'No cleaners at this hour of the day?'

'Not in the mornings. They do the offices after five at night.'

'Anything missing, Mr Weatherby?'

'Not as far as we can tell.'

'Did anybody see Sir Jeremy here in his office during the evening?'

'I checked with the gateman's records; they're supposed to keep a register of people going in and out. They don't always bother with management, I'm afraid, so I've just phoned the evening security man at home. He tells me that Sir Jeremy came back in at around nine-twenty p.m. The night man didn't see him, and there's no record of him going out.'

'What about his chauffeur and the Rolls-Royce?'

'He drives himself. He uses his Discovery out of office hours; it's still in the carpark outside.'

'Is there an internal security patrol at night?'

'No. They're supposed to stay on the gate.'

'Anybody on the premises at all?'

Weatherby shrugged. 'Twilight shift in the factory until ten o'clock. Management are in and out from time to time, but the office staff go home at five; we don't have that privilege, of course.' He smiled thinly, the responsibilities of high office. My heart bled.

'What time do people start to arrive in the mornings?'

'Long-distance deliveries can start any time after five a.m. Depends.'

'And there's always a man on the gate?'

'Supposedly.' He sounded doubtful. 'Twenty-four hours a day. Two in daytime, one in the evenings and one at night.'

An overnight static guard: he must be bored out of his skull. Familiar with the ways of glorified night-watchmen, I wondered how many hours of paid sleep he'd accumulated overnight.

'What time does the factory start up?'

'Eight o'clock.'

'Damn!' It was five minutes past. Faintly, I could hear the clang and clatter of some sort of conveyor on the move. A factory full of people, and we'd got a search on our hands.

'What about the offices?'

'Nine o'clock, but Jack Causley, the manager's, here already. No vandalism in his office; it was locked.'

I turned; in the doorway a strange, Martian-like figure lurked. The Compleat Cyclist from helmet to skin-tight Lycra suit in black and yellow. It smiled nervously; tall, thin, middle-aged, a subservient kind of wasp.

Weatherby stared briefly, scarcely acknowledging the smile; apparently undecided between exasperation and polite contempt.

'Jack,' he said, 'enjoys the exercise; he usually cycles to work. Changes into a suit the moment he arrives,' he added pointedly. The apparition promptly withdrew.

I looked at Paula; her division, her baby now. 'The whole office block will remain closed,' she said firmly. 'I'll go and have a word with Mr Causley.' The mind boggled; I sincerely hoped she was going to give him time to get changed.

'Sorry, but that's the way it is. I'm sending for our Scenes of Crime Department, and a forensic liaison officer. In the meantime, we'll need additional officers to conduct a proper search.

'Can you speak to your factory management and make sure that if anybody spots anything, er, unusual, they're instructed not to touch, and to report it straight away?'

All good, brisk, let's-get-on-with-it stuff, and without waiting for a reply, she left the room. Detective Inspector Paula; I suppressed a grin. The new broom, efficiently sweeping clean.

Simon Weatherby had lost his aggressive bounce; even to the casual observer he looked slightly green about the gills.

'You surely don't think . . .' he said.

The remaining police contingent looked from Weatherby to the sticky pool and back. He was taking naïvety, stupidity or a wilful refusal to face facts just a little bit too far.

'Lady Blatt,' I reminded him, 'phoned you. She must have been pretty worried to call you at that time of day.'

He didn't appear to react; he stared at us stolidly for a moment before the penny dropped.

'Yes,' he said. 'Right. If he's not at home and he's not booked out, he's got to be somewhere here . . .'

His voice trailed away and he took another tentative look at the blood. His logic was impeccable. Never one to mock the afflicted, however, I personally forbore to remind him of his former references to Sherlock Holmes. Momentarily, Pat looked as if he were going to supply one of his familiar *bons mots*, but having had enough for one morning, I awarded him the grade-two Glare, and stiffened him in his tracks.

'Yes, yes – well, no point in standing around, is there?' The Director (Frozen Products) made a beeline for the door.

Silent for once, uninstructed, our junior rank accompanied him from the room with the over-virtuous air of a yeoman warder escorting a candidate from the dungeon to the block. Over-optimistic on the evidence available so far, but on current performance, Simon Weatherby did not exactly impress.

'Oh, just one thing.' He was back, hovering by the door, a curious little smirk on his face.

'Yes?'

'I almost forgot. Hacker, is it, that friend of yours?' He'd obviously retained his talent for insult, disaster or not. 'He should be along to help you soon. He starts work today.'

No possible response but silence. In the background, even Patrick Goodall appeared to have lost his penchant for the snide remark. His mouth opened slowly, while his shoulders definitely drooped.

7

***

'But I had an appointment with him at nine!' He glared at me accusingly. It was all my fault. I glared right back at the brand-new suit, the blue silk handkerchief peeping coyly from his breast pocket above his security tag, and the tightly knotted Force tie set against his made-to-measure shirt. Ronald Hacker, the man we loved to hate, swept and garnished for the fray. It was like telling a juvenile delinquent that Santa Claus had fallen victim to the Mob.

'What are you going to do about it?' he said, oblivious to the members of the Scenes of Crime Department, the CID men, the forensic liaison officer, me, Paula, Pat and exactly half the strength of the Force Special Operations Unit searching the Daisy Dew premises, all busy beavering away.

'Perhaps we ought to send for a dog van,' hazarded Pat. It's amazing how cheeky they get when they're dealing with ex-senior officers, once they stop being scared.

Thick, but not that thick; Ronald Hacker blistered him with a single glance and Paula gave him a silent dose of her *Just you wait till later, sonny*. Quite right too; I'd already trotted a somewhat similar remark past Derek Rodway at the scene of the battery-house fire. It doesn't do to let the juniors steal your lines.

'We're searching the premises,' I said superfluously, 'and we've got a call out for an artic and the three vans. Detective Inspector Rodway is over at Trippe Hall talking to Sir Jeremy's wife.'

'What vans?' asked Hacker distantly, plainly wrapped up in thoughts of immediate unemployment. Not even started work, and somebody had borrowed his boss.

'They start early around here,' I explained. 'An articulated lorry was booked out at five forty-five this morning, and three delivery vans were on the road by half past six. We'll stop them and have 'em searched. Whatever happened, it doesn't look as if Sir Jeremy's still here.'

'But they're refrigerated. Surely, he won't be riding around in one of those?'

'Not by choice, Mr Hacker,' said Pat.

Nothing if not consistent, Ronald Hacker hung around and moaned. After that he gave the Scenes of Crime Department ten minutes of his undivided attention, and moaned some more. Then he went looking for the sergeant in charge of the search teams to give him the benefit of his professional experience, prior to embarking on an exhaustive tour of the premises, inside and out. Twenty minutes later he was back, flourishing a set of wire-cutters in one handkerchief-wrapped hand.

'I found these myself,' he said grandly, 'next to a hole in the perimeter fence, Sergeant. Get a grip!'

The Special Operations sergeant fixed him with a cold and jaundiced eye; Hacker and his ruddy handkerchief; he'd probably wiped off any latent prints.

'Thank you, sir,' he said, aiming for the maximum psychological damage. 'One of my lads had left them *in situ*, ready for packaging and subsequent examination by Scenes of Crime.'

Impervious to criticism, Silver simply stared; Latin was probably beyond his grasp.

By this time I'd had more than enough. I discovered the whereabouts of his shining, newly decorated office with its three executive telephones and the fancy intercom, and led him none too gently away. I didn't see him again for the rest of the morning, but he apparently spent his time making telephone calls to Force Headquarters and making life miserable over the intercom for the men in the security hut.

Personally, I too had plenty to be miserable about. The forensic man, ably assisted by a civilian from Scenes of Crime, had taken a sample of blood. Among it, he'd found what appeared to be tiny slivers of bone, skin and the occasional human hair. If the Daisy Dew chairman had been clobbered, I was prepared to bet that by this time he wasn't feeling very well.

That wasn't all; apart from the wire-cutters, an SOU man found a short, rusting case-opener in the long grass outside the security fence.

More bad news; no fingerprints, but the flat end was smeared with blood. Weatherby claimed that case-openers, clippers and similar toys were frequently left lying around in the loading/unloading bays.

'Careless buggers,' moaned Causley, the office manager. 'I'm forever doing orders for new bits and pieces; tools.'

And alive or dead, there were no signs whatsoever of what the local radio station was to describe as the self-made millionaire, well-known philanthropist, flamboyant entrepreneur and ex-county councillor, Sir Jeremy Blatt.

'She's not a bad sort.' Derek Rodway sounded just that touch patronising. 'A bit of a gold-digger, perhaps. Redhead; ex-model, thirty years younger than him.'

'How old does that make her?' George looked interested; very much married, he still falls victim to middle-aged male fantasies from time to time.

'Twenty-eight.'

'Gee whiz!' Sarcasm rather than admiration on Paula's part. Having said it, she glanced uneasily around the room; I knew why. Paula, blonde, attractive, thirty-three, diamonds and sapphires on the third finger of her left hand, was engaged to Detective Constable Andy Spriggs, aged twenty-five, and recently transferred out of the immediate range of his fiancée-boss. An Easter wedding was on the cards, but the phrase 'toy boy' had been employed in certain quarters, and detective inspectors who live in glass houses should not lob conversational bricks. George contented himself with a cynical grin.

'Anyway' – I would never have accused him of it, but Derek's eagerness to hurry forward might have had something to do with tact – 'he went out again after an early dinner, at about seven forty-five last night. Said he was going back to work.'

'Isn't that unusual?'

'He's done it a lot recently; during the past month.'

'Why?'

'One, he's obsessed – thinks somebody's out to do him down. Two, he's a workaholic in any case.'

'Go on.'

'We-ll . . .' Derek drew out the word with a degree of self-satisfaction. 'According to Christine' – he paused again for effect, the man on first-name terms with the presumably sexy Lady Blatt – 'he's always had what you might call a suspicious mind; doesn't trust anybody very far. She thinks it might be something to do with the way his first marriage worked out.'

'She buggered off with an estate agent,' translated George. 'She said he might be into chickens, but he looked, lived and loved like a pig.' Remarks relayed by kind permission of the Sarah Caunt intelligence service, I presumed.

'This is the former Sylvia Peters, is it? The ex-Mrs Blatt? Died just before Christmas, right?'

'Yeah,' conceded George. 'Dead at fifty-four; imagine that. You catching up with the Eddathorpe gossip, boss?'

I refrained from enquiring into the details; George's next birthday was very much on the cards. It would, I believed, be tactless, all circumstances considered, to go into that.

'Gossip? Yes, some of it: you might have told me that his first wife was related to Kevin Cooke.'

George looked faintly abashed; his sources had obviously let him down. I felt absurdly pleased; local colour, a whiff of scandal even, and he didn't know.

'Yeah.' Derek sounded faintly irritated; people were spoiling his show. 'Christine says his first wife was a bit of a cow, and the son took his mother's side. When she died a few months ago, she left Sonny Boy a bob or two, and that's really put the cat among the pigeons; Jerry junior and the old man are at each other's throats. A few quid in his pocket, and he's started chucking his weight around.

'Now the lad's cleared off somewhere, and Blatt also blames her for that, dead or not. Makes him a bit short on trust in general and family feelings in particular, according to Chris.'

'What about all this "doing down" stuff? What's that about?'

'Profits haven't been too healthy in the frozen food division, lately. That's all she knows. Then there's the fire, the theft of the lorry and the vandalism and all.'

'Conspiracy theories; persecution mania,' murmured George.

'Somebody seems to have conspired to whap him over the head,' I pointed out. 'Fatally, perhaps.'

'If it was him that got whapped. Maybe he's cleared off because he's committed GBH on somebody else.'

'Nobody else missing,' I said.

'Nobody else *reported* missing,' sniffed George. 'Doesn't mean a thing.' Blatt the criminal as opposed to Blatt the victim held definite attractions for George, and he hadn't even had to sit through his mess night speech.

'OK,' I said hastily, 'point taken; but it doesn't seem that likely, does it? Let's stick to what we've got so far: no domestic trouble, no problems at home?'

'Not so far as I know.' Derek Rodway shrugged. Thinking about it later, his eyes might have lingered on my face for a fraction of a second too long when be said that.

'So, he followed a recently established pattern last night and went back to work. He suspects that somebody is committing a series of thefts, or some sort of fraud?'

'Yep.'

'He drives himself to the factory, he's seen going into the premises by the gateman at nine-twenty last night, and despite there being a twilight shift in the factory until ten, he's never seen again. How many on the shift?' I turned to Paula.

'Including the foreman and the charge-hand, sixteen.'

'And they all left shortly after ten o'clock?'

'According to their time cards, yes. We've got all the names and addresses, but we haven't got around to visiting everybody at home. Anybody we miss should be back at work at six o'clock.'

'What exactly happens at ten?'

'The production line stops; lights off, power off, apart from the freezers. The offices, of course, are on a separate switch. Everybody clocks out, the foreman locks up, the keys go to the gate and everybody goes home – mostly by car; some dropped off by a battered old minibus hired by the firm.'

'So somebody could have done Jerry Blatt before ten p.m. and stuffed him in the back of their vehicle?'

'Could have, if they'd managed to leave the factory floor and visit the offices during their shift. They'd have to do him and secretly load him into their car, prior to going home. Not very likely, is it?'

'What about the hole in the fence? And the jemmied door; that indicates a burglar, surely?' Paula liked everything to be nice and straight.

'Fence clipped, door forced,' I agreed. 'But no obvious theft; vandalism

57

but no apparent search. Somebody, presumably Sir Jeremy, clobbered; lots of blood and absolutely no signs of him leaving, or being dragged out via the hole in the fence.'

'So that could leave the vans.' She consulted her list. 'We've got details of the three van drivers, their clocking-on times, the times they left the premises and details of today's journeys. Same with the articulated lorry, although there's a bit of a problem there.'

'Oh yes?'

'We've, er, traced two of the vans; one in Leicester, delivering to a supermarket. One in Stoke on Trent. They've been searched. Nothing untoward.'

'OK.'

'The third one's on its way to Newcastle upon Tyne. Two drops on the way; we've missed it so far, but it should be all right when it gets to its final destination. Besides, nobody's started shouting and screaming yet, so it's fair to assume there's nothing nasty inside.'

'All these vehicles,' I said idly. 'I assume they were pre-loaded last night? All the drivers had to do was clock in, get in and drive away. Right?'

'Yes, boss. All they did was clock on, pick up the keys from the board in the cabin at the loading dock, collect their documentation, get in and drive away.'

'An unsupervised cabin?'

'Yep; the only night security is at the gate.'

'Fine, now tell me the exciting bit; the one you've been saving up.'

'We-ll, I've been expecting news of the lorry,' she said, puzzled. 'I should have heard by now.' She made a gesture towards my telephone. I nodded, she picked it up, dialled and had one of these brief, unsatisfactory conversations with somebody. The kind you have when everything has gone wrong.

'What d'you mean it's no longer there? Where is it, then?' Her temper was going; she flushed.

A muffled voice at the other end of the line quacked briefly. Apologies were being offered; she remained unimpressed.

'They must be a load of complete idiots,' she said. 'If it didn't pass them, it must have already been on board. Doesn't take a genius to work that out!' She slammed down the phone.

'We've got a problem with jurisdiction with the artic, boss.'

'I know that; same with the vans,' I said equably, not knowing what was coming next. 'From the look of the evidence we're unlikely to have either a missing from home or an injured man. He's likely to be dead, and murder enquiries start where the body is found. Difficulties with coroners' jurisdiction, liaising with another force; a rare old-time all-round—'

'Worse than that, boss.' She cut the soliloquy short. 'I didn't worry you at the factory because I thought we'd been in time.'

'In time for what?' Guts lifted; heart sank. There are times when I curse my Scottish ancestry; all this malarkey about the second sight.

'I sent a message,' she said defensively, 'but somehow Aylfleet cocked it up at the other end. The Aylfleet ferry, boss; it's sailed. That lorry is at sea right now, and it's on its way to Rotterdam.'

Silence: the news, the extent of the disaster, sank in. An international cock-up. Policemen, senior policemen, senior *Dutch* policemen: marked displeasure being shown.

Then for the first and last time in the course of the meeting, our most junior rank opened his mouth. 'It's all right,' he said. We were not completely reassured.

'Why's that?' George, unthinking, fell.

'All that fresh air,' said Detective Constable Patrick Goodall, pushing his luck far, far beyond the reasonable bounds even of constabulary taste. 'A long sea voyage will probably do him the world of good.'

A dockside meeting; two superintendents of my acquaintance watching the *North Sea Trader* inch its way back into its berth. Both quietly blaming me for their troubles, and not exactly the best of friends. Junior ranks, uniformed and CID, milled around in a separate group. Being kept, despite their insatiable curiosity, well out of earwigging range.

'Run that past me again,' said Thea to Teddy with an air of chilly constraint.

'It's your crime.' Teddy was in one of his obliging moods. 'Once we get the body back, it's all yours.'

'Rubbish! The factory's on your division, he was obviously killed there. Eddathorpe's got another murder; that's the third in less than two years, not counting—'

'No.' Teddy appeared to be enjoying this. 'The enquiry belongs to wherever the body is found. That's why we recalled the ferry. Silly, having a crime in England and a corpse in Holland.'

'The corpse,' said Superintendent Dorothea Spinks grimly, 'was found on the high seas, wherever they were when they opened up that lorry, and outside territorial waters; so the place of discovery doesn't count. The killing obviously took place on your division.'

'It's a British ferry, this is its home port, and once it lands the body is in your jurisdiction. Right.' A statement, not a question. They both turned to me.

'Yes,' I said.

'What do you mean, "yes"?' Dorothea's voice was dangerously sweet. Nice try, but I was the meat in their sandwich once again.

'It's yours, I mean mine. According to the book it's an Aylfleet crime. It doesn't matter anyway, does it? Same coroner's area, same investigating officer, same Force. The point is, we got them to open the lorry, and we persuaded 'em to turn back.'

Not the point at all, and it mattered to her all right. Aylfleet now had a murder according to the book. Baring's revenge: and nothing, absolutely nothing she could do.

Eddathorpe one, Aylfleet nil, and he wasn't even hiding it. We could both see his expression. Teddy, with male chauvinist self-satisfaction plastered all over his face.

'Good job they opened up the lorry straight away,' he said comfortingly, rubbing it in. 'Poor chap might have frozen to death. If he hadn't been dead already,' he added.

Ignoring this final slight, Thea turned her attention to me, looking as if I was something oozing and nasty she'd recently discovered adhering to the sole of her shoe.

'Home Office pathologist?'

'On his way, ma'am.'

'Good.'

Transferring the whole of her attention to the ferry, she watched the bow doors open, the ramp crash into position and a thin line of commercial vehicles make their hesitant journey back on to the Aylfleet dock. Finally, freed at last from the ruck, the Daisy Dew truck appeared. The event was greeted in total silence; no applause.

Life, death, police work, can be so unfair.

8

'I suppose I'd been expecting it,' said Christine Blatt bleakly, 'from the moment Inspector Rodway told me about the vandalised office and the blood.' Three hours since Derek Rodway and a policewoman had delivered the news. She was holding together more than well.

Red-gold hair, blue eyes and a full, high-breasted body that told you straight away that she'd not enjoyed a career as some fashion jockey's clothes-horse, whatever other sort of model she might have been. Very pale skin; but then I noticed the touch of telltale pink about the eyes. Tears and a touch of shock.

Not that she was giving much away; a slight tremor to the hand holding the teacup, a tiny, not unattractive hesitancy in the voice from time to time, and that was about all. How much, I wondered, had this been a marriage of convenience, and how much did she lament the passing of the late Sir Jeremy Blatt?

She looked me squarely in the eye, crossing her legs with a promising rustle of pale blue, pleated skirt. 'Whatever you think, he had his points, you know. He was always very good to me.' A bit of a mind-reader on the side.

'I, er—' I said. Not among my best, my most eloquent speeches. She was obviously satisfied with the effect.

'Oh, I know what you're thinking. Detectives or dustmen, men are pretty much the same. Sexy model meets elderly businessman; a marriage made on the stock market rather than in heaven, hmm?'

I smiled at her; not too much though. She was probably making some sort of insulting equation there. 'Yes.'

'And to some extent you'd be right. I wouldn't have married him if

61

he'd still been living in a council house; not at his age.'

It was a bit much for me; all this honesty towards the end of a very long day. I spared a second or so for the room; too much again. Nineteenth-century panelling, antique porcelain and reproduction antique furniture covering three hundred years and half the cultures in the EU, plus a Chinese carpet. A combination that did everything but talk: none of your poncy interior designers here, but buckets and buckets of cash.

'I'm sorry to have to intrude at a time like this, but do you feel up to answering a few questions, Lady Blatt?'

'It's probably better if we get it over now.' No hesitation there; could that have been a note of asperity in her voice?

'I'd like some background information, if you don't mind. How long have you been married, Lady Blatt?'

'Just over two years; it was – it was a Christmas wedding.' Hurry up, give her something else to think about. Oh dear.

'And had you known your husband long?'

'About four months.' She paused for a moment. 'There was no sense in waiting; we both knew our minds.'

'I see.'

'If you want to ask about his first wife, I'm quite prepared to tell you. She left him six or seven years ago; I wasn't the happy home-wrecker, you know. Except in Jeremy junior's eyes, that is. She died towards the end of last year.'

'Jeremy junior; his son?'

'His son,' she confirmed. 'Mummy's boy, spoiled rotten, according to Jerry. Fifteen years old, and at a very vulnerable age when they broke up, according to common sense. Besides, it's only natural; he saw his inheritance going down the drain once I came on the scene.'

'And he's, what – twenty-one, twenty-two now?'

'Twenty-two.'

'And what happens now?'

'I'm sorry?'

'The, ah, inheritance?'

'He's not been cut off with the proverbial shilling, if that's what you mean, despite them falling out. My Jerry isn't a complete bastard, in spite of what they say. Hard; but how many softies do you know who manage to get everything they want?'

And had she? Got everything she wanted, either then or now? All the same, I felt more than a twinge of sympathy for her. I'd noted her automatic use of the present tense. Despite her news, she wasn't thinking like a widow yet.

'Do you know the present whereabouts of his son?'

'I don't know, Chief Inspector. Around. He turns up occasionally to have a row with his old man. What is this, anyway? You surely don't thi—'

'I'm just taking a look at the background, Lady Blatt.'

She turned to Derek Rodway seated by the open fire and busy admiring a pair of Royal Worcester urns, leaving all the spadework to me.

'What is this, Derek? You surely don't think that Jeremy junior would break in to his own father's factory and vandalise it, do you? He can walk in through the front door any time he likes.'

Interesting: a strictly self-censored version of events. Vandalism was the least of our current troubles. A strong, determined young woman, but not inclined to take unpleasant speculations too far? Or was this a touch of family loyalty; what the old man might have wanted of her on behalf of his allegedly spoiled son? Finding Junior's address and paying him a visit was high among the fairly urgent things to be done.

'Can you tell me something about your husband's business worries?' I said. Not the most tactful way of putting it, but I wanted to know if there was anything else going on.

She flushed. 'That implies some sort of financial problem, doesn't it? Nothing of the sort; the business is very sound. Family-owned and very solvent, thank you very much!'

'Perhaps I put it badly.' And perhaps not.

'His worries, as you call them, consisted of a conviction that somebody was probably responsible for organised thefts of frozen food. He'd been going through the stock records in particular, and the recorded sales.'

'And had he come to any firm conclusions?'

'Not so far as I know; not yet.'

'I understand,' I said carefully, 'that despite the factory security, there are leakages from time to time – employees taking stuff home?'

'The company takes account of that – Jerry was prepared to accept anything up to one and a half per cent, averaged out over the year. It happens everywhere.'

Not the dumb adjunctive to the ageing tycoon; a lady who could talk facts and figures. Took an interest in Hubby's doings, then.

'And this was something different?'

'He said it was more like a couple of vanloads scooting out of the back door every week.'

'And those were his exact words?'

'Yes.'

'Did he know who was doing it?'

She almost smiled. 'You didn't know my husband, Chief Inspector?'

'Not very well.'

'Not well at all. He said he was going to barbecue the bastards slowly, like chickens on a spit, once he'd found out.' She spoke with obvious pride. 'I don't quite think he meant that literally, of course.'

'Did he, er, confide in anyone about this?'

'Me.'

'Apart from you?'

'He isn't – wasn't – the confiding type.' A correction this time, but still that touch of pride: *I was married to a hard, hard man!* Derek Rodway stirred uneasily in his seat.

'What about his managers?'

'Simon and David?' OK, then; one director, and a *general* manager, eggs.

'What other managers are there?'

She ticked them off on her fingers, 'Factory manager, sales manager, office manager – he's a glorified clerk; managers at each of the two egg farms and the poultry production units. Then we've got retail managers at the Daisyfayre frozen food outlets. They're scattered all over the place.'

'Yes, thank you.' Gloom descended: lots of people to see.

'Then,' she said, 'you've also got the new security adviser, or manager, or whatever you want to call him. I think you know him.'

'Yes,' I said cheerlessly, 'I know him.' Ronald Hacker; one official day of employment. I could, thank heavens, eliminate him straight away if some sort of fiddle was involved. A new boy. Lack of opportunity rather than shining integrity, I had to admit.

'Your husband didn't trust any of these people?'

'People outside the factory didn't count; they could hardly be involved in the thefts. And,' she said, 'you don't do people any favours by trusting them too far; puts them into temptation's way, doesn't it?' Another gem from the Jeremy Blatt anthology of popular sayings, no doubt.

Just over two years of marriage to a man twice her age, and she seemed to have wholeheartedly embraced the philosophy along with the man himself. Svengali and Trilby? Or a slavish acceptance of the good old fashioned motto, money talks?

'Er, Christine . . .' Derek Rodway had woken up. 'There's no easy way of saying this, but who benefits from your husband's death; companywise, I mean?'

She bridled, 'Companywise, assetwise, everywise: me.'

'What about . . . ?'

'OK, Derek, you and your colleague seem quite determined to . . . to go all the way with this. I should have thought a straightforward burglary and a murder were quite enough for local police to handle, but there's nothing to hide.'

Not the conventional grieving widow, then: plenty of energy left to put us down. Still, the Derek and Christine stuff was worth a passing word, once we got out of here.

'Daisy Dew is a big operation, but it's strictly family. No outsiders, apart from Simon and the company secretary, and they hold a minority of shares.

'Nominal capital one hundred pounds, and one hundred shares issued for cash. Jeremy owns – owned – sixty; I own twenty-five. Jeremy junior owns nine; Simon and the secretary have three apiece, purely to qualify them for the board. The nominal value of the shares has got nothing to do with the real value, of course; that's something astronomical, by now. Satisfied?'

'Who's the company secretary?'

'About Jerry junior. You said—' We both jumped in together, Graham and Rodway, a confusion of sound. There was an awkward silence; none too patiently, she sighed. Then she made her decision; senior officers first.

'The company secretary is Jack Causley, the office manager; he's been with Jerry for years.' I raised my eyebrows: so much for the glorified clerk.

'My husband made a new will when we married; three hundred thousand net of taxes for Jeremy junior; a lump sum for me and any children we might have had' – her face twisted momentarily – 'the rest, including Jerry's shares, in trust for my lifetime. Then it was back to the kids . . .'

'No other relatives?'

'The Peters clan? That was her maiden name. She was taken care of when they divorced: got her hands on a lump sum. Never married again, so Jerry inherited her bungalow and her settlement, whatever was left. As for the rest of 'em, you have to be joking!'

'Family feud?'

'The Peters family? They're not important enough to feud with. You know about her sister's son, Kevin Cooke?'

'Yes.'

'There you are, then. Shows what happens when you try to pick people up out of the gutter.'

An interesting point of view. No time for council house dwellers, and agin the rackety Cookes in their Eddathorpe terraced home. Christine's version of the underclass, whose vices and ingratitude apparently barred them from possessing reproduction Louis Quinze furniture, as well as decorated Royal Worcester urns at three or four thousand pounds the pair.

Derek Rodway, still smitten, smiled sympathetically. Echoing the hard-headed cynicism of the late lamented, I stayed neutral: more interested than convinced.

'What about his other enemies?'

'I beg your pardon?' The high horse, now.

'Sir Jeremy,' I said, spreading flattery like axle grease, 'was a highly successful self-made man. He's bound to have attracted some animosity along the way. People he, well . . . left behind, for example?'

'Nobody who wanted to kill him, Chief Inspector, if that's what you mean. Personally, I think you'd be better off looking at some madman from among these animal rights campaigners, or perhaps some panic-stricken thief. Businessmen don't behave like that.'

Of course not. And pigs have certainly been known to fly. Nevertheless, she had a point. Graffiti, a fire, a drive-away and vandalism; followed by burglary, more vandalism and an elderly man with a bashed-in skull. Sir Jeremy and his suspicions might well be totally irrelevant to our murder enquiry, but it was a damn good place to start. The chain of events suggested sustained hatred; obsession, rather than a rational dislike. The one thing we almost certainly hadn't got, however, was spur-of-the-moment panic on the part of a casual, frightened thief.

Time to disengage, express the conventional sympathies. Had she anyone to stay with her? To help?

She smiled faintly, dismissively, and shook her head. Her parents, apparently, were on their way. She too was anxious to wind up the interview while remaining polite, almost perfectly self-possessed.

Iron control? All very admirable until it broke. Or the jackpot winner, about to celebrate the moment we stepped outside? Not in my book: she gave every indication of being something better than that.

We'd arrived; we departed; nothing much had changed. Lady Christine Blatt was still something of an enigma. Outside, I eyed the solid Victorian architecture, and Derek Rodway kept his slightly goofy smile.

I was already into gatehouse records, chilled, well-travelled corpses, Jeremy junior and the hole in the factory fence.

The murder room was crowded, and the two DCs were strangers to me, both drafted in for the duration; very young, and very chuffed. The tail end of the shift, time to go home, and after a certain amount of aggro, apparently, they'd secured their particular prize.

'Took some getting, did them,' said the first, removing the Daisy Dew gatehouse register from his briefcase, and carelessly throwing a sheaf of statements into a filing basket. 'Security staff? I've shot 'em. Pah!'

'Specially when that mate of the boss turned up; hung around like a vulture on a power line,' said the second. 'Scared 'em silly about keeping their jobs; the bloody old fool.'

'What mate of mine, young man?' A remark calculated to make me sound like Methuselah, and it's sneaky, attacking from behind. If they want to be detectives, however, lippy juniors should cultivate eyes in the backs of their heads. He jumped.

'Oh, er, Superintendent Hacker,' he said. 'Sorry, sir.'

'Ex-superintendent,' I said flatly, indicating the precise degree of matiness involved. More, and I would have been currying favour with sprogs. They both eyed me anxiously for a moment; no incoming flak. They visibly relaxed.

'We've taken statements from the security men,' ventured the first.

'How many?'

'Four in the last twenty-four hours; one man for each shift, plus a nine-to-five. Six a.m. till two; two till ten, and a man on nights. We had to see him at home. The day man doubles up for part of the morning shift, and part of the afternoon. That's when the gate's busy. Apart from today's morning man, they're all a waste of space.'

'The morning man?' I was disappointed, 'The retired cop?'

'Yeah; Alec Chamberlain. He's OK; at least he writes things down.'

'The afternoon man's a prat. Reckons that management movements are a waste of time, so he never books 'em in. Or out.

'Visitors, goods and the occasional random search of employees; that's his lot. Nobody ever checks the book. He's given us some names and the times they left, so far as he can recall. Remembers the big boss coming back at twenty past nine last night.'

'And the night man?'

'No ruddy interest whatsoever: moaning his head off about cups of tea. They had a bit of a fire in the security hut about six months back, so they're not allowed to brew any more. Goes backwards and forwards feeding the tea machine with his wages, half the night.'

'To the office block?'

'Sorry, boss.' Hope died. 'The machine he uses is in the foyer by the loading bay at the back. Besides, he's a ruddy moonlighter; got another part-time job. Seems to think the Daisy Dew mob pay him to go to sleep.'

'And he never even noticed the jemmied door?'

'Nope.'

'OK.' I was reduced to sarcasm. 'What about these vital trips backwards and forwards for tea? Surely he passed it; no signs of a sodding great hole in the fence?'

'Sorry, boss.'

'Don't exactly blame him at three forty-five an hour,' muttered the first DC. 'Pay peanuts, an' you get monkeys.'

Unoriginal. Exposure to the Alec Chamberlain experience, I supposed. It was late, I was tired; cock-ups, corpses, widows and post-mortems had cluttered my day. And what's more, the sun had practically risen on that remark.

'Did you borrow that one from a simian's statement?' I snapped.

Silence; I turned away. The first detective constable sounded puzzled. 'Who's a Simian, anyway? I could'a sworn he was British, boss.'

And all said in such a spirit of honest enquiry. I think.

9

'No, it wasn't a joke,' said Kevin Cooke, exploiting a grievance. 'I'd have told you properly, but you couldn't get rid of me fast enough at the time.'

I remembered; getting rid of Kevin was one of the things I did best. Interview, get the story, kick him out and become more usefully employed. I can't say I liked him, I didn't even sympathise with him very much, but I had dragged him down to the police station again; something like conscience struck. Our first meeting had been curtailed. Uncle Jerry; he might well have got round to telling me more about his family relationships, given time.

The oily, acned, overalled figure looked at me, gloom and apprehension written all over his face. Dragged away from important duties associated with motorcycle maintenance and never having heard of Zen, he was now mixing it with the cops.

Murder enquiries now; little or no possibility of mutually beneficial arrangements, or a shower of ten-pound notes. It was pretty obvious he would have preferred to keep his head down, his mouth shut and to stay far, far away from Eddathorpe nick.

'I suppose,' I said grudgingly, 'it wasn't your fault.'

'Right on, ma—'

I shook my head warningly; whatever else I might be, I was definitely neither his man nor his mate.

'Anyway,' he said hastily, 'Auntie Sylvia was his first wife, and Jeremy junior's me cousin, OK? That's why I got the job. His old man was all over me when I started; said I could go to college and get a GNVQ qualification in poultry stuffin' or something.'

'So, he gives you a job and you reward him by dropping his company in the mire with the Ministry of Ag?'

'Aw, c'mon, Mr Graham; you saw the place. It stunk like the arsehole of the world. How would you like to spew up your ring every time you went to work, and all for eighty-five notes a week?'

'Plus one day a week at college for the National Vocational Qualification, eh?'

'That didn't come off, did it? Next year, he said, if I settled down. Slave-driving old git.'

'Nevertheless . . .' I said.

'Nevertheless nothin'! You don't get it, do you? He was only after one thing, and once he'd got it I'da got the heave anyway, so I got mine in first. Right?'

'He wasn't after your body, was he?'

He appreciated that one. 'Na-aw.' He gave me a gap-toothed grin. 'He was strictly hetero; he'd screw practically anything in skirts. He just wanted information, mate.'

I still had this burning ambition not to be Kevin's mate. Nevertheless, in the interests of justice and a well-filled cell block, I was prepared to let the occasional slip-up pass me by.

'What sort of information?'

'He wanted to pump me about Auntie Sylvia and cousin Jerry, that's all.'

'Why?'

'Because he thought they was going to take him to the cleaners before long. At least, Jerry was going to do it on Auntie Sylvia's behalf, her being dead and all. He thought he was using me to keep his ear to the ground: a sorta spy.'

'Terrific. Kevin Cooke instead of James Bond?'

So it was plots, conspiracy theories, spies. With Kevin's track record I could well be wasting my time. One conviction for arson already. Definitely unstable: an overactive, not to say diseased, imagination at work?

'All right, don't believe me, if that's how you feel.'

'Supposing I do believe you, Kevin; what about a bit of the why and how?'

'Eh?'

At the back of the room Derek Rodway stirred, cracked his knuckles, rolled his eyes heavenwards in exasperation, and pantomimed dissent. Keep it simple, he was saying. Boss or not, you're introducing unnecessary complications here. You are a detective, he is a mindless yob; use nursery language, backed by the occasional threat of a thick ear. Derek, I was beginning to discover, would bear a spot of close supervision now and again.

'Why was cousin Jerry going to take him to the cleaners?'

'Because of her shares.'

I waited patiently.

Kevin gave a heavy sigh, 'The shares in the business were divided between him, me aunt, and me cousin; right? Oh yeah, and Weatherby and that little creep in the office had one or two. Then they got divorced, Auntie Sylvia got a bit of a settlement, but cousin Jerry reckoned that her shares had mysteriously gone kaput. OK?'

Another version of a familiar tale. But the wife's shareholding belonged to Christine, not Sylvia Blatt.

'How did that happen?'

'He flogged 'em, or transferred 'em or something. Ask Jerry; I dunno.'

Unspoken; but Kevin appeared to know more than a little about the life and times of cousin Jeremy Blatt. Shares rightfully belonging to Mum had been lifted; so that was the tale.

'Sounds like a great idea. Where is cousin Jerry now?'

Kevin treated me to a look of pity, heavily laced with weary contempt. 'You did go and take a look at them New Agers I told ya about? You didn't just let it slide?'

'They made the enquiries from Aylfleet, thanks.'

I looked across at Derek Rodway, who shrugged and shook his head. Enquiries made; Jerry junior, apparently, not on site. Kevin, I decided, should have been walloped, hard and often, as a kid.

'Well, he was there, wasn't he? Got a caravette and a girlfriend on the site, last time I heard. Goes *in* for things, does Jerry.' He paused, then with the air of a man conferring a favour on the terminally thick, he added, 'He's anti-establishment. Believes in a new and freer society, an' that's only the start of it; right?'

Derek teetered dangerously on the edge of his chair. I thought he was going to choke.

'Seems to me you're just stirring things up, my son.' His voice acquired an edge of effortless menace. 'First you give us a load of old malarkey about low-paid cleaners and suggest they might have a motive for arson, then it turns out you're related to Sir Jeremy Blatt.'

'I would'a told—' said Kevin.

'Shut up and listen!'

Kevin shut up. He tried to look at Derek over his left shoulder. Disconcerting, when the nasty half of the team has eyes boring into the back of your head.

'Next' – Derek warmed to his theme – 'you tell us that Jeremy Blatt junior is living with the very people you fingered as suspects for the fire. Something else you kept quiet about: you're either a prize pillock or a prize liar, or both.'

'Hey! Just a minute,' said Kevin.

'Just a murder, you mean.' Derek Rodway had the bit well and truly between his teeth. 'You'd better start coming across with the full story, my lad. You were employed by your uncle, you grassed on his company, then you got the sack. There's a fire, an unlawful taking and vandalism to a lorry; a burglary at the factory and your uncle ends up with a crushed skull.'

Wonderful: Detective Inspector Rodway, the man who lays it firmly on the line. Only one thing wrong. Technically, Kevin was a volunteer. A person being interviewed at Eddathorpe police station. Not cautioned; not under arrest. Hard and soft is a tried-and-tested game, but the Home Office *Codes of Practice* don't leave you much room for manoeuvre, once you voice your suspicions out loud.

Was Kevin a genuine murder suspect at this stage? A vandal, a taker of lorries without owner's consent, even? Almost nothing in the way of evidence: I preferred to think not.

'You've got it in for me,' muttered Kevin, 'just because—'

'Got it in for you? I haven't even started yet. You think you can faff us around, don't you? Tell us bits and pieces when it suits you, eh?

'Your uncle's dead, sonny, and he didn't die of an overdose of his lousy junk food. Play games with us and you could end up counting bricks in an Eddathorpe cell.'

Short fuse; big mouth. He reminded me of somebody else I knew. Never mind, the damage, if any, was done and just for once it might be worth going along for the ride. I could always give him a round of applause later, once Kevin was out of earshot. In the meantime, my way, his way; if we got a result, who cared? Kevin Cooke wouldn't like Mr Policeman any more? Oh, well . . .

'Hey,' said Kevin without much conviction. He paused, then added with an accession of crazy courage, 'You've tried threats already, Mr Rodway, and it didn't do you a lot of good!'

Derek Rodway turned bright red; his body stiffened, his leg muscles flexed; he was almost on his way. Then he took one look at me, suddenly recalled the difference between three pips and two, and stayed put. There are moments when you forget whose side you're on. Left to myself I could almost have dished out a VC; I barely stopped myself from grinning at Kevin Cooke.

'Come on,' I murmured instead, 'you're helping yourself. If there's any more dirt to dish, now's the time.'

'I dunno.' Kevin was still busy deciding whether there was anything approaching him from behind. Spoke volumes for Aylfleet investigative methods, did that. Something to bear in mind. 'There's the houses, I suppose.'

'Go on.'

'Bit of sharp practice here an' there. He wasn't liked.'

Derek Rodway opened and shut his mouth; his fingers flexed. He twitched. Oblivious to this performance, Kevin gathered his thoughts.

'We-ll, y'know the houses up by the old gas-works at the top of our street.'

'Yes.' A couple of dozen Edwardian terraced houses next to eight or nine acres of derelict clinker, surrounded by a wire fence.

'Me uncle bought them for next to nothing, years ago.'

'Good for him.'

'Practically got the Labour Party to pay for 'em, too.'

'Eh?'

'Used to boast about it; have a bit of a laugh, like.'

Stout Conservative county councillor screws the opposition party; I could well imagine that.

'Years ago,' said Kevin. 'The last Labour government; before I was born. High inflation,' he added wisely. This must be one of Kevin's A-levels; twentieth-century history. Count me out.

'Anyway . . .' Kevin had been watching my face carefully; he grinned. 'Because of inflation the government allowed businessmen to roll their tax liabilities forward so they could purchase stock. OK?'

I nodded in a half-stunned sort of way. And this stuff was coming from *Kevin*, the chicken-turd kid? You certainly live and learn. I looked

73

at him with something approaching respect; Derek Rodway, unreconstructed, was still doing his homicidal twitch.

'Yes, but what has this—'

'Got to do with Uncle? Well, he was buying property at the time. He
persuaded the Inland Revenue that houses were business stocks, 'cos he
dealt in property. So he rolled over his tax liability, an' bought more
houses with the money. Good, innit?

'Fine; so you reckon that Tony Blair was out for revenge, or something?'

'Put out a contract, huh?' Derek Rodway was happy at last.

'No need to be sarky; I'm just trying to help. He got these houses,
then he rented 'em out; hardly spent a penny on repairs. Council enforce-
ment notices, writs, the lot.

'Hardly anybody knew he owned them; he used to collect the rents
through the estate agent that ran off with Auntie Sylvia. Anyway, if the
tenants found out, there'd be another load of people to hate his guts.'

'So Auntie Sylvia ran off with an estate agent, huh?'

'Yep. Not that it lasted long. She lived with a labourer on a North Sea
oil rig for a bit, after that.'

'Was she seasick?' asked Derek. Then, seeing the expression on my
face, he tried for an explanation, his voice trailing away as he made
matters worse. 'Y'know, living on an oil rig . . . Sorry, never mind.'

I began to feel a sneaking sympathy for Dorothea Spinks: ignore the
bugger and perhaps he'd go away. Concentrate on Kevin, instead.

'How would you know all this?'

'Jerry, me cousin, told me.'

Even Derek was impressed. 'Busy sort of bastard, your uncle. Bet you
take after him,' he said.

It was, as usual, a highly professional report. Professor Andrew Lawrence,
Home Office pathologist, had demonstrated his effortless superiority over
all us lowly plods and plodesses, once again. Jeremy Blatt was apparently
a well-nourished middle-aged male, one point six-seven metres tall,
eighty-seven kilograms in weight, suffering from the early stages of fatty
degeneration of the heart. An excellent beginning; enough to remind me
of my reluctant presence at the post-mortem, and all the disgusting bits
laid bare under Lawrence's knife.

The deceased had not, I was marginally disappointed to learn, succumbed to this complaint, thus letting us all off the hook. Nor, surprisingly, had he died from the single, crushing blow to the right side of his head, which had splintered the skull, although the blow had almost certainly been delivered by the rusting case-opener found outside the factory fence in the long grass.

Professor Lawrence, a neat chart outlining problems associated with the cooling of bodies in refrigerators well to the fore, had plumped for a combination of violence, followed by coma, and the effects on the victim of almost immediate cold storage at something approaching −15°C.

Cautiously, keeping the margin uncomfortably wide, he placed the time of death at some time between 2 and 6 a.m. He did not speculate on the time of the actual attack. He might have survived the blow, he concluded, had he been fortunate enough to receive treatment straight away. Oddly, uselessly, as it turned out, the rapid decline in body temperature might well have contributed towards a prolongation of the victim's life. One of fate's little ironies, hinted Lawrence: the sort of irony that makes some of us lesser mortals feel pretty sick.

Poor old Jeremy. *Bizarre Ice Coffin Tragedy: Mugged and Frozen Alive!* It was the stuff of journalistic dreams; the material of nightmares for the rest of us. I could be grateful for small mercies, though. However the poor old sod had died, he'd done it before the artic had been loaded on the ferry: just. One muted cheer for that. No criticism winging its way in the direction of bungling coppers for killing the man by failing to search the ferry down at Aylfleet dock.

Jack Causley, company secretary, office manager, or that little creep, according to taste. Not so little, however; around five foot ten, fiftyish, skinny to slim; wiry and pale in a double-breasted navy blue suit and a nondescript tie. Not exactly the bold, buccaneering personality, but he obviously kept himself fit. Efficient, I soon decided, self-important, slightly smug.

He looked at me slyly through half-closed eyes and fiddled with the fountain pen on the stamped leather blotter positioned in the exact centre of his desk.

'I'll do everything possible, of course,' he said, 'but I don't really think—'

'Really, Mr Causley,' I cut him short. 'It isn't exactly confidential, is it? Every company has a method whereby its share register can be inspected. Anyway, it's a matter of public record: I can soon get details from Companies House.'

He sighed, relaxing marginally in a gentle hiss of breath. 'I suppose you're right. One has to be so careful, you know. In my position one has to balance so many conflicting . . .'

He let his voice trail away into an ambiguous silence. He still looked worried; a man who'd apparently assumed an immense burden, nobly borne. The lonely figure at the very heart of an industrial empire.

My detective sergeant, seated to the left of Causley's desk, cleared his throat. There are those among us who have absolutely no conception of the weight of responsibility that high office confers. Their sympathies are not aroused. In any case, George frequently eyes the reluctant witness in the same light as an ageing predator eyes an unexpected pre-lunch snack.

'When, sir,' said George, 'did Mrs Sylvia Blatt transfer her shares?'

Causley rose to his feet; even the subordinates were snapping at him now. Gathering the remnants of his dignity around him like a cloak, he stalked over to the huge, old-fashioned fire safe which graced one corner of the office, reached into his jacket pocket, selected a narrow key from the bunch he carried in a leather case and opened the door.

After fumbling inside for a few moments he returned in dignified silence to his seat, ceremoniously balancing a single green-bound book on the palms of his hands.

'The company minute book,' he announced, 'and share register combined. Would you, er, care to examine it with me, Chief Inspector?'

A graceful surrender? Not on your life: a snub directed at George, who, for some inexplicable reason, failed to take it as a serious blow to his professional self-esteem. He waited until I'd positioned myself behind Causley's chair, watched him open the book and said, 'One other thing Mr Graham was going to mention, sir; there's no record of you leaving the premises that night.'

'What night?' Causley's head snapped back, his hand frozen in the very act of turning a page. He stared fixedly at George.

'The night your employer was murdered, Mr Causley. There's no record of you ever going home.'

Nasty. Underhand. Grossly unfair. The gatehouse book, as we had already discovered, was an eccentric, unreliable mess. Lorries in; lorries out, OK. Visits, people, times and dates of appointments; not too bad.

76

Factory employees clocked in elsewhere; their comings and goings were recorded on the clock cards, so the workers merely flashed their ID to whoever was on duty at the gate. Clerical staff were supposedly booked in and out as a Health and Safety precaution, in case of fire. They signed a book in the general office; sometimes. Ultimately, they were Causley's responsibility; in practice, it was another cock-up; they didn't clock on or off at all.

Management arrivals and departures, however, seemed to be recorded at the whim of whoever was on security duty at the time. Records formed little more than a casual diary of events, kept intermittently, either to satisfy the gatemen's authoritarian leanings, or, more probably, to keep boredom at bay. Nobody seemed to care much about the possibility of fire or missing personnel.

Security, impressive at first sight, had turned out to be something of a bad joke. Blatt was important, the top dog, so his arrivals and departures were often faithfully, if uselessly, recorded. Others – company secretaries, divisional managers, factory managers, visiting retail managers and any other middle-ranking staff you cared to mention – were sometimes booked in, and appeared to remain incarcerated on the premises for days on end.

Perhaps, if the gatehouse records were accurate, they'd flown over the security fence at some unspecified time and date, only to have their names recorded when they decided to return to the premises by more conventional means. It added an element of excitement, not to say uncertainty, to any internal enquiries we cared to make.

Causley finally turned the page. 'I've already made a statement regarding my movements, Sergeant,' he snapped. 'I worked late, but I left before seven o'clock.'

George treated him to a slow, sad, understanding smile. 'I know; we've got statements from practically everybody, sir. The trouble is, we were rather relying on the gatehouse book to confirm whatever people said. In your case there's no independent record of your going home.'

'Apparently,' said Causley tensely, 'you haven't got very much of a record at all. Weatherby wasn't booked out; neither was Lang. As for the office staff . . . in any case, we wouldn't have thought that our movements would have mattered one solitary damn.'

George, I think, was inclined to take offence at the Thatcherite plural. Self-important bureaucrats are not his favourite type.

'Oh?'

'It's obvious, even to the meanest intelligence. Somebody cut through the security fence, vandalised the offices and attacked Sir Jeremy with a jem . . . sorry, case-opener.' Oh good, he'd noticed it just in time, an unfortunate juxtaposition of sounds to say the least.

'Oh, it's obvious, is it? And to the meanest intelligence, too?' George playing parrot. He looked at his victim with a practised sympathy traditionally hidden under a face-mask on Tower Hill. 'And which particular intelligence is responsible for ensuring that the gatehouse records are properly kept?'

Causley stared back, stiffening slowly like a rabbit in the presence of a stoat. Personally, I'd seen it all before. One remark too many and you suddenly found yourself on George's extensive list of subjects for persecution and revenge.

'Me. I suppose you know that perfectly well. I end up being responsible for supervising almost any damn job around here. I do eventually manage to get around to doing the impossible, given time.'

'OK, so you're busy; burdened with far too much to do.' George gave him just enough time to relax before he struck. 'Just one little problem, pal.' A permanent demotion, I suspected, from 'Mr Causley', and company secretary or not, he'd have to cherish a fading memory of having ever been addressed as 'sir'.

Mesmerised, Causley awarded him a reluctant nod.

'Perhaps you could help.'

Another infinitesimal movement of the head.

'Tell me,' George asked with heavy sarcasm, 'about the fence. Was it cut by a burglar on the way in, or a staff member on the way out?'

Impatient George. Especially when a highly paid forensic scientist was prepared to formulate his own carefully constructed hypothesis on this very subject, in his own good time.

10

<hr />

Teddy Baring looked grim. Methodical, orderly, almost fanatically tidy himself, he didn't take kindly to people turning his personal environment into a working model of a rubbish tip on a windy day. I watched with interest as statements, photographs, action forms and sections of my report spread themselves remorselessly over his office floor.

Tidy, unfortunately, was something that Detective Chief Superintendent Peter Fairfield, our bulky, bucolic head of CID, just didn't do. From his grey suit, which reminded his fans of an elephant's ancient, crumpled skin, to his size eleven brogues, which probably last saw polish in honour of the CID Christmas bash, he was the antithesis of the well-dressed man.

To top it all, his behaviour towards my carefully assembled murder file gave the casual observer the distinct impression that his mission in life was to search and destroy. Every time he finished reading a page he grunted; whenever he came to the end of a statement he threw it on the floor. Occasionally, for the sake of variety, he skimmed a wedge of paper halfway across the room to start a new pile. This, I gathered, was the Fairfield filing system at work.

Even when matters were skinned down to essentials, I'd managed to produce a formidable file. Fairfield, therefore, was making a pretty spectacular mess. I wasn't totally enamoured of what he was doing to my personal copy of the magnum opus, but from the expression on his face and the growing chaos in his polished and garnished sanctum, I was counting on Teddy to initiate an unseemly brawl between senior officers before very long.

'Well,' said Fairfield at last, 'you've got a right witches' brew on your hands here, huh?'

'Not quite.' Teddy skipped in straight away with his version of the rules of this particular game. 'This enquiry is the exclusive property of Dorothea Spinks. Body, incident room, enquiry teams, the lot. In fact' – he surveyed his newly desecrated carpet with distaste – 'other than to meet Bob at his permanent base, there's little reason for you to be here.'

'Oh, come on, Edward, we both know the book. On a technicality, it's down as Aylfleet's crime, but we both know where—'

'It happened?' Teddy finished.

'Yes.'

'We had a burglary,' he conceded, 'and an assault. It's anybody's guess where he died.'

'Eh?' Fairfield scowled. He didn't like chopped logic, and he didn't care for divisional commanders who passed the buck.

'It's true, you know.' Teddy rose and delicately picked his way between the scattered remains of my carefully assembled information. Unerringly, he reached down and collected half a dozen sheets, the pathologist's report.

'I know.' Fairfield waved a dismissive hand. 'The poor bastard died in the truck.'

'He died, according to Professor Lawrence, some time between two and six a.m. And that's a very approximate estimate, at best. Sticking the dying victim in a freezer doesn't exactly help us to calculate the exact time of death.' Teddy paused to gather his forces, ready to deliver the final self-justifying blow: Jeremy might not even have died on his division, after all.

'Bloody good job!' Our Detective Chief Superintendent cut him short. No need for the rest; I knew what was coming, even if the Eddathorpe boss hadn't yet caught on.

'If,' Fairfield continued sourly, 'we knew the exact time, Edward, heads might roll. Supposing,' he added nastily, 'we added another hour or two to that *approximate* time?'

Teddy still looked puzzled.

'Some incompetent idiot at Aylfleet let 'em send Blatt's body to sea, didn't they? Thought about the consequences of that, if he'd still been alive?'

Press, television, the Police Complaints Board; not to mention the man himself, unconscious, bundled into a freezer lorry, unnecessarily dying alone.

It hadn't happened; almost, but not quite. My stomach turned over. Heads rolling: the incompetent idiot, yes; but what about the scatter-gun effect? The inevitable witch hunt for scapegoats which always takes place when it all goes wrong. Supervisory officers, Paula Baily, me . . . According to the odds, you can't be right all the time, but when the wheel comes off, when you make a mistake, even when you're standing on a nearby street corner innocently twiddling your thumbs when it happens – Bloody Hell!

'Fortunately, the situation does not arise.' For once Teddy looked taken aback. He might have looked slightly ashamed. In his eagerness to score over Dorothea, he'd managed to let himself down.

'No; it's nasty enough as it is, and I suppose *we*' – Fairfield put a touch of emphasis on the word – 'have plenty to do without worrying about the might-have-beens. Let's just worry about something worthwhile instead; what about the time of the attack?'

'Lawrence,' said Teddy primly, 'won't speculate. He's prepared to run some tests on the time blood takes to coagulate; that's all.'

'He's relying on the state of the blood on the office floor?'

Teddy nodded, 'He reckons it's going to be very approximate, even so.'

'Rock me gently,' said Fairfield, with a smirk. Something to do with the well-known Baring antipathy to obscene language at a guess, and an oblique comment on scientific caution and straight-laced people in general, both at the same time. Nothing the boss could put his finger on; nevertheless, he scowled. The smirk, especially constructed to score a point, broadened into a knowing grin.

He turned to me. 'What about these security men, Bob? They don't seem to know who they're letting in and out of the premises, half the time.'

'They concentrated on deliveries in, and loads going out.' I shrugged. 'The visitor system appears to have been OK, but they couldn't care less about management and staff.

'There was some sort of instruction at one time to record staff, as opposed to workers, in and out. It's just like that ex-copper said to me at the start – pay peanuts and you get monkeys. That just about sums it up.'

'Ex-copper?'

'Statement of a guy called Chamberlain; he was on the day shift, unfortunately. Records everything; he's one of the few reliable security staff they've got.'

'Oh, yeah.' Fairfield reached down and picked up three sheets of A4 paper. 'Doesn't do us a lot of good, knowing who came to work the next day. We need to concentrate on movements during the evening and the night he went missing. I see there's a gap.'

'Yessir; Blatt got home around seven p.m.; he was out again by a quarter to eight, but he didn't arrive back at his factory until twenty past nine.'

'And the only bugger they even halfway cared about is the boss.' He skimmed Chamberlain's statement back to one of the untidy piles. 'Traced all Blatt's movements yet?'

'We're working on it.' CID-speak for an admission; I hadn't got a clue.

'So I should hope.' He gave me one of his straight, none-too-friendly looks before he passed on. 'Busy little feller, Blatt. Never made a single enemy when six would do!'

I smiled; tried to look confident, relaxed. It was a bit of a strain.

'He wasn't deeply loved,' I admitted. 'It gets worse, the more enquiries we make. He was mean to casual employees; he sacked people right and left. His managers were scared of him; some of them hated his guts. He played Jack the lad with anything in skirts; his business dealings verged on the crooked, he was a rack-rent landlord on the side, and to top it all he reckoned his company was the victim of some sort of mysterious scam.

'Apart from that, if you leave out the animal cruelty, the vandalism, the fire and the war he was having with his son over his ex-wife's estate, he was a model citizen.'

I waited for a couple of seconds to allow the gloom to settle. 'Oh, I almost forgot; last year he even managed to offend the Chief.'

Teddy, who knew the story, looked marginally pleased. Peter Fairfield stiffened momentarily; then, playing the sportsman, he laughed.

'Every cloud has a silver lining,' he said. 'If you promise to read him his rights, I might let you interview the Chief Constable first.'

Market day in Aylfleet closing down; the streetlights coming on and a thoroughly miserable afternoon slowly drawing to its end. I wished, fervently wished, that I'd never let Derek Rodway talk me into this. Why us? Or, being selfish as well as precise, why, especially, me? If Derek wanted to play detectives by himself, he was more than welcome as far as I was concerned.

Drizzle, dusk, a shop doorway; watching women laden with shopping bags, a gaggle of market traders starting to strip their stalls. Half a dozen idiots in anoraks, accompanied by a girl dressed up as a pantomime dog, were distributing soggy leaflets from a trestle table by the side of the Town Hall. Keeping observations, they call it; something usually reserved for a couple of junior detective cons, or even that lowest form of constabulary life, a CID aide.

I turned up the collar of my Barbour and moved reluctantly forward into a stream of rainwater from the damaged guttering, as a window-shopping harridan barged me to one side. The drizzle turned to a downpour, right on cue.

'Sorry,' she said, displacing me in the shop porch and taking an entirely spurious interest in the trays of cheap watches on display. Derek, a chauvinist to the backbone, gave her a look to blister paint. Umbrella, handbag, sharp-edged shopping basket or not, there was no way she was usurping his dry, relatively sheltered place. She shuffled a few inches too close, giving him the full benefit of a well-placed spoke.

'You bought the lease, then, missus?'

'Eh?'

'The way you shove people around, I thought you'd taken over the shop.'

'You shopping or sheltering? I've got as much right to be here as you.'

'You stick me with that brolly again, and I'll show you how to open it in some place you aren't goin' to like!'

'Hey!' She turned to me. 'Did you hear that?' Then, getting no response, 'Call yourself a gentleman!' I hadn't. She lumbered off.

I resumed my place in the doorway. Derek Rodway spared me a single patronising glance.

'She's probably gone to find herself a cop,' I said, trying to re-establish myself.

'And the best of British luck; she'll never find one. A good policeman never gets wet!'

He never even glanced at me when he said it, but he has this way with him all the same. Makes you wish you'd never opened your mouth. It continued to rain, hard.

'D'ya reckon,' he said by way of conciliation, 'that the fat one with the glasses is a girl?'

Speculatively, I eyed one of the dumpy, leaflet-flourishing figures across the road. It was still bravely waving its bundle of soggy paper, still in good voice despite the wind and wet.

'Sign the national petition against vivisection! Support a new parliamentary bill! Sign up here today!' The words carried faintly across the square above the sound of revving Dormobile engines, the crash of boxes being loaded and the curses of disgruntled market traders preparing to go home.

'Female,' I said judiciously, 'by the sound of the voice.'

'You sure? It looks more like Michelin Man to me. I like the beagle, though; she's got big tits.'

'I hope,' I said crushingly, 'that you haven't dragged me out here just to indulge your fantasies of kinky sex.'

He was, however, right. There was something more than clinging nylon fur and a drooping, puddle-soaked tail to the young lady across the street. Now and again, that dog skin definitely *moved*.

'You ever hear the one about the Welsh Baptist, the ventriloquist and the sheep?'

Just about all I needed; lurking in shop doorways with an exponent of bestiality jokes, with nothing between me and Siberia except a couple of thousand miles of windswept European prairie and the cold North Sea.

'Yes; about twenty years ago. And it wasn't funny then.'

Sullenly, I watched the last, most persistent show in town begin to pack up. There is a limit to what even the most fanatical animal rightser is prepared to do for the cause. Anoraks, nylon over-trousers, even plush-fur fancy dress will not keep out the East Coast variety of wet and chill on a typical winter day.

They took their banner off the trestle table; they collapsed its legs. Somebody put the remaining leaflets and the remnants of their soggy petition into a Marks and Spencer carrier bag. I could practically hear it squelch. Prospects for a happier Graham future re-emerged. No score; but if they went home, I went home. It was as simple as that.

'Told you so,' said Derek, starting forward as a broad beleathered figure on a flash red motorcycle roared up. He loves being right almost as much as I hate being wrong.

The anthropomorphic beagle promptly flung her arms round the new arrival's neck while he struggled to dismount from his machine. It might have been my imagination, but the rest of the workforce, wet, cold and probably bored at the end of a largely unproductive afternoon, appeared to be viewing him with less enthusiasm.

'Jerry, darling! I've been waiting for *hours*!' A hound making a fair stab at a Roedean accent; unusual in these parts. Nice one, though: it went a good way towards confirming the identity of our boy.

'And where the bloody hell have you been?' The over-bundled female with the glasses appeared to be far from chuffed. Her fellow animal enthusiasts put up something like an approving growl.

'That,' said Derek Rodway airily, joining the party and deploying his nasty grin, 'is something us nosy coppers would like to know too.' He flashed his warrant card aggressively. 'Jeremy Blatt the younger, I presume?'

'Oh gawd,' heckled an anonymous background voice, 'it's Stanley, fellers: Dr Livingstone lives!' Derek flushed and clenched a formidable pair of fists. A short fuse: he alone was licensed to do the jokes.

The figure in leathers removed its helmet; black with a white lightning flash down one side. The face beneath was young, beefy, set. Despite a difference in height and shape, he was definitely his father's son. Another graduate of the Adolf Hitler school of diplomacy too; just like his dad.

'Wrong,' he said coldly. Then, scarcely pausing for breath, 'You must be Rodway; I'd heard you were pretty thick. Jeremy, yes, but not Blatt; it's Mr Peters to you!'

It was obvious right from the start; never mind the alias, Derek had finally met somebody as suave, as tactful, and as open-hearted as himself.

11

‘Every cloud has a silver lining,’ said Detective Chief Superintendent Fairfield sententiously. ‘Dorothea Spinks is doing her nut.’ I didn’t share his pleasure; I was even prepared to sympathise to a certain extent. First she’d been landed with a murder enquiry, now one of her officers was the subject of a serious complaint. The greater part of my available sympathy, however, I reserved to myself. Peter Fairfield was beginning to haunt my dreams.

He sat back and we both eyed the two piles of boxed magnetic tapes occupying the top of my desk. One pile contained my interview with Jeremy Peters, otherwise known as Blatt. The second, consisting of two tapes, was the Derek Rodway version of the smoking gun, and for once Fairfield was failing to deploy his slightly stupid boozer’s smile. He had, I noticed, once again brought himself and his news to Eddathorpe nick instead of seeing me at the Aylfleet murder room. Was he scared of Thea on the quiet?

‘Can I hear the additional tapes, sir?’

‘All in good time. I want to know what you’ve got to say about the original interview first.’

‘You’ve not listened to my tapes yet?’

‘Bits,’ he admitted, ‘but I haven’t had a chance to go through three hours of the first Peters interview, *and* these.

‘By the way’ – he stared at me blandly – ‘I wouldn’t take it kindly if Complaints and Discipline got to know about our little chat!’

We both took a further slightly guilty look at the second pair of pariah boxes on the desk. The original tapes had obviously been abstracted from the Aylfleet archives, copied on a strictly unofficial basis, and the master tapes replaced in the store. Not the sort of thing that rule-book coppers did. Not when they provided heavy evidence for a police complaint. None of Fairfield's business, and he must have a very trustworthy, very tricky friend with access to the Aylfleet tape store to have pulled a stroke like this.

Two interviews, two sets of tapes. The first, straight down the line: me, Derek and Jeremy Peters, firmly rejecting the patronymic of Blatt. The second, an hour after I'd left: Detective Inspector Derek Rodway, Detective Constable Patrick Goodall (it would be!) and a prisoner who was now claiming oppressive conduct and assault. And that wasn't all.

'What do you want to know, sir?'

'Just a quick run down of events; what went on.'

'We-ll, we nicked Jeremy junior, whatever he likes to call himself, in the market square and took him to Aylfleet police station; suspicion of criminal damage and the freezer lorry TWOC.'

'You had some evidence, I suppose; or was this just your idea of fun?'

'There was a motorbike at the scene of the fire; the lorry drivers saw a red motorbike and a man in leathers and a lightning-flash helmet at the café prior to the lorry being taken, OK?' Silly, hostile question: I felt entitled to be curt.

'Yeah.' Fairfield only pretended to be dumb. 'Just testing, Bob. You might soon be asked by nastier buggers than me; best have your answers ready, eh? What was his attitude on arrest?'

'Very truculent, lots of mouth and he seemed to have it in for Derek Rodway, right from the start.'

'In what way?'

'Sneering at him; a few sarcastic remarks about his sources of information. That sort of thing.'

'Anything specific?'

'No, but for the son of a murder victim he was acting pretty tough. No shock, no sympathy. One bastard less on earth; that was his line.'

'Did he explain why he hadn't come forward over the last two days?'

'Yes. He said he was deciding what to do.'

'Did he now!' Fairfield managed to look happy and predatory, both at the same time. It wasn't difficult to read his thoughts. We were about to wrap up a murder enquiry; no need to bother then about the police complaints. Typical CID boss.

'It's a bit complicated,' I said, wondering where to start.

'I'll bet.'

'According to him, Sylvia Peters – his deceased mother used her maiden name – was a bit of a dizzy cow.'

'What's that got to do with anything?'

'She used to own twenty-five shares in Blatt's company. Twenty-five per cent of the whole shooting match, that is.'

'And?'

'By the time her divorce was over, she didn't own any at all, but Jeremy junior still has nine; all shareholders are nominally on the board and they draw directors' fees. He draws eighteen thousand a year from Daisy Dew. Christine, his stepmother, never told me that.'

'Less than twenty grand for a directorship in an outfit that size? Is that all?'

'It's not so bad, considering he's only ever attended a couple of board meetings in his life.'

'Pocket money for a middle-class hippie, huh?' Fairfield relaxed so far as to give me the hint of a cynical grin, 'It's a wonder that the genuine scruffs have anything to do with him. Capitalist fink!'

'His mother wasn't supposed to own any shares, but she showed him her old certificates a few months ago. They're worthless pieces of paper now. She reckoned that her ex-husband transferred 'em out of her name without her consent. Jeremy junior says his father forged the share transfers prior to the divorce and blew her out.'

'So Sonny Boy went in for a spot of vandalism, theft and eventually murder to get even with his dad? Is that what you're saying?'

'No; he's admitting nothing, apart from painting the slogans on the sheds a few weeks ago. Giving the old swine a spot of grief, he calls it. Part of his campaign.'

'Campaign?'

'He was leaning on his old man; he'd seen a lawyer to get the share transfers examined at Companies House, but he thought he'd try and short-circuit the system by bringing pressure to bear and giving his old dad a hard time.'

'Painting slogans and nothing else,' jeered Fairfield. 'He must have thought you'd fallen off the Christmas tree!'

'That's his story and he's sticking to it. Claims he knows nothing about the fire, nothing about the taking of the freezer lorry, and absolutely zilch about the death of his father. Says he was in London, anyway, at the time.'

'Doing what?'

'Consulting his solicitor, would you believe.'

'Ye gods!'

'He gave us the address he was staying at; some sort of squat. Says he's got lots of friends; Aylfleet, London, Timbuktu. Crashes out wherever he fancies at the time.'

'I'll bet. No names, no corroboration. It sounds very much as if he's up shit creek without the proverbial paddle, my son.' Fairfield looked at me slyly to see how I took his last remark. He simply enjoyed being crude.

'Or at least he would have been,' he added sourly, 'if it hadn't been for Derek bloody Rodway and your idiot DC.'

'We'd given young Jeremy a three-hour trot,' I admitted. 'And I'd arranged to have him detained overnight. Derek was supposed to leave him for the statutory eight hours' rest.'

'Well . . .' Fairfield's tone was dry. '*Derek* didn't think too much of your methods, Chief Inspector. He waited until you'd gone home, collected the most irresponsible detective constable he could find, and talked the custody sergeant into taking your suspect out of the cells to have another go.'

'Did he get anywhere?' I was pleased with the way I'd said that. Cool, the professional approach. I'd served with people who'd have had to have been scraped off the ceiling after hearing news like that.

'Not yet.' Our caring, sharing DCS had been waiting for an opportunity to shine. 'But he's *getting* somewhere all right. All the way to court on a charge of assault, followed by a disciplinary hearing and the dole queue, I shouldn't wonder!' He closed his jaws with a snap and treated me to a long, dramatic pause before the punch line winged its way. 'Jeremy junior's bruised, the incident's on tape and Rodway and Goodall are both suspended pending an investigation.

'Oh, and I almost forgot.' Suddenly I caught a totally unexpected nuance. Absolutely inappropriate, I would have thought. 'That's not all; guess who's been bedding the grieving widow, Bob.'

'Derek Rodway and Christine Blatt?' Incredulity raised the pitch of my own voice to a self-betraying squeak. Not the elegant ex-model and cocky, stocky Derek, the pride of the working class? Never in a million years.

'Lady Christine Blatt to you, laddie. Nothing but the best for our lad.'

I was right; I'd caught the tone. Another Fairfield silver lining to a second scandalous constabulary cloud. Ridiculous as it seemed, he was basking in the reflected glory. The snobbish old devil was feeling proud of one of his boys, despite having turned a detective inspector into a murder suspect at a single stroke.

'It's getting on for twenty-four hours since you arrested him,' said Dorothea Spinks, 'and that's your lot.'

A consultation, she called it. Huddled in one corner of the custody suite at Aylfleet nick with Jeremy junior and his solicitor smirking at us across the room, and the custody sergeant eyeing the wicked CID like a virgin in fear of rape. Popular we were not.

'You could,' I insinuated, 'keep him in custody for another twelve. The arson alone is a serious arrestable offence; we don't need to take him before the magistrates for further detention until—'

'Thank you; I do know the provisions of the Police and Criminal Evidence Act, Bob, and the answer is no.'

'We could keep him while we conduct further legitimate enquiries,' muttered George.

'You can make those while he's on police bail, Sergeant Caunt. Besides, if you've got some custody time in hand, you can always bring him back once you've got additional evidence. *If* you get any additional evidence,' she concluded nastily.

The end of a perfect day. Suspects and solicitors smiling; coppers on the rocks, and Superintendent Dorothea Spinks taking all her frustrations out on us. She'd been lumbered with a murder enquiry on a technicality, the Aylfleet reputation had been tarnished by a police complaint, and she was now, I suspected, busily insuring herself against any blunders on the part of the feckless CID at my expense.

'We can charge him with criminal damage,' said George, making a last desperate throw.

'On what evidence?'

'He admits painting the slogans, ma'am.'

'Really?' Acid etched her voice. 'He's a director of the company, isn't he?'

'That doesn't give him the right to damage its property. Companies are separate entities from—'

'Yes, I know that law, too. I suggest you release him on police bail pending further enquiries and report him for summons for the slogans. Leave the decision to the Crown Prosecutor, if you insist on making a fool of yourself over trifles. *Painting things on walls.*' She stared witheringly at George; a matter of form. Message received and understood. I knew perfectly well that I was the real target of her contempt.

Not the most productive of days; an absolute waste of time. Nothing but a conscientiously completed custody record and reels of magnetic tape. Stout denials all the way down the line, and a steady wearing out of shoe leather and floor tiles as we trudged backwards and forwards; cells to interview room, interview room to cells.

Yes, he'd got a motorbike, a red Triumph 1200; nice, innit? Doesn't mean to say he was within spitting distance of the egg farm on the night of the fire. Same went for the freezer lorry: lots of thieves, lots of red motorbikes around. Lots of sets of expensive motorcycle leathers and helmets with lightning flashes too. A friend with a burgundy anorak? Nothing and nobody came to mind. Identity parade? You have to be joking! My solicitor advises against it 'cos there's nothing so uncertain as a police ID.

Sure, he was out to recover twenty-five per cent of the Daisy Dew Group. His by right, OK? *Legally recover*, right? Sure, he'd scrawled a few slogans on a wall; that was weeks ago. He *might* have encouraged his cousin to grass on the late unlamented with the Min. of Ag. His old man had tried to use cousin Kevin; he'd managed to use cousin Kevin right back. A spot of legitimate grief being delivered. Serve the old bastard right.

Here's how we stood; OK? His father was an unmitigated old pig. His father's latest wife – sorry, widow – was a smooth-talking, high-class tart. That other copper was having it off with her, and when he mentioned, just *mentioned* his stepmother in passing during his second interview, he'd received a smack in the mouth.

All recorded on tape and in front of a witness too, although he didn't expect that snotty detective constable to admit what had happened. All coppers are bast . . . Well, no, sorry; there are exceptions, all right?

Anyway; no arson, no lorry, no paint on frozen chickens and nothing tipped in the mire. He hadn't been near the Daisy Dew factory at all; he'd been in London the day Papa was killed, and he'd stayed overnight. His London solicitor could confirm the visit; this gentleman here was acting as his local agent, by the way. The local agent smirked again; Jeremy junior smirked. Syncopated smirking. They'd both done a lot of that.

The climax came about twenty past four; after the third or fourth session of coffee and biccies. The solicitor vanished for half an hour; Jeremy had retired to the cells. On his return the solicitor produced half a dozen sheets of fax. One letter from the London firm confirming Jeremy's appointment on the afternoon prior to the murder. It proved nothing by itself.

The other documents were copies of copies, purporting to come from Companies House. They included one share transfer; twenty-five shares from Sylvia to Jeremy Blatt in June 1991, and a second; twenty-five shares from Jeremy to Christine shortly after their marriage. Not necessarily the same shares, but the London solicitors were alleging that the original transfer document was a forgery. Would we care to investigate this serious criminal offence?

It was the only happy moment of George's day. No, he'd said indiscreetly to the local dogsbody, we wouldn't. No longer a criminal enquiry, he said; a purely civil matter now. In any case, we were unlikely to find an officer able to interview Sir Jeremy down there: too hot.

George, older, wiser, more devious than some, had not voiced this opinion on tape. Not the sort of remark to enthuse a lawyer, all the same.

We had to take part in the usual sad little ritual though, in the end. Releasing the suspect; it tugs at the heart-strings every time. Breaking the plastic seal on the envelope; giving all the cash and property back: the comb, the dirty handkerchief, the bunch of keys, wallet, miscellaneous correspondence and twenty-five pounds ninety-two pence in cash.

'Where's my crash helmet?'

'With your motorbike, in the garage at the back. Sign here for police bail.'

It's not so much the return of the property, it's the restoration of the self-satisfied grin to a previously worried face that tends to upset the average member of the CID.

Then there was Dorothea, a lady of considerable wit and charm.

'Best pull your finger out,' she said about a millisecond after he and his smiling brief had passed through the charge office door. 'You can both start by leaning on his girlfriend and all his scruffy pals. Don't just stand there picking your nose, Robert; there's a parricide on the loose!'

'Parricide,' said George disgustedly, well out of earshot of Boudicca.

'Yep; as in one who kills his dad.'

'I know it, you know it,' muttered George. 'But I bet she had to find a dictionary to look it up.'

'Maybe she's right.'

'There has to be a first time, I suppose.'

One of those conversations you hold in the bleak safety of the carpark, well away from Aylfleet loyalists equipped with flapping ears and big, malicious mouths.

12

Keith Baker, the bulky, ageing landlord of the Links Hotel, lifted the flap and leaned tentatively forward, keeping the latched bar door between himself and any immediate harm.

'Nice doggie; good little chap!' He held out a conciliatory packet of crisps, while Joe, my eighteen-pound Lakeland terrorist, rumbled contemptuously and, crisps or no crisps, turned his back.

'They're a sort of Anglo-Irish breed with a shot of Welsh,' I explained with a grin. 'Originally. His Irish side probably remembers Cromwell, and he certainly ain't going to forgive you!'

'Aw, c'mon,' said Keith pleadingly, dropping in the meantime the open packet of prawn-flavoured temptingly close to the chomping end. 'I didn't mean it; anyway, it was months ago.'

True enough: in the course of a genuine misunderstanding with Keith, involving the abrupt withdrawal of a proffered snack, an escaping suspect and a brief preview of the third world war, Joe had found himself insulted, assaulted and barred by the landlord of our favourite pub.

Not a dog to take these things in his stride. Nearly six months later, he still managed to combine the pleasures of successful blackmail with all the satisfactions to be derived from a vigorously prosecuted blood feud. Joe, Uncle Joe, alias Stalin in ascending order and depending on his mood, is not your average cuddly pet.

'Personally,' I said, sampling the top of my pint, 'I wouldn't bother. Cut off his supply of crisps, if he's going to be like that.'

'You really think so?' Casually, Keith picked up a tray and unlatched the bar door; empty glasses, he signalled mendaciously, were about to be cleared. Sliding through the gap, he made as if to pass Joe, reached down, snatched at the packet and the overwhelming majority of the crisps, and rushed to safety just as an irate terrier body slammed against the wood. Joe, paws scrabbling against the varnish, swore.

'Bloody hell! That was close.'

'I was advising on future conduct,' I said thoughtfully. 'Not sending you out on a suicide mission. You very nearly earned yourself a post-humous award for gallantry there.'

Joe quivered with rage, then, having measured the unassailable height of the bar, he was reduced to hoovering up the remnants of the lost packet. Practicalities taking precedence over revenge.

'I'd sell up and leave town now, if I were you,' I said sadly. 'Or he'll very likely get you in the end.'

He stared thoughtfully at my disappointed mafioso. 'I reckon you're laying it on a bit; you like having an animal with a bit of a rep, and he just plays up to you, that dog.'

'OK.' I adopted my casual, neutral tone. 'Suit yourself. Time we cleared up this little misunderstanding, anyway. I'll put him on his lead, and you can come out and make friends.'

Keith stayed firmly on his own side of the bar; Joe, tail twitching expectantly, grinned.

'Another pint, please, Keith.' The voice, familiar but, for once, unex-pectedly subdued, came from the far end of the bar. I turned to face the owner. Slight embarrassment all round; Pat Goodall, my recently sus-pended DC. Thou shalt not communicate with sinners under investigation according to the rules.

'Evening, boss.'

'Pat.'

Ears straining, the local news service and purveyor of unreliable information went to draw the beer.

'A word?'

Cautiously, I weighed up the odds. Early evening, an otherwise empty bar. Keith was a gossip, but Keith was also an ex-probationary constable, if only for a few months and thirty years ago. Besides, it's see all and say nowt, if you want to keep the lucrative CID custom, pal.

'Sure.'

Pat gathered up his beer and moved back to his place in one of the high-backed booths in the far corner of the room.

'What's up?' No get-together; no convivial chat at the bar. Mine host was all agog.

'You've not heard yet?'

'Some sort of trouble?' Our mate Keith; he really ought to have radar aerials sticking out of his ears.

'You could say that. Remember what George said, the last time we had a bit of a confidential CID chat?'

'Eh? What? Head down, mouth shut, you mean?' Exactly; and George hadn't been entirely joking. On a previous occasion we had been sharing secrets after hours, but prior to doing so, George, semi-seriously, had acquainted Keith with the unfortunate consequences of a loose mouth.

'Not a word,' he said. 'You can rely on me.' He'd no idea what was going on, but he was chuffed to bits to be in on it all the same. Very easily pleased and impressed is Keith.

I took my pint and slid into the booth opposite Pat. Big, well muscled, blond, he usually oozed self-confidence, a quality not always justified by performance if honesty was the name of the game. No doubt about it, a first. Patrick was looking pretty pale and wan. Depressed.

'I've been suspended from duty.'

'I know.'

'Told I can't even visit a police station without permission and ordered not to communicate with colleagues.'

'I know that too.'

'Thought I ought to tell you, sir. You're taking a risk.'

'I know how they operate, thanks all the same.'

Faintly, the dimmest of lights began to glow midst his encircling gloom. It might have had something to do with the hint; them, and hopefully us.

'That dirty louse-bound little bastard,' he said.

'Probably; but it doesn't help you a lot.'

'We never laid a finger on him, boss.'

I'd listened to Peter Fairfield's copy of the interview tape. My turn to feel depressed.

'You never said that, did you? I've heard the tape.'

'I haven't said anything yet. Told Miss Spinks that I was going to consult the Federation, and I reserved the right to keep quiet.'

'What did she say?'

'She told me that an independent investigator would be appointed from another division, and I needn't think that I could get together with Derek Rodway and hone up a convincing story. She advised me to put the blame on him.'

The devious old cow! It had been obvious she didn't like her detective inspector, right from the start. Now she was out to ditch him; priority number one. On the other hand, from what I'd heard, it wasn't altogether bad advice. Not much of a choice for Pat, though; defendant or Judas, in a case about to wing its way to the Police Complaints Authority and the DPP.

It's all very well promoting the fearless, clear-eyed integrity stuff, but they don't easily forgive and forget on this job, if you end up dropping people in the mire. Criminal crime is one thing; batting a stroppy prisoner is not regarded in some circles, however, in quite the same uncompromising light. Shock-horror from the reading public? Too damn bad!

'There's one thing certain; you can't go around telling investigating officers how innocent you both are.'

'Nobody touched him, boss. The conniving little swine set us up!'

'Pat,' I said patiently. 'I've listened to the tape; I've also seen young Jeremy junior's face. He's got the marks to prove his point, and I presume, from the racket that was going on in that interview room, that he's got other bruises on his body as well.'

'Very likely,' he muttered sullenly, 'the way he threw himself around. He was having a one-man fight with himself; thrashing around all over the floor.'

'Yes, I've also listened to Derek Rodway's little speech at the end of the tape. All very calm and collected; the prisoner who assaulted himself, and that's what he reported to the custody sergeant, too. D'you really think they're going to buy that?'

'It's true; Jerry junior set us up. The interview was going OK apart from him denying everything except the slogans, and putting Kevin up to grass his father with the Ministry of Ag. Then he starts accusing DI Rodway of having a hidden agenda; having good reason for wanting him out of the way. Said it was all a bit too convenient, and our case would all fall to pieces once the truth about him and sweet little Christine came out.'

So far, so good. But I was waiting for him to talk his way out of the rest of the show.

'He starts sneering, wanting to know whether Derek's girlfriend's anything special in bed. That's when DI Rodway started to get shirty.'

'And that's putting it mildly,' I said.

'OK, so he lost his rag, and as soon as he started shouting, Blatty started to scream blue murder. "No, no, and keep your fists to yourself, you bastard!" Then he sent the chair flying and threw himself on the floor. He was rolling around and yelling like something not right!'

'And?'

'I went to grab him, but he was thrashing about so much he banged his face against the table leg, and I had a hell of a struggle to calm him down.'

'And what did Derek Rodway do while this was going on?'

'Nothing.'

'Not quite.' That's the problem with tapes; a selective memory isn't going to do you a lot of good. 'He was still yelling, wasn't he? A real gem "Serve him right! Leave the little shithouse down there where he belongs," or words to that effect.'

Patrick did not appreciate the prosecuting-counsel touch. It reminded him, all too vividly, of the place where this little episode was likely to sort itself out.

'He saw him bash his face; that's what he meant.'

'Once upon a time there were three coppers under investigation,' I sighed. 'Their prisoner had gone flying down a set of stairs.

' "Well," says the superintendent. "What happened to him?"

' "He tripped," says the first.

' "He wasn't pushed," says the second.

' "I never touched him," said the third. "Attempted suicide: the silly bugger threw himself off the steps!" '

'I trusted you!' Patrick Goodall stared at me with a mixture of misery and venom twisting his face. Not so very hard boiled after all; young, perhaps a shade too young for the CID. 'I thought you could help me out.'

'That story,' I said flatly, 'is going to come unstuck; it's a Derek Rodway special. Not too bad for a spur-of-the-moment job, but—'

'It's God's honest truth.'

Something to stop me in my tracks; I'd never figured Patrick as the man from the Sally Ann. Or was this something along the same lines as the lying suspects who always swore on their mothers' lives? They never offered up Daddy in the same context; either they'd never known him, or they thought it better not to remind the rozzers of somebody already in jail.

'Let's get this straight; you and Derek ran this strictly kosher interview?'

'Yes.'

'And Jeremy junior deliberately wound him up by having a go at his relationship with Christine Blatt?'

'That's right.'

'Then, when Derek Rodway lost his temper, young Blatt, or Peters, or whatever he likes to call himself, screamed assault, flung himself off the chair and you were fool enough to help him out by trying to grab him and contributing to the din?'

He nodded.

'What about the bruise on his face?'

'Accidental. The table leg, I think.'

'So, either you and Derek Rodway are a pair of definite no-hopers, or Jeremy is a cunning, devious bastard who's looking for a way out on a murder charge.'

'DI Rodway doesn't reckon he killed his father; says he's probably the arsonist, and he almost certainly twocked the lorry, and all we've got to do is find his mates and whoever was with him on the bike at the transport café. He's got other candidates for the killing.'

'Who?'

'Weatherby for one; Kinsley for another. He says old man Blatt, at one time or another, was screwing both their wives.'

'How the hell did he discover that?'

Detective Constable Patrick Goodall simply stared.

'*She* told him?'

Strictly non-verbal. To grass up a colleague, simply incline your head.

On the other side of the room, Keith Baker, crisp bag well to the fore, had cautiously ventured three or four steps forward on to the wrong side of the bar. Poised before him, balanced on his haunches, tongue lolling, tail wagging, Joe was wearing his silly, sycophantic grin. Personally, I blame the Eddathorpe air; it's softened him, undermined his doghood. May even have turned him into a bit of a canine creep.

13

'I've been giving your little problem a bit of thought. That's why I've asked you here today.' Ron Hacker, smiling, wearing yet another improbably expensive pale blue suit, drooping silk handkerchief and matching tie. I couldn't see 'em. but I was prepared to make a substantial bet about the colour and material of his socks. The colour-coordinated boy.

I knew perfectly well why he'd summoned me; in part, at least. He wanted to sprawl behind his big executive desk and play the boss, the superintendent, still. He did not wish to sit in Eddathorpe nick, civilianised, patronised and barely tolerated; another old warhorse still sniffing the scent of powder, well after he'd been driven out to grass.

'Good of you, Mr Hacker.'

'Ron, please.' He waved one expansive hand. 'After all,' he said generously, 'the past is over and done with, it's all whisky under the bridge.' It's one way of describing our former professional relationship, I suppose. I'd have plumped for arsenic, myself.

George, his face inscrutable, found something fascinating about the distant view from the window, far, far beyond the confines of the factory fence. George is within a couple of years of retirement; security jobs in industry, however, do not beckon George. Regrettable, but there are indications that my detective sergeant might be something of a snob.

Outside, it was cold, it was drizzling, it was bleak. Somewhere, below and beyond Ron Hacker's office, we could hear the distant clank and rumble of the production line; the endless chain interspersed with hooks, each bearing a potential Sunday luncheon on the move. Inside, Ronald gloried in his newly decorated den: the immaculately painted walls, the Monet prints in shiny steel frames, the new carpet. Ronald had his central heating turned extremely high. Ungratefully, both George and I began to sweat.

'I realise,' said our new friend expansively, 'that it's only one minor line of enquiry, but it's nice to think I've been able to clear it up on your behalf.'

Congratulations were obviously in order: miserable George refused to play. A detective sergeant, a latter-day Trojan even, being wary of Greeks bearing gifts.

'You've cleared something up for us?' George transferred his attention from the distant view; his tone was somehow incredulous. Nothing you could pin down, but there was the tiniest hint of an unspoken extra line; *if that's true, it's for the first and only time in your life!*

'Oh yes.' Peace, love and bonhomie for all. 'You needn't worry about the so-called thefts from the factory. Nothing major at all; a few employee leakages, but I've had the screws tightened down on the buggers, believe me.'

'Sir Jeremy Blatt was wrong?'

'About major thefts through the factory gates? Worrying about nothing, poor old chap. Spot of executive stress, maybe. So that's one line of enquiry we can all forget.'

'You've followed the system through, er, Ron?' My eyes travelled almost involuntarily to the grey-cased computer screen on the trolley beside his desk. On the basis of previous experience, I would have had him down as a paper-and-pencil man myself; better still, give him a big frame and rows of coloured beads.

He followed my gaze. 'Nothing to it,' he said. 'They're very user-friendly, once you know how; dunno why coppers are so reluctant to adapt. Born conservatives, total stick-in-the-muds, I suppose.'

And this from the man who thought that the standard method of interrogating a computerised criminal intelligence system involved twisting its electrodes, and removing the mattress and all the blankets from its cell.

'I see, Ron; could you, er—'

Diffidence, I decided, was the name of the preliminary game.

'Of course, of course.' He removed a bulky pink file from the top right-hand drawer of his desk. 'A quick run-through, eh? And you can take a copy of the print-outs away with you, if you like.'

I did like; somebody, somewhere, was going to have a very careful, very sceptical, look through those.

'First,' he said, adopting a pontifical air, 'I had a go at the purchase ledger; actual and notional. Actual purchases are deliveries of live birds from contractors against invoices. Notional are deliveries from our own sources: together they make total input. Follow?'

I tried the admiring nod; George eyed the file and the untidy rolls of paper in a way that suggested he might like to tear something up.

'I then compared these with the processing records for slaughtered birds and, er, the various portions – whole breasts, boned fillets, legs, oyster thighs and so on. Now these are subsidiary items and really, they . . .'

He droned on, and on, and on. Lessons in chicken-chopping I could well have done without. Still, he was enjoying himself, demonstrating his newly acquired grasp of the business, and to be fair, he seemed to have done a good job. Obviously a man with a mission; I'd never seen this side of Ron Hacker before. Police pension, plus commutation cheque, plus an additional salary had transformed him into the eager company man.

'So,' he concluded, 'taking into account rejects, a standard percentage processing wastage, and an actual less than one per cent for leakage by theft, it all works out, more or less. Got it?'

Getting it included those ominous words, *more or less,* but why alienate a new-found friend? Until I had proof, of course . . .

'Yes, thanks; that's great. I seem to remember an allowance of one and a half per cent for leakage. That right?'

'Far too generous, in my opinion. I'm happy to say it's less, and I intend to get it way, way down. I'm already putting rockets up bums around here, you can count on that!'

I was happy for him; tough on the workforce, though. The Chief Chicken replaced by Hacker in his role of Chief Porker, and the whole place turning into a latter-day version of *Animal Farm.*

In the meantime, the local spoilsport had returned to window-gazing. Enough to put the rest of us off. A very low boredom threshold; the cynical, unhelpful old sod. It was only much later that I asked Hacker the simple question that I should have asked at the time.

It was – is – a very nice house, and anyway, who am I to mock? It might not be my particular version of gracious living, but you pays your money and takes your choice, from the white shag-pile carpet in the lounge, to the highly coloured collection of Napoleonic china soldiers balanced precariously on individual wooden plinths in Simon Weatherby's den. Home sweet home, and guests were invited to remove their footwear in the hall. I kid you not; it was just like visiting a mosque.

Karen Weatherby, slim, pretty, mid to late thirties, expensively blonde; cornflower-blue eyes, and all the delicate charm of a captain in the SS. Mentally, I cursed Jeremy junior and the only piece of information he'd volunteered: she was not, to my mind, the ideal mistress for his dad.

'Come in,' she said. And, 'Would you mind leaving your shoes over there? Carpets, you know.' Minding was obviously something only the brave, not to say the suicidal, ever did. She'd even laid out several pairs of outsize camel-coloured slippers beside the cupboard at the foot of the stairs.

Professionally, I have to admit it; we were a bit taken aback. Imagine how silly we were going to look if we ended up arresting her old man: little boys changing back into outdoor shoes under the eye of the missus, and us with a captive husband in tow.

'Simon,' she announced, leading us into the lounge, 'is in the shower. Five minutes. Would you like China tea?'

She allowed George and me to sink into a pair of very low, very soft, very chintz armchairs prior to awarding us a brace of the smallest, thinnest, most delicate teacups we'd ever seen. No sugar, no milk and exceedingly full. Once the enemy were sufficiently embarrassed and engulfed, she perched herself on the edge of something considerably higher while she made stilted conversation and waited for the constabulary to crush or drop her cups.

'Isn't it simply awful weather?' she said. And, 'Have you come far?'

Five minutes; it seemed more like five hours, and when Simon Weatherby finally appeared she made absolutely no effort to relieve us of our porcelain eggshells as we struggled out of the chairs to follow our host. It was a lesson in psychological warfare at its worst.

Weatherby led us next door; not a library, not a study, it was his den. Just to prove it he had some sort of animal skin on the floor. He followed my eyes.

'Bear,' he said. 'There's the head; I was always tripping over it, so I cut the damn thing off.'

Waste not, want not. The inconvenient bit, teeth bared, gazed down at us from the wall between a Simpson print of the First (King's) Dragoons attacking Chinese infantry in 1860, and the 10th (Prince of Wales) Royal Hussars providing the rearguard against the French in 1808. Bruin, decapitated and minus his undress uniform, looked a bit out of place.

Somebody had been spending money hand over fist. A glass-fronted Victorian bookcase occupied most of one wall; the carpet, reds and blues and blacks, looked genuinely old and Asian, set against polished boards. He had a leather chesterfield, a high-backed armchair, a state-of-the-art stereo stack and a reproduction partner's desk. The drawn deep red curtains hung so heavily they looked as if they could have been carved. Den: a place to which he could retreat from the world, from his troubles; from his lady wife?

'Smoke?' We occupied the chesterfield; he indicated a gun-metal cigarette box on a coffee table in front of us.

'No thanks.' George shook his head.

'We've been going through your statement, Mr Weatherby,' I said. 'There're just one or two points I'd like to clear up.'

'Oh no there aren't.' He lifted himself in his armchair, thrusting out his belly, and scowled. 'Think I don't know why you're here?'

Go for the high ground. 'You do?'

'That malicious little scumbag, Jeremy, rang her up. Told her he'd spilled the beans about her and his old man. For Chrissake, it was years ago.'

'What?'

'The spot of rumpy-pumpy with poor old Blatt.'

Poor old Blatt? Not the sentiment I would have expressed in connection with a man who'd had an affair with my wife. Not the sort of sentiment I *had* expressed, come to that. Mentally, I compared the fate of the Chief Chicken with that of Angie's ambitious ex-lover, Superintendent Clive Jones. Clive, onwards-and-upwards Clive, was now a staff officer to one of HM Inspectors of Constabulary; Jeremy, stiff and stark, had drawn the short sea trip.

My interest sharpened. Who was he trying to kid? Were Company Directors (Poultry) of a finer, more forgiving nature than cops? Law-abiding citizen or not, there had been occasions when this particular husband would willingly have placed Clive and Jeremy senior side by side on the same slab.

Beside me, George stirred. 'You mean, sir, that Jeremy junior telephoned your wife to tell her that he'd dropped you in the mire with the police?'

Not exactly the way I'd have said it myself.

'He has not,' replied Weatherby distinctly, 'dropped me in the mire. Tried to embarrass me, and that's as far as it goes.'

When in doubt, switch tactics, quick.

'Can we go back to the circumstances of the murder, please? What time did you leave the factory the night before?'

'Some time around eight o'clock. The cleaners had gone.'

'Some time after Causley went home?'

'Probably, yes. I'm frequently the last to go.' Another one making his bid for executive of the year.

'But you weren't booked out?'

'Apparently not.'

'And that wasn't unusual?

'How the hell should I know? It's none of my affair; chasing up security men at four quid an hour.' And that was erring on the generous side, from what I'd heard.

George sniffed, 'Not much wonder they're lax, the amount they get paid.'

'None of your business, is it? The taxpayers fill your pockets; we've got a business to run.'

George was not the man to take that one lying down. 'Nevertheless,' he said, 'there's no record of the time you left work, but we know what time Sir Jeremy came back – twenty past nine. Sure you didn't see him, sir?'

'Quite sure, absolutely sure; it's already in my statement. Right?'

'And you have no idea why your employer came back?'

'The company employs me. As an individual, Sir Jeremy did not.' Nit-picking; my detective sergeant had definitely got under his skin, and Weatherby, unsurprisingly, sounded sore.

'But you'd no idea why he returned to work?'

'No; but it wasn't a unique occurrence. Clock-watching,' he added nastily, 'is only for factory hands and clerks.'

'Sir Jeremy,' I said, 'was unhappy about some aspects of management; you didn't know that?'

'Sir Jeremy,' he retorted, 'thought somebody had their fingers in the till. I did not know that then; I do know now.'

I raised my eyebrows interrogatively

'Your ex-colleague,' he said bitterly, 'the lovely Ron, has been blundering around like a cross between the chief of the Gestapo and the wrath of God. If I hear one more word about his expertise with a computer, there'll probably be another murder done.'

Odd, how you can warm to the most unlikely people all at once. Interview situation: not done, therefore, to let your sympathies show.

'Anything in his suspicions?'

'Son,' he said coldly – he was barely five years older than me – 'one thing you learn in this game; there's always a mouse gnawing away in the woodwork, OK? Sir Jeremy knew that as well as I do. The only thing that surprises me is the fact that the old bugger didn't pass the information on. Therefore he must have suspected a bloody big rat.'

'A management rat?'

He shrugged. 'Could be.'

'And you didn't have any particular cause to love him, yourself.'

Read the instructions carefully, light the blue touch-paper, and retire. I waited with interest for the bang.

He leaned back in his chair and gave me a shark-like grin instead. 'Not bad,' he said, 'not bad at all for a plod. Just one thing wrong; in the first place, there's no evidence of any major theft having taken place at all, and in the second, I earn damn near twice as much as you. I've no need to steal.'

'Forgive me,' I said with total insincerity, 'but the victim had an affair with your wife. You continued to work with him, so it might have been nice to get a slice of your own back, eh?'

'Steal his marbles, and once I'd been found out I could bash him over the head with something blunt? And you've got the crust to sit in front of me in my own house and say that?'

'Just exploring the possibilities,' I said.

'I ought to throw you out. You're lucky you aren't exploring the possibilities of a concrete path against your teeth, young man.' He was still grinning; still harping on the difference in age. Somehow, he still seemed to think it secured his position as top dog.

'That's a denial, I take it,' I said.

He didn't deign to reply.

'Tell me again about the discovery of the body.'

'I got to work early; Christine had rung me about him being out all night. Frankly, it didn't altogether surprise me. I thought he was probably out on the tiles.

'Anyway, it was no skin off my nose, going in first thing. Some of us have routine work to perform, even if we're away from the factory for the rest of the day.' Another jibe, presumably, at the mythical civil service hours worked by the police.

'And you *were* booked in that morning,' said George.

'Yes; there was a conscientious ex-policeman on the gate.' He made it sound as if the security man were suffering from some kind of disease.

'I unlocked—' he started, but I wanted to take him through it step by step.

'So you took the factory keys from the security box?'

'No; I've got a master key of my own; so has the office manager and David Lang. So, come to that, had Jerry Blatt himself.'

'Yes,' I said. His keys, I recalled, had been in a wallet in his trouser pocket, undisturbed.

'OK, then. I was first there. I went through the inner doors into the main office to go to the lift. First I saw the damage to the VDUs; then I noticed the stationery trolley from upstairs on its side, by the fire doors. That's when I knew that we'd had a burglar.

'I saw the lift doors were open; the control panel had been smashed. The floor was running with water, so I went upstairs to see what other damage had been done. Some offices were still locked, but there was blood on the floor in Jerry's office, and his computer and CCTV screens had been broken up. That's when I called security and the police.'

'You didn't think of calling them immediately from downstairs?'

'No; I wanted to find out exactly what was going on.'

'You could,' murmured George, 'have walked right into the intruder. Did you ever think of that?'

'I just assumed he'd left by the fire door. It never occurred to me there'd still be anyone around.'

'What next?'

'Nothing.'

'Nothing?'

'Oh yes, your uniformed patrol arrived, followed by the CID. Then Jack; totally useless. You saw him trotting around in that silly cycling outfit, just like a big kid.'

'Jack Causley, the company secretary,' I said.

'Yeah,' he said slyly, 'bit of an old woman; ageing bachelor; you know the type.'

'Nobody seems to rate him, eh?'

'He's good at his job, so far as that goes. He's an old buddy of Jerry, OK? Office manager is right; the company secretary title is pretty nominal. He doesn't interfere with proper directors or divisional managers, that's all.'

'Jeremy Blatt ran the show?'

'The last of the great dictators, Jerry Blatt.'

'Which brings us back to—'

'Yeah. Look, I'll admit it, we're not exactly faithful unto death, Karen and me. Jerry's wife walked out; he and Karen had a bit of a fling. It was a bit awkward, but we got over it. End of story, OK?'

'You make it sound very unimportant.'

'It wasn't quite like that at the time, but it was five or six years ago. It wasn't long before it petered out. I'm hardly likely to wait all that time to bash him over the head, don't you think?'

'And you didn't?'

'Didn't what?'

'Bash him over the head and put him into cold storage while he was still alive?'

The traces of the grin vanished; his face lost its carefully arranged touch of objectivity. 'You're a callous bastard, aren't you? You can't half lay it on the line.'

I didn't blink first, and I didn't repeat the question a second time.

'Jerry spread it around a bit,' he grumbled irrelevantly. 'Karen wasn't the only one, you know. Do the initials PK, or more specifically Mrs PK, mean anything to you?'

Interesting; but not what I wanted, all the same. When in doubt, continue the inflexible stare and wait for a proper reply.

'No,' he said finally, 'if that's what you want to hear. I did not kill Sir Jeremy Blatt.'

Better, much better; now we could get back to Paul Kinsley and his coyly lisped initials, as well as a Director (Frozen Foods) deflecting attention by trying to drop some other poor devil in the cart.

Once outside, George slid behind the wheel of the CID car and chuckled.

'Was he right, boss?'

'About what?'

'About what you wanted to hear. Sarky bugger; I'd like to get an admission, wrap it up, and haul him off to court.'

'You think so? What about Jeremy junior and his games?'

He started the engine. 'Ah, well, him too. He's still as good as anybody. Sod Dorothea's luck; how about dragging them all down to the nick, then?' Helpful George.

14

'Wife all right?'

'Yes, thanks.'

'And the baby, er, Laura, isn't it?'

'Flourishing; fine.'

Teddy, the weak winter sunlight flooding his office, his back half turned, seemed to be conducting an earnest study of the street below. All this apparent solicitude; not Teddy's style. Good news; bad news? Something was apparently up.

'This, ah, enquiry at Aylfleet,' he said finally. 'Quite inadvertently, I seem to have embarrassed Miss Spinks.'

'Oh dear.' I hadn't intended the irony; it just came out.

I had, however, done something right. Superintendent Edward Baring gathered his forces, turned, and resumed his seat. He gave me the merest hint of his downturned smile.

'Not my fault,' he said. 'Headquarters moves in mysterious ways its wonders to perform. What do you think of Jeremy Peters, Bob?'

'Devious,' I said. 'Nasty piece of work.' I was puzzled; the connections he was making were pretty obscure.

'Did he do it?'

'The murder? I don't know. He's on the front row for the arson, the TWOC and the vandalism; that's for sure.'

'What are you doing about that?'

'Looking for his girlfriend; making enquiries to trace the lad with the burgundy anorak from the café. Interviewing his mates.' I'd almost said 'persecuting', but that wasn't Teddy's style either. Not his kind of joke.

'Girlfriend?'

'Margaret Gilmour; twentyish, public school-educated; lives in a caravette.'

'New Age *and* animal rights,' he said distastefully. 'I'd heard.'

In that case, why ask me? Making conversation? A lead-in to something else?

'So; Miss Gilmour has disappeared?'

'Not exactly; she's gone walkabout. Left the travellers' encampment on the estuary, but she shouldn't be too difficult to find. Not with a ruddy great psychedelic-painted van.'

'Keeping out of the way?'

'Probably.'

He sighed. 'I don't suppose she's relevant to my enquiry,' he said.

Came the dawn: Teddy was investigating the Derek Rodway complaint in his capacity as a superintendent from a separate division. But not entirely independent, I would have thought. Surprise, surprise.

I assumed my earnest, slightly puzzled look. 'You're investigating the allegations against DI Rodway, sir? What about the connection with Goodall? He belongs to us.'

'DC Goodall? They're having second thoughts. They feel,' he added slowly, 'that somebody was a bit too precipitate there – jumped in too quickly, so to speak. Rodway was the supervisor, after all.'

So now they wanted Pat as a witness, not a victim. Somebody's version of softly, softly catchee monkey: divide and rule.

'The, er, Police Complaints Authority, sir—'

'Have been informed.'

'Yes, sir.'

'I don't wish' – Teddy being subtle – 'to embarrass you, of course, but you may possibly have spoken to Mr Fairfield about this?'

Hell and damnation: he knew about the very unofficial tapes. And Teddy with a puritan conscience that made Messrs Knox and Calvin look flexible, even soft. Not the moment to be precipitate myself. Not the occasion for the full and frank admission. Wait.

'Tell me; what does Goodall have to say about all this?'

The Chief Constable of Eddathorpe, they called him; the man with the personal private radar system. The bat-like ears and the crystal ball. Whenever Teddy put his mind to it, all us petty conspirators, we poor little rule-benders, never stood a chance.

'Are you asking officially, boss?'

'Perish the thought.'

'In that case Pat Goodall says that young Jeremy set them up.'

Teddy fiddled with the lid of his silver inkstand, one of the luxurious fittings that went with his heavy Edwardian desk, relics of the days when Eddathorpe had a genuine Chief Constable for its Borough Police, long, long ago. 'A bit unoriginal, wouldn't you think?'

'That's his story, and he's sticking to it. Jeremy junior wound Derek Rodway up by mentioning his affair and slagging off Christine Blatt; then he faked an assault by rolling around on the floor, and yelling blue murder for the benefit of the interview tape.'

'And the injuries to his face?'

'Accidental, or self-inflicted during the performance.'

'His motive?'

'Presumably to get himself off the hook. He's succeeded, partially at least. He's now on police bail.'

'You didn't, of course, suggest yourself . . .'

'Definitely not, In any case, Rodway chipped in with something similar for the benefit of the tape, once they got Jeremy junior back on his feet. It's a lousy story, anyway. I wouldn't be seen dead inventing that.'

'Of course not.' His voice was super-dry. 'I have a very high opinion of your ingenuity, Bob.'

And I could take that in any way I liked.

'You wouldn't by any chance be using me, Bob?' David Lang smiled pleasantly. So it was Bob, now. On the strength of a couple of phone calls, one witness statement and our meeting at the Mess Night from hell, were we really such intimate friends?

'Gathering information, David,' I said. 'It's what policemen do.'

Well, some policemen anyway. Others stare around their host's office, rudely clocking the furniture and the decor in general with a distinctly critical air. Detective Sergeant Caunt did not, apparently, approve of spindly steel and glass set on a wheat-coloured carpet, supplemented by a low-seated settee and soft armchairs, nor did he altogether appreciate the two Chagall prints.

Lang followed George's eye. 'It all comes with the territory,' he said defensively. I can't take him anywhere; George looked smug.

'Background,' I said hastily. 'That's all we're after. I thought you could help us out.'

'So I'm off the hook, am I?' He still looked pleasantly amused.

'Left the factory at four,' I said. 'Went to see Kinsley about the demolition of the damaged poultry unit. Got home about six-thirty and stayed at home all night. Alibi, the wife and two teenage kids. All right?'

'It's nice to be in the clear.'

'Nicer still when we can get this sorted out. Clears the air; business life can go on.'

He laughed outright. 'That must be Simon Weatherby talking: such a subtle, sensitive soul.'

'You don't like him?'

'I don't have to like him; we both get paid to do a job. His job, my job, and never the twain shall meet. We've got a gentleman's agreement; we don't tread on each other's toes.'

'At the Mess Night,' I said, 'You, er . . .'

'Gave the wrong impression? Made the occasional anti-Blatt remark, and embarrassed my loyalist friend?' He paused and considered me for a moment, not exactly displeased at the prospect of laying it on the line.

'Yes. OK, Bob; I'm the outsider around here. Not the convinced company man. I've been here four years; I do the job, I collect the pay. I didn't play happy families with the old fart, and if I hadn't been efficient, I'd have been on my bike. That what you want to know?'

'Happy families,' I said. 'Mr Blatt the bonker; that's what I thought.'

'Ha! Sir Jeremy Blatt rogers Simon Weatherby's wife? Not talked about, but known. According to the best information available, however, it was before my time.

'Tell you one thing, though. If it had been my wife, he'd have been found face down in the chicken shit a long time ago. Not that it's likely; my wife has absolutely perfect taste in men.'

Just as David Lang, naturally, had perfect taste in wives. Not exactly hiding his ego under a bushel, wasn't Dave.

'How did you find out?'

'Executive washroom secrets, Bob.' He winked.

'Lots of gossip, is there, around here?'

'It's a bit of a closed society; something like the police force, I should imagine. Isolated spot; family business; hothouse atmosphere. Everything revolving around one man.'

'But you didn't know anything about Sir Jeremy's suspicions about the thefts?'

'We-ll . . . I wouldn't quite say that.' Not exactly reluctant; working out, I suspected, the best way of pushing somebody else over the cliff.

'But not your problem, huh?' George looked wise. 'Not with you not wanting to tread on somebody else's toes?'

Lang stared admiringly at George; it's not every day you come across syntax like that.

'True; but only to a limited extent. The old devil never asked my opinion; he hardly ever confided in me, but problems of that kind affect us all. If profitability on frozen products is down, it's not something you can look at in isolation. It affects the whole group.'

'And profits are down?'

'Marginally.' He shrugged.

'What's marginally?' George was still plugging away.

'A guesstimate? Nothing to pin down, but there's a discrepancy somewhere between production, sales and global stocks. Perhaps six hundred a week.'

'Nice work if you can get it,' said George.

'And what's Simon Weatherby's attitude to all this? Now it's out in the open?' I said.

'Relief.'

'Eh?'

'Your Mr Hacker assures him that there's nothing wrong. Product in; product processed; product out. Orders in; orders delivered; invoices sent, and payments received. And it's all as sweet as a nut.'

'But you don't believe a word of it, yourself?'

He yawned ostentatiously; then he grinned. 'I admire the police force; I really do, but—' He allowed his voice to trail away.

My feelings exactly: Ronald Hacker with a computer was like the proverbial chimp with the typewriter. He might end up with a perfect copy of the plays of William Shakespeare, but don't hold your breath.

'Do you,' said George, 'still think that your colleague could be having it away with the company's gear?'

'You,' said Lang flatly, 'are covered by Crown privilege for defamation; I am not.'

'Educated guess?'

'Not even an educated whisper, Sergeant.' He was grinning again at

George. 'You've got the print-outs, from what I hear. Spend some taxpayers' money; a decent accountant will cost you about sixty quid an hour.'

'Plus VAT.' I was grinning back.

'You've got to speculate to accumulate,' he said. 'Is there anything more I can tell you right now?' Not a man to stick his head right over the parapet; time for him to try the busy-busy ploy.

I shook my head. George looked surprised, but he went along with my not-too-protracted farewells, and waited until we got outside.

'I thought you were going to milk him for gossip?' George was definitely puzzled. The plan had gone awry. Something had been left undone.

'I did.'

'What about the Paul Kinsley story? Lang must know him pretty well; he's the divisional manager for eggs.'

'OK, but how would you describe our new-found friend?'

'Manipulative.'

'And how far would you trust him?'

'About as far as I can spit.'

'Exactly; so the more he knows, the more he'll take advantage to serve his own ends. Besides, he only answers questions; he doesn't volunteer. Maybe he doesn't even know. We're better off talking to the man himself.'

15

Not the ideal place to hold a briefing; hardly room to swing a cliché, let alone a cat. Cramped, old-fashioned; Aylfleet police station was undoubtedly tiny. It was also falling to bits, and nobody, least of all the Police Committee with its overstretched budget, cared.

It was, to be fair, the sort of building where you could shelter out of the rain, type a statement, or even lodge a drunk. Nevertheless, it was not the place to house a major enquiry team with its incident room, computers, cars, files, feeding facilities and back-up. People, especially the locals engaged in routine enquiries, were being pushed into odd corners to do their work. Tempers frayed; competition turned into conflict in zero flat.

'Bugger them, and bugger their briefing. Bugger their whole damn murder enquiry come to that. I suppose' – I could hear the voice through a half-opened door – 'they'll be wanting us to move the offices of the poor bloody infantry into the piss corner next!' This, I gathered, was the local uniformed inspector sounding off.

'I wouldn't mind,' a second voice chimed in, 'but they're running round in ever-decreasing circles. Any minute now their detective chief inspector should be vanishing up his own—'

'Not if he can help it,' I said, poking my head around the door. The grievance committee, consisting of one uniform inspector, one shift sergeant, one custody sergeant and a highly embarrassed PC, tried to distance themselves from each other as far as the limitations of space would allow. They also tried to look as if they'd been discussing somebody else.

Nobody likes criticism, but I could see their point. The office, such as it was, originally belonged to the Local Intelligence Officer, the embarrassed LIO. All his indices had been piled box on top of box and banked up against one wall, and some genius had managed to wedge three extra desks, a tangle of telephones, a large, elderly typewriter and a couple of filing cabinets into the cleared space. They'd almost managed to force a rucked-up sample of holey rug on to the only available spot of empty floor. A gem of its kind; a practical example of how not to promote health and safety at work.

'I'm sorry,' I said to the slowly reddening inspector, 'that space is at such a premium. It must be pretty rough.'

The custody sergeant, absent from the cell block and obviously underemployed, looked as if he would like to slide away. Circumstances, and his own not inconsiderable bulk, stood in the way of an unobtrusive exit. Three guesses as to who'd made the ever-decreasing-circles remark.

'Nothing personal, sir; it's just that we've—'

'Got a police station to run,' I finished. 'And we've pinched space for an incident room, space for me and the duty DI, space for CID men doing paperwork, and now we've nicked your parade room for a briefing. Only temporarily; OK?'

'Yes, sir.' The uniformed man was inclined to conciliate the strange DCI. Youngish, newish; otherwise he wouldn't have been quite so free with his sirs.

The LIO, rankless, with greying hair, was prepared to play the village Hampden; at his time of service he figured he'd got nothing to lose. 'It took us hours to push all the PCs' lockers out of the way in the parade room; just for a bit of a briefing.'

I stared at him with interest. 'Hours?'

'Sir,' he added.

Making the point is fine; labouring it is self-defeating. Especially when I wanted the locals on my side. It was bad enough having a female superintendent simmering away upstairs like a kettle with a cork in the spout. Dorothea Spinks still thought she'd been lumbered with somebody else's enquiry, and Dorothea had a talent for staying mad. Life could become impossible if her attitude was reflected by her troops on the ground.

'This enquiry,' I said cautiously, 'isn't just down to a CID team, you know. Personally, I'd welcome any input from the lads and lasses on the streets. How about the subdivisional supervisors and the LIO joining the briefings, and spreading the good word to the rest of uniform staff?'

Transparent, maybe; something to keep the kiddies quiet, or that's what they might think. Nevertheless, I should have done something of the sort before the grousers had made a start.

All too easy to tread on toes when you're working in a strange place. Back at Eddathorpe I'd got used to seeing everybody from superintendent to civvy clerk as part of the same familiar gang; they tended to put in their own two penn'orth as a matter of course. Nobody found it necessary to sulk because they hadn't been separately consulted, or to stick out their feet to display their highly sensitive sets of corns.

Here, among comparative strangers, I ought to have invited a bit of co-operation, promoted a spot of interdepartmental camaraderie, long before this. A printed crime bulletin and a few instructions to do that and not to do this was no substitute for a touch of the face-to-face. The success of the trick, apparently, depended on keeping all the balls in the air at once.

'I wonder,' I said, addressing the duty inspector, 'if you'd like to attend our briefings, or send one or two members of your shift to find out what's going on. Always grateful for new ideas.'

'Er, yes; things to do myself, but I'll send somebody along.' His eyes fastened on his uniform shift sergeant, who promptly stared meaningfully at the solitary PC. Rank not only has its privileges, its holders have this unerring instinct for passing the buck.

Satisfied, I closed the door on the voice of the proponent of liberty and democracy raised in the inevitable, the unavailing protest against the malignancy of fate.

'But you're not the only one who's busy, Sarge,' it was whining. 'Why me?'

'They always do it at Christmas,' said George.

'True.'

I sank back in the passenger seat of the CID car; fairly happy, slightly smug. The disgruntled Aylfleet constable had come up trumps. Shows what a spot of uniform/CID co-operation, let alone DCI's revenge, can do. Man management, I could call it; making the system work.

Gratefully, I clutched the LIO's contribution to our murder enquiry; four lines of ill-typed text on a tatty piece of card. He hadn't enjoyed our briefing, but it had set his file-burrowing instincts to work, and hey presto, he'd come up with a domestic dispute. Ruth versus Paul Kinsley, a treble nines call from the midst of nowhere, last Christmas Eve.

Finding the Daisy Dew sign, George swung off the road and began to pilot the CID car slowly, cautiously, along the twin concrete ribbons of track towards Lowbarrack Farm. It was worse than I'd remembered; self-congratulations were in order. Mileage allowance or no mileage allowance, I was glad I wasn't destroying the suspension on my own car.

'The first time I went to a domestic disturbance as a probationer was a Christmas Eve.'

'Oh yeah.' This was meant to convey my supreme lack of interest in combat stories. Not that it ever does me any good. I was a captive audience; another chapter from *The Memoirs of George Caunt, His Life and Times*.

'Yeah; we'd had a hell of a night. Fights, road accidents, stupid three-niners, the lot. Then, when I arrived to sort out a husband and wife at this bungalow, a feller in the street outside gives me twenty-five quid.'

'Novel,' I conceded. 'What did you do, arrest him for attempted bribery, or pocket the cash?' Insult, outright defamation; the only possible way to keep him down.

'He wanted me to be stake-holder for his fine.'

'What fine?'

George grinned; he had me hooked.

'He lived next door to this drunk who was always belting his wife. Whenever this bastard hit her, she cried. Whenever she cried, she went next door looking for sympathy, and that made this other feller's wife cry too.'

'Wearing,' I said.

'Yeah; Christmas Eve, kids in bed waiting for Santa, and bugger-lugs starts to perform. Shouts, assault, tears. Sure enough, Madam comes round to share out the grief, so this guy gets totally dischuffed. First he rings the police; then he stands outside with the money in his sweaty little fist, awaiting me.

'He hands over twenty-five notes, and tells me he's going next door to banjo the drunk for spoiling his Christmas. After that, I can arrest and bail him, and the money's for the magistrates once the courts reopen after the break. Naturally' – George was in virtuous mode – 'I refused.'

'Naturally.' Irony of this kind is usually lost on George.

'Anyway, I go inside and find this animal hiding under the dining-room table, blubbering for police protection against the man next door. So I arrest him for assault on his wife and drag him off to the police station. He's only wearing a pair of socks and a string vest.'

A trifle informal, I conceded, even for Christmas Eve. But not, I would have thought, essential to the plot.

'Our section sergeant,' said George bitterly, his indignation undimmed by time, 'was the idlest, most indecisive copper I ever met. He refused the charge and ordered me to take the prisoner home. I'd have seen him in hell first!'

'So?'

'So I waited till the gutless old swine went upstairs for his meal before I explained one or two bits and bobs about wife-beating, and then I threw meladdo into the street. Two in the morning, and he'd got about half a mile to walk.'

'In his vest?'

'In his little vest and socks; dangling his great hairy—'

'I think I get the picture, thanks.'

Difficult to put your finger on it, exactly; but legally, constitutionally speaking, it wasn't altogether unlikely that George had been riding roughshod over the liberties of the subject somewhere along the line . . .

The undamaged battery houses, or percheries, or whatever you like to call them, were still there, but the fire-damaged building had been demolished. Nothing remained except a huge expanse of scrubbed, patchily blackened concrete upon which tightly strapped bales of bricks, stacks of timber and a cement mixer squatted as an earnest of good faith. Of the builders themselves there was no evidence whatsoever, and no signs of any Daisy Dew employees around the yard.

'Typical,' I said.

'Never there when you want one,' agreed George. He eyed the hundred-and-fifty-yard strip of ash-covered pothole, rut and mud dividing us from Paul Kinsley's cottage. Very doubtful, very dodgy indeed; but I didn't fancy a pair of filthy shoes and the price of a dry-cleaned suit. We lurched ahead at a steady five miles an hour.

Kinsley was waiting for us on the front porch of his cottage, wearing his foxy grin. 'Never thought you'd make it in one piece,' he said. 'Sooner your suspension than mine. Have you found the arsonists yet?'

'We could give one good guess,' muttered George bluntly, 'and so could you!' Nothing, in George's opinion, like starting as you mean to go on.

'This is Detective Sergeant Caunt,' I said, but names seemed superfluous, somehow, after an introduction like that.

'You'd better come in.' Neither upset nor embarrassed, he waved us inside; he even retained a vestige of the grin. 'You wouldn't expect me to lose my job over a bit of idle speculation, now, would you, Chief Inspector?' I promised myself an adequate return for that.

He ushered us through a small, dark, central hall with a single door on either hand, into a cluttered kitchen. No need to ask about the whereabouts of his wife; definitely not there. The pine table in the centre of the room was cluttered with unwashed pots; so was the sink.

The kitchen boiler, front open, was smoking sullenly. I noticed a scattering of clinker upon the concrete surround; one or two bits had fallen forward, leaving burn marks on the linoed floor. A poker had been thrust inexpertly between the bars to break up the welded mass still in the grate to encourage the fire to burn. You didn't have to be a detective; the whole room – the piles of newspapers on chairs, the smell of greasy food, the air of general neglect – told its own tale. Mrs Kinsley had decamped. Or, to introduce a slightly sinister note, that's what we hoped.

Generously, he cleared a couple of chairs and we sat down.

'Coffee?'

'No thanks. I'm surprised you're not out there.' I nodded towards the window and the poultry units beyond.

'Having an hour to myself; only got one pair of hands.'

'What about the other employees?'

'What others?' He gave a short, bitter laugh. 'I've got a team of female packers coming in three times a week. Apart from that, I'm lumbered. I'm supposed to have one full-time labourer, but—'

'You mean you're left to run this lot by yourself? I thought you were the manager around here.' George might have been deploying a spot of sympathy; personally I put it down to sheer lack of tact.

'Well . . .' Kinsley stared at him coldly. 'I suppose you could say I'm managing myself, OK? Anyway, I'm sure you don't want to hear about my troubles; I suppose you've come with some more questions about the fire?'

'Not exactly; we've got some new questions about you and Sir Jeremy Blatt.'

'Oh.' He pulled out a kitchen chair and sat facing us. Just like last time at Aylfleet nick; the strained, wary look. Very tense.

'Why didn't you tell us about the slogans and the fire?' Deliver the bad news, then flick back to the expected question.

'I didn't know who'd done it; still don't.'

'But you could guess. Kevin Cooke,' I said, 'is Jeremy junior's cousin. Common knowledge, of course?'

Reluctantly, 'I suppose.'

'Slogans on walls; and your operation getting grassed up to the Ministry of Ag?'

Silence.

'The cousin works here, and Jeremy junior was having a running feud with his old man. Was that common knowledge too?'

'Up to his father to tell you, if he was going to tell you; not me.'

'The motorbike,' I said, 'in the early hours. Followed by arson. You knew Jeremy junior had a bike, eh? Put two and two together? Is that why you stayed safely in bed?'

'No.'

'What the eye doesn't see, the heart doesn't grieve over?'

'What's that supposed to mean?'

'Well, it *could* be something to do with you not wanting to get too close to your chairman's son and his shenanigans, because of your job. On the other hand, how recently did you find out about your wife and Sir Jeremy himself?'

'You bastard!' He erupted from the chair; George and I stood up.

'Were you scared, Mr Kinsley? Physically scared that night, or scared of seeing too much and compromising your job?'

'I didn't know it was young Jeremy; it was only after I thought—'

'Or perhaps,' said George, 'you weren't bothered about the slogans, the potential prosecution, or even the arson. After all, Jeremy, if it was Jeremy behind it, was helping you out, eh? Helping you get revenge.'

'It was up—'

'—To his father to tell us; so you say. Up to him to tell us about his relationship with your wife, too, eh? He must have wondered; a son with one grievance, an employee with another . . .'

Somebody cut Paul Kinsley off at the knees; he dropped back into the chair. He'd been scared before, for all his bluster. He was terrified now.

'You're playing with me, aren't you? It's obvious, you know all about it.'

'Really? All about what?'

'You know all about the old man being here that evening. The row with Jerry Blatt.'

Wrong, as it happened; nobody had issued the CID with a crystal ball. But say what you like about us, we're always willing to learn.

Midnight, the witching hour, when we finally kicked him out. This time, at least, we did it of our own accord, and without the assistance of Dorothea Spinks.

'No joy?' asked the custody sergeant, with no discernible trace of a smirk.

'No,' said George. 'He reckons they had a bit of a discussion about his missing wife on the evening of the murder, that's all. He's not seen her since Christmas, but he never went to the factory; never laid a finger on Blatt.'

'Left him, did she?'

'So he says.'

'For that old goat? Casanova rides again.'

Kinsley stood there dumb. Not the nicest, most sensitive of things, your intimate affairs being discussed as if you don't exist.

'Police bail,' I said firmly, cutting them short. 'For further enquiries: six weeks.'

'Another one?' The smirk surfaced at last. The Aylfleet sergeant with attitude: I remembered him.

'It's our life's ambition,' said George with a distinct trace of frost in his voice. 'We're arresting the entire male population of Aylfleet, one by one; then we're letting 'em all out on police bail just to annoy you.'

Unjust, regarding George as your typical, totally callous cop. He can, I realised, be very caring, if a trifle over-sensitive, at times.

16

'Mother rang,' said Angie. I didn't even twitch; instead I dandled Laura in a non-committal sort of way. Reserve your fire, and wait for the enemy to advance.

'That's nice.'

'She wants us to go over for the weekend.'

This was easy, too easy. 'I can't; not in the middle of an enquiry like this. Lucky if I can take one rest day just now.'

'We didn't go over at Christmas.'

No, we didn't: a minor engagement in a lifelong campaign. I did not dislike Maria Hervey, and please note the posh spelling of the name. Put it this way; we were simply better apart. Twenty-odd years of social skirmishing among her fellow army wives had turned her into something to frighten the SAS, and here we have to be talking majors and above.

And it wasn't that she didn't like policemen. People to keep away from, of course; but you could smile and show them your driving licence before waving regally, and continuing on your merry way. Or, in extreme emergency, you might invite them as far as the kitchen and offer them a cup of coffee – or do such people confine themselves to heavily sugared Indian tea?

Three of the great disappointments of Maria's life: Angela had gone to Essex University; Angela had become a teacher in the state-run sector; Angela had married a cop. Not that she said it aloud. To be fair she'd even tried to like me at first.

My name helped. Something to do with a spineless, semi-coverless copy of Debrett she'd dug out at a jumble sale for seventy-five pence. She looked up Graham, and she almost wet her knickers when she found it was the family name of the Dukes of Montrose. I should, at least until after the wedding, have confined myself to the occasional mysterious smile. How was I to know that she hadn't got a sense of humour; that on the subject of lineage she positively did not joke?

Instead, I'd treated her to an embroidered history of a totally unconnected Graham clan; ragged, trouserless, seldom washed. A gang of landless, thieving, robbing Borderers with a talent for arson and receiving, interspersed, for the sake of variety, with a spot of gizzard-slitting and rape. It's not as if I've a shred of evidence connecting me to either lot, but somehow the spark of friendship died.

In some obscure way, as blood will out, the disclosure seemed to affect her view of the integrity of rozzers as a class. Common, I was led to infer, without the additional taint of inherited criminality, would have been quite bad enough.

Still, live and let live. Mrs Maria Hervey, sixty-eight and widowed. is perfectly entitled to her point of view. As long as it's expressed in Derbyshire, and I remain on the East Coast. Both of us healthy, both of us happy; may she live for ever. Fair enough?

Not, apparently, tonight. 'She doesn't see much of her granddaughter.'

True. I temporised by growling at Laura; playing bears. Laura was delighted; but not the determined wife.

'We *ought* to go.'

'I can only manage one day at most. It's a hundred miles or more; hardly worth it, all that way and back. And things are pretty hectic at the moment; I can't even guarantee which day.' An appeal to professionalism rather than patriotism; the last refuge of a scoundrel, all the same. Dr Johnson hadn't quite thought things through.

'You don't want to go, do you?'

'Not exactly, no.'

'Is it anything to do with . . . I've never said a word, you know. She knows we went through a rocky patch, that's all.'

'She knows we lived apart; and she's not stupid. She can count up to nine, and she probably smiles when she does it too.'

Angie came over and sat on the arm of my chair, sliding one arm across the back and looking down at us both.

Wistfully, 'She looks a lot like you.'

'Your mother?'

'You know perfectly well who I mean. Anyway; times, dates, visits,' she said vaguely, dropping her wrist, twisting my ear. 'I think I've misled Mother a bit.'

'Women are a devious lot.' I felt about a thousand per cent happier, all the same. Reasons, feelings, excuses; I pushed them to one side. You can't choose your relations, not even your in-laws; not once you've made a choice over far more important things.

'You'll come, then?'

'I'll see what I can swing.'

Or whom, with a bit of luck; this was a murder enquiry, after all.

It happened on the Saturday night, and we didn't get back until Sunday afternoon. Never mind: not a lot of time wasted. He didn't regain consciousness until after three o'clock.

We arrived home at twenty past four. 'I'll just pop down to the nick,' I said.

Angie smiled. Duty done, all was sweetness and light. The barbarian had been on his best behaviour; I'd even helped Mother to wash up after Sunday lunch. Domestically speaking, therefore, we were definitely cooking on gas.

Not so Paula Baily, found brooding in the Eddathorpe detective inspector's glass-and-plywood hutch, contemplating an absolutely empty CID general office beyond.

'Glad you got back,' she said.

'Trouble?'

'You could say that. Last night; somebody did for Kevin Cooke.'

People, even friends; they do that to you from time to time. Try to see if they can get your heart to jump right into the back of your throat. She watched for the reaction, then, satisfied with taking about five years off my life, she let me re-start my pulse.

'One of the beat men found him in a back alley just before midnight. He'd had a good kicking, but he's come round now.'

'No permanent damage?'

'They think not; nasty, though. They've done a scan, and they're keeping him in for a few days.'

'Street robbery?'

'No.'

'Any idea who did it?'

'I'm hoping he's going to tell us that.'

Kevin occupied an amenity bed, that is to say another glass-and-plywood hutch in Eddathorpe and District Hospital, all to himself. His head was swathed in bandages, and from what I could see, his face was one solid bruise. His right arm, extensively bandaged, was artistically arranged on top of the folded-down sheet. Mrs Cooke, née Peters, was sat beside his bed. She ignored me, clocked Paula and glanced down at her lap. She appeared to be running a mental competition as to the relative length of their skirts.

She fancied men, but not policemen, did Kevin's mum. A carefully preserved lady in her forties with lots of legs, she had a stinging line in repartee, and we had met before.

'Hello,' said Paula.

There was no need for introductions. 'You took your time.'

'How are you feeling, Kevin?'

'And a fat lot you care; he could have died!'

'Do you feel up to answering a few questions?' I joined the band.

'And do you feel up to fucking off?'

'Mum!'

Delicately, she applied a handkerchief to the mascara on a perfectly dry eye. 'Where were they when I was sitting here worrying all night beside your bed?'

'We,' said Paula flatly, 'had a constable here all night. And, as I recall it, when we sent somebody round to tell you, you were out. You arrived here some time after six a.m.'

'I'm entitled to a bit of fun now and again. What is this, a police state?' She turned towards me in an indignant flurry of cheap face powder tinged with the faint but unmistakable aroma of last night's gin. I was not inclined to help.

'The constable who visited your home,' continued Paula remorselessly, 'met Kevin's little brother; he was by himself. How old is he; nine, ten?'

Paula's skirt was longer; Paula's temper shorter. Kevin and I kept out of it: we seemed to be witnessing a spot of inter-female tetch.

The door opened abruptly, and the ward sister appeared: a dark blue avenging angel with her lips tightly compressed.

'I can hear you next door in my office,' she snapped. 'If you intend to quarrel, please do it somewhere else. I will not have my patient disturbed.'

Paula subsided; Jane Cooke stormed to her feet. 'I didn't come here to be insulted,' she said ludicrously. 'See you later, Kev. As for you' – she

128

turned on the sister – 'I hope you've got rid of the smell of pig by the time I get back!'

Kevin watched his parent depart through one half-closed eye. Difficult to tell, but his expression might have been one of relief. The ward sister left too; she appeared anxious to have another word with Mum. Personally, if she'd been anything like her sister, I could sympathise with the husband of the first Mrs Blatt, womaniser, chicken-chopper, tax-evader, slum landlord or not.

'You all right, Kevin?'

'Flat on me b-back. with me head busted open, covered in bandages, with this arm an' three or four cracked ribs? You ought to be a detective. you.' Lots of dressings; a purple, swollen face and slow, painful speech, but the Kevin we knew and loved was definitely at home and functioning, somewhere in there.

'Sorry about your mum.'

'Not as s-sorry as me, mate.' Force of circumstances compelled it; I'd been promoted to an acting rank. I was finally Kevin's mate.

'What happened?'

'What's s'posed to have 'appened? I got elected Miss World.'

'Congratulations; I like the bandaged crown.'

The figure in the bed moved. 'Don't; it hurts when I larf.'

'What about it, Kevin? Are you going to help us make this guy laugh on the other side of his face?'

'I w-would if I could.'

'Somebody been warning you off?'

A slow, stiff inclination of the head.

'Your cousin?'

'Might – mighta been. He d-don't like me talking to coppers. Not him who did it, though.'

'Who, then?'

'Dunno.'

Paula sighed; a single, impatient rasp of breath. She is not the credulous type.

'If I s-say I dunno, I dunno.' He roused himself; almost tried to sit up. His voice rose to a whining, indignant slur. 'You find him, an' you c-can give *him* a good kickin' from me, but I never seen him before, OK?'

'OK. Tell me what happened, then.'

'H-had a few bevvies at the Railway; not drunk. Saw some mates, tha's all.' The Railway Arms, a back-street pub, two or three hundred yards away from his home. 'Walkin' back by meself.'

'Nobody else around at all?'

'Don't think so. No.'

'And?'

'This feller came runnin' up behind me, an' bang!'

'Can you describe him?'

'Chunky.'

'And?'

'That's about it. Oh, yeah, and he stunk like a f-ferret. Musta almost never had a bath; tha's what I remember most. H-hadn't got a chance to take photos, had I? Mighta been the one I saw in the pub, though.'

'I thought you said you'd never seen him before.'

'Not before I saw 'im in the – y'know what I mean.'

'Yes, OK. Describe the man you saw in the pub.'

'Starin', he was; starin' at Mickey's girlfriend, too. Twenties. Big belly; long arms. Too big for his clothes.'

'Mickey?'

'Mickey Donovan.' Mickey I had met before. I might almost have known. The girlfriend, too, bore a famous family name from Eddathorpe's top estate. One of Paula's minions could go out and get a couple of witness statements, and the best of British luck.

'Is that it?'

'Trainers, he was wearing. Trainers and blue jeans. One gold earring; brown hair, I think.' And there I was, wanting something distinctive; hoping for green.

'Nothing else?'

'Sorry.'

Kevin's statement later. A proper interview, but by the look of him, much, much later on. One or two professional platitudes, a few more words of consolation, and we prepared to depart.

'These jeans he was wearing,' said Paula. 'You say he was too big for them; so they'd shrunk?'

'Nah, not the jeans. The anorak.'

'What anorak?'

'The o-one he was wearing. A whatya call it, darkish red.'

'You mean burgundy?'

''Sright; a burgundy one.'

130

'I'll get somebody to see Mickey and his girlfriend this evening,' promised Paula. 'They might do a better description than Kev. Then it's back to the anorak and the stink.'

'Two and two make twenty-two,' I replied cryptically.

'Coppers.' She shook her head sadly. 'Jumping to unwarranted conclusions. Not very politically correct.'

It was dark outside. I thought about the state of the place I had in mind; the piles of rubbish to trap the unwary; the flat, squelching landscape; the gelatinous mud.

'First thing tomorrow morning,' I threatened, 'I'll broaden your experience; treat you to a visit to the New Age travellers' camp.'

17

It was not your average jolly holiday scene. Two hundred yards away, the vehicles huddled miserably around the remains of a Second World War anti-aircraft post, a wilderness of crumbling concrete set in a flat brown landscape, with the waters of the estuary slapping unhappily against the foreshore beyond. The caravans and buses had been arranged in a rough circle incorporating the remains of the gun site, and somebody had dumped several loads of sand and shingle into the central space in an attempt to create a relatively mud-free zone. Add the piercing wind and the low, grey, rushing sky, and you wondered why anybody, however desperate, stayed.

'They love it.' Behind me, the Aylfleet detective sergeant leaned forward and peered through the windscreen with gloomy satisfaction. 'They reckon that it's a haven of sanity, spirituality and peace.'

'Do you come here often?' asked George in a conscious imitation of an adolescent at the Palais de Danse. Roger Prentice, Derek Rodway's sidekick, glowered. Ho, bloody ho!

Sidelined, left to run the local shop while the rest of us gloried in the big-time excitement of a murder enquiry, he was making it plain that he was not truly our friend. He should have been grateful; nobody was chasing him for results. Besides, a song, a smile, a merry tale; anything to relieve the depression of a day, a scene like this.

'You came here with Inspector Rodway last time?'

'I come with him every time,' he said. 'He, er, chases 'em a bit.' Did I detect the merest hint of anti-Rodway criticism in his voice?

I craned my neck over the back of my seat. 'Oh yes?'

'Inspector Rodway,' he muttered, 'seems to think they're Gypsies, or sum'mat. Expects to find the place crawling with stolen property. Either that, or they're smuggling drugs.'

'Hello, sailor,' suggested George. 'Chuck us a small waterproof packet as you're sailing past?'

'Fat chance of that, I'd say.' Not the humorous type; not at this time of a cold, raw, end-of-winter day.

Slowly, not to say uneasily, our second car breasted the muddy rise behind us, and George eased the CID car into gear as we slid rather than moved towards the encampment in a procession of two at an unsteady five miles an hour. One of those occasions when the forward planner ought to have sorted out the whereabouts of a cheap car-wash for use on the way back.

George, with his unerring instinct for the dramatic, pulled up outside an Indian tepee set beside an elderly single-decker bus.

'They said they were goin' to set up a totem pole just here, but they haven't got around to it yet.' Roger Prentice was determined to give us the full conducted tour.

I simply couldn't resist it. 'Why?'

'They're a tribe.' He sounded pleased to be asked. 'They want a symbol of tribal unity and strength to set beside their sweat-lodge.'

'Don't tell me,' begged George, opening the driver's door, 'this Red Indian thing is the sweat-lodge, an' it's a place where they sit around an' smoke pot while they share bodily odours to their hearts' content.' Unreconstructed Tory, with built-in totalitarian tendencies, that's George.

'It's for ritual cleansing, and to promote community bonding and good health.' Prentice sounded almost aggrieved.

'I'd sooner use senna pods, meself.'

By this time we were out of the car, and Paula's party, consisting of herself. a uniformed driver, big Malcolm Cartwright from Eddathorpe and one of Roger Prentice's DCs, got out of their vehicle.

Early morning; two dogs sniffing around a bucket beside a caravan fifty yards away. One of them barked, its voice echoed by half a dozen other animals concealed inside the vans. Apart from that, nothing; and despite the slamming of car doors, nobody appeared. As a display of utter and absolute human indifference to our arrival, it was quite impressive in its own right.

'Go on,' said Paula, 'choose a door, any door, and knock.' Eddathorpe's crime; committed on Paula's patch, and therefore Paula's shout, with

Roger, the local representative from Aylfleet, merely along for the ride. Nothing much to do with my murder enquiry either, so far as I could see. I was simply there in my official capacity; the nosy, interfering boss.

Diffidently, almost reluctantly, the big raid got under way. No warrants, no aggro; not unless we found somebody fitting the general description – anorak, brown-haired, an earring, aggressive and chunky with very long arms.

Roger Prentice strode purposefully towards the nearest battered bus; he seemed to know what he was about. I chose an elderly orange-painted caravette; curtains drawn all round. I tapped on the windscreen with a coin. The nearside door slid back.

'I've got me road tax, and an MOT; also I'm insured, OK?'

'OK,' I said amiably. 'How did you know I was from the police?'

'It might be me psychic powers,' said the large, unbrassiered woman at the door. 'On the other hand, it might be the sight of that prat in the blue uniform over there. I got a GCSE in the filth.'

I kept on looking pleasant; no point in turning ratty, just because you've made yourself look a mug. Besides, I'd seen this lady, more adequately clad for the weather, somewhere before.

I took in her current attire and shuddered, doing my best not to let it show. About an acre of sloganised yellow tee-shirt over pink nylon knickers. Casual, but not the Benetton look; not if you're five foot four and approximately twelve and a half stone. I had my doubts about the favoured wording, too. Unusual, off-putting, confrontational even, at twenty minutes to 8 a.m. MARRIAGE IS LEGALISED RAPE!

'What d'you think you're looking at?'

Not a question I felt equipped to deal with all at once.

'I, er . . . haven't we met before?' Then, hastily, just in case this expression of male panic was taken for a lustful, if clichéd, sexual ploy, 'The animal rights petition: Aylfleet Town Hall square, right?'

'It rained.'

'Yeah, it rained all right.'

Having, in the inimitable manner of the English, fulfilled the social niceties, she seemed more disposed to talk.

'Wait,' she said, 'while I get me kecks on, and dispose of the worm.' The door slid shut; I could still hear her, loud and clear.

'Jacko, get your backside out of that bed, and stop polluting me space; the Queen's comin' to tea.'

'For Chrissake, Bernice, what's got inter yer now?'

'Visitors. I've told you – out!'

A series of groans, protests, metallic scrapings and muffled thuds accompanied the folding of a bed, and the preliminary measures accompanying the disposal of a no-longer-welcome guest.

'Don't I even get a hot drink?' The male voice sounded plaintive.

'What am I supposed to be running around here, a café? If you want tea with it, matey, you can book us both into the Ritz!' Another late-twentieth-century instance, literally as well as figuratively, of girls on top.

Eventually, an undersized male in his late twenties or early thirties, with wild, uncombed hair, torn jeans and shirt tails flapping beneath an old bomber jacket, was ejected from his night's abode.

'Mornin',' he said, striving for nonchalance, succeeding only in stumbling on the step of the caravette.

'Morning.'

'Watch it,' he warned over his shoulder, making for a converted ambulance a dozen yards away. 'They ought to have put a gov'ment health warning on her.' Oddly enough, the thought had already crossed my mind, but by this time the troops all seemed to have vanished, and it's so undignified when detective chief inspectors are seen to scream before they're hurt. Still, a chaperone might have been nice.

'Come in,' she said. I was not entirely eager, but we are, after all, trained as well as paid to do this sort of thing. It was, I figured, an occasion where the wise copper takes a deep breath, enters, says it all as quickly as possible, and gets out prior to being overcome by a rampant female or noxious fumes.

I'm not often right, and I was wrong again; the inside of the vehicle was not only tidy, it was scrupulously clean. The bed, folded into a padded bench, was fresh and chintzy, and over the miniature sink and cooker, beside the fitted wardrobe, swung four china mugs on hooks. Relieved, I also noticed she had squeezed herself into a pair of tight, stonewashed jeans, clasped around with a beaded belt.

'You're making the place look untidy; siddown.'

I sat.

'Coffee?' Do not make excuses; refusal so often offends.

'Thanks.'

'Still looking for Scumbag, are we?' Noisily, she filled the kettle and slammed it down on the hob. 'Devious bastard, that.'

'You mean Jeremy?'

'Jeremy,' she confirmed. 'We didn't know, y'know. The little shit.'

'Know what?'

'About his old man, an' the business an' everything. No idea that he was a rich bastard using us for his own ends.'

'Actually,' I said. 'I was looking for—'

'His girlfriend, huh? He's way ahead of you lot, mister. Got her out from under, straight away. Probably got her working in a brothel in Venezuela by now.'

'Really?'

'You retarded or something? Not really, no. But he won't let you lot get his hands on her in a hurry. Stands to reason, OK?'

'Why?'

Instead of replying she turned towards the cupboard beneath the miniature oven and hob, reaching for a screw-top jar. 'Coffee, you said? Sugar and milk?'

'Come on, you're not his closest friend, are you, Bernice? Why does it stand to reason, love?'

'Sorry to get you all excited, sunshine. Blabbermouth Bernie rides again; nothing else to say.'

'Not even about his using you lot here?'

'Oh, I don't mind talking about that; common knowledge. Surely you must have heard?

'He persuaded some of the girls to go and work at that stinking egg unit for next to nothing an hour. Nobody knew his proper name and his relationship to the old bastard at that time. He said it was all for the good of the cause.'

I checked her for irony: nothing. So far as she was concerned causes were sacred. You worked, you demonstrated, you wore slogans across your chest and perhaps you burnt down the occasional wooden hut. Your cause; their cause; anybody's cause: you did not manipulate the crusaders, and you never, ever, took the mick.

'Anyway,' she continued, 'he had some reporter lined up ready to do a story about low wages, and the atrocious conditions. Then he chickened out.'

Not to be encouraged, but a humorist after all; ho hum.

'Jeremy junior?'

'No-o; the ruddy reporter, of course. Reporters have got bosses, and the bosses have got . . . friends in high places, shall we say?'

'So Jeremy junior arranged the paint job, and fixed up a spot of trouble with the Ministry men, as part of plan B?'

'Yeah.'

'What about the fire?'

She half turned away from me, spooned the instant coffee into two mugs, applied boiling water and shrugged.

'And the vanload of frozen poultry, followed by the vandalism at the factory and the murder of Sir Jeremy Blatt?'

'Don't know; don't know, and I don't know,' she said. 'Add a don't care at the end, if you like, but it's nothing to do with any of us. We're all dedicated to non-violence here, and I've already played both sides of this particular tape to Aylfleet's very own Keystone Kop.'

So much for Derek Rodway; not entirely respected in New Age circles, I gathered.

'Did you work at the egg farm, by any chance?'

'No. I'da probably gone and crucified the bastards within a couple of hours if I had. Too much imagination for my own good.' Not, then, entirely committed to love and peace and doing good to your neighbour, after all.

She poured the milk and gestured towards an earthenware basin of raw cane sugar. I shook my head; she picked the mug up by the handle and passed it across, cooking my fingertips in the process. Far, far too hot to handle. I winced; she smiled.

'What can you tell me about the assault on Kevin Cooke last Saturday night?' Delicately, I transferred my grip on the mug, forbearing to groan.

She watched my performance unsympathetically. 'Who's Kevin Cooke?'

'Jeremy's cousin.'

'Oh, him; yeah. The amateur grass.'

'Oh. yeah, him,' I mimicked. 'He's pretty non-violent, too. Didn't stop him getting his head and ribs kicked in by somebody about twice his size.

'Biggish feller; Godzilla type. One earring, long brown hair, and a burgundy anorak short at the wrists; stinks. How many of your peace-loving friends look like that?'

'None,' she said promptly, 'and if they did, I wouldn't tell.'

'Thanks.'

'Never said anything about enemies, though, did I? Stinks like a polecat, huh? Sounds familiar; one of Jerry's little helpers, but he's not one of us.'

She'd made up her mind already, but she paused deliberately for a few seconds, nevertheless. It was all carefully calculated to wind me up. Strictly verbal teasing; the lone DCI was in luck.

Suddenly, her face cleared and, squat, cheerful, malicious, she grinned. 'Drink your coffee, and I might even give you an address, who knows? Then again, I might only want your body!'

I'd been afraid of that all along.

She paused for effect; the grin widened as she studied my face. 'No sex? OK, lover boy, relax. I'll settle for a bit of a laugh about a copper with asbestos fingers and a blistered throat.'

18

It did not take all of us to bring him in. That's only the unfortunate impression we created when the majority of the team crowded into the custody suite, grasping bits and pieces of prisoner as they arrived. Modestly, Paula, Roger Prentice and I brought up the rear of the procession. From a strictly personal point of view, the less I had to do with Clifford Darren Housley the better. Hell's Angel rather than New Ager, after all; Kevin, Bernice, the rest of his fans had been right: bathing was not among his talents, and the custody sergeant was not a happy man.

'Let the dog see the rabbit,' he muttered grimly. The escort fell back. 'Whose body is it anyway?'

'Ours.' Malcolm Cartwright and George retained their grip. 'Clifford Housley, Sergeant; arrested at Aylfleet for grievous bodily harm with intent.'

'In that case,' said the custody sergeant, ignoring the supervisors, giving his olfactory senses a treat, 'you could have taken him to Aylfleet nick for interview, instead of lumbering him on us.'

'No-o; he's definitely ours . . .' Explanations followed, courtesy of Big Malc. The prisoner, bulky, stooping, sullen, dressed in a studded motorcycle jacket and at least two pairs of black, holey jeans, did his best to stare through the wall behind the custody sergeant's head. The custody sergeant stared stolidly back.

Roger Prentice gathered up his detective constable and the Aylfleet uniform man, folded his tents, and stole silently away. An Eddathorpe crime, Eddathorpe's business; under no circumstances was he taking responsibility for any of this.

Nor, for the time being at least, was I. Winking at Paula, I closed the door of the custody suite quietly behind me as I went. Prior to my further involvement, I vainly hoped, somebody might think of swilling Clifford down.

Teddy Baring was pleased in a sarcastic sort of way. 'I see you've got your priorities right,' he murmured gently. 'Eddathorpe first, and Thea and her murder a very poor second, if at all.'

'I was coming to that, sir.' I could do smooth and silky on Monday mornings just as well as him. 'I ought to see Derek Rodway as soon as possible. You're the investigating officer as far as the complaint is concerned, and I, er, wondered if . . .'

'It's a bit tricky, Bob.' He gave me his wide-eyed innocent look. Teddy being devious again; probably preparing to boot something into touch.

'Yessir,' I said. Sounds great; means nothing. A useful catch-all phrase.

'For one thing, you've got my complainant on police bail. I've not talked to Jeremy junior yet, and you know the usual policy; no comprehensive complaints investigation until other proceedings have taken place.'

'But—'

'I have, of course, taken certain measures.' If Teddy wanted to sound like William Ewart Gladstone, it was no business of mine. 'I've sent that interview tape for forensic examination. Amazing what they come up with from time to time.'

'You've got it back?'

'Not yet.' Ah, yes; flying a kite. Teddy living in hope.

'I have, however. spoken to the police surgeon who examined young Blatt.' He opened the right-hand drawer of his desk and pulled out a slim manila file. 'He was good enough to provide me with a statement at once. A very helpful man.'

The tone of voice, the slightly self-satisfied air; conscience kept Teddy on the straight and narrow, but I was prepared to bet that he'd worked out something to the distinct disadvantage of the junior Blatt.

He skimmed through Jeremy junior's injuries; bruising and a slight contusion to the right shoulder and the right side of the face; complaints of pain and stiffness in the lumbar region. No hospital treatment necessary . . . Surgeon present to direct the taking of photographs of the alleged injuries by Scenes of Crime, blah, blah, blah . . .

'Oh, yes, here we are . . . "I am unable to form a definitive opinion as

142

to the cause of the patient's injuries. He has made positive complaints to me of police assault. The injuries sustained, however, are not inconsistent with the patient having suffered a heavy fall. In particular the facial bruising may not be wholly consistent with a blow from a fist. It is not inconceivable that these latter injuries, of a superficial and minor nature, are the result of the patient coming into violent contact with some hard inanimate object.

' "I have examined the furniture, consisting of a four-foot-square wooden table and four metal-framed, plywood-seated chairs, as well as a wooden side table containing recording equipment, in the interview room at Aylfleet police station.

' "I am in a position to say that the injuries are such that the patient may have come into contact with one or more similar objects. I cannot, however, speculate further as to whether the object or objects in question formed part of the furniture of this room." '

'Who took the statement?' I said.

Teddy surveyed me with his cold, expressionless grey eyes. 'Dr Harris is a very competent, very experienced man. He never allows anyone to set down his medical opinions, other than himself.'

'I see.'

I did. Well, I thought I did. And if I'd been working as an investigative jounalist, it is barely possible that I might . . . But Teddy was looking at me in a way that would have made George Washington's father flinch. *If you say you didn't do it, Georgie, then by heaven, you didn't do it! And anyway, who cares about a rotten old cherry tree, son?*

'Tell me, Bob . . .' His face was still giving nothing away, 'how familiar are you with the Police Disciplinary Regulations?'

Involuntarily, I grinned. It all came back. Ladies Night in the mess in my former force; the music, the dinner jackets, the temporarily improved accents, the posh frocks. Followed in short order by one right hook, and the sight of Superintendent Clive Jones, Angie's ex-boyfriend, sprawled on the highly polished floor.

Back in the here-and-now Teddy did his thought-reading act. 'Yes,' he said coolly. 'Apart from that.'

'The, er, technicalities, boss? Not a lot.'

'All I have,' he said, staring distastefully at his file, 'is a written formal complaint covering the alleged assault, and a vague allegation of what might amount to discreditable conduct.

'Jeremy Blatt, or Peters, or whatever he likes to call himself, is on unrestricted police bail, and he's chosen to make himself unavailable for interview by me. I've no statements, no detail and I'm in no position to take my investigation any further, apart from requesting a personal explanation from the officers involved.'

Teddy was upset. Nothing obvious, but whenever he was rattled he started talking slowly, precisely, just like the speaking clock.

'I have,' he said, 'served written notices of the complaints, and asked if either Rodway or DC Goodall wishes to make a written or oral statement. Goodall, at least, was polite.'

'I suppose that Pat Goodall wants to take Federation advice?'

'I could only wish' – Teddy was still doing his mechanical voice – 'that Detective Inspector Rodway had said the same.'

'What did he say?'

He abstracted a single sheet of notepaper from the file, handling it delicately at the edges, almost as if he were afraid of smudging any latent prints.

'After careful consideration,' he quoted, 'I have decided to make a brief written statement regarding your notice of complaint.

'Firstly, your complainant is a devious, lying, manipulative little toe-rag, who will almost certainly end up in jail. I did not assault him; Detective Constable Goodall did not assault him. Looking back on the incident, I only wish I had.

'Secondly, my relationship with Christine Blatt is none of your business. Our private lives are our own affair, and we will both take legal advice with a view to action against every individual and organisation involved if you dare to suggest that my conduct, and by implication hers, is in any way "discreditable", whatever that is supposed to mean. Queen Victoria is dead: your disciplinary notice is defamatory. Grow up!'

Teddy stretched back in his chair, those protuberant eyes fixed challengingly on my face. No time, I decided, for a light-hearted probe into the workings of the puritan conscience. Not the moment to discuss his considered opinion of late-twentieth-century sexual mores, perhaps.

'About the murder,' I said. 'Does that mean I can now go out and see 'em both myself?'

Down in the custody suite, war had been declared. The uniform staff lounging about, happily supping their tea, were thrilled.

'Where's the prisoner?'

The custody sergeant gave me a swift jerk of the head. 'Still in the interview room,' he said impatiently, unwilling to miss a single syllable of the row. 'Malcolm Cartwright's looking after him while them two have it out.'

No real need to question either who, or precisely what, was coming out. Paula and George, and I could hear the raised voices drifting down the cell block corridor and through the cunningly half-closed charge office door. Scandal; dissension in the CID; the custody sergeant, not to mention his minions, were enjoying a real-life soap.

'If you're going to give me a job, why don't you leave me to it, instead of poncing around like a female elephant tiptoeing over a crate of eggs?' The clear, if distant, voice of George.

'That's it, isn't it? Nothing to do with the job: it's me being female that gets right up your nose. You're a bloody dinosaur, George. As far as women are concerned, you never got beyond 1936.'

'Fancy that; dinosaurs in 1936.'

'Why don't you act your age?'

'Why won't you leave me to do my own interviews in my own way?'

'I was making a suggestion, that's all.'

'Teaching your granny to suck eggs.'

'I've got every right to—'

'Pull rank.'

'Yes, Sergeant Caunt, if that's the way you want it, I certainly have!'

Time to bring this particular piece of unscripted entertainment to an end before things got really out of hand. Carefully closing the charge office door upon three disappointed faces, I moved in on my disaffected troops.

'What's wrong?'

'She said that I should—'

'She? Who's *she* when she's at home?' Paula was still giving it a touch of volume. 'She's the cat's aunt!'

George, I noticed, looked neither apologetic nor impressed. *She*, apparently, could play the cat's aunt or the dog's dinner or any damn role she pleased. No skin off his nose, and he wasn't taking kindly to a comment he'd probably first heard when he was about six years old.

'Good,' I muttered, quickly putting a second door between the action and the eager audience beyond. 'And now we've settled that, d'you both think you might tone it down a bit and stop giving the neighbours a treat?'

Paula flushed. George looked uneasily towards the door, then his expression became about one degree less grim.

'Sorry, boss, but this has been coming for some time.'

'Just clearing the air.' Paula tried for the jaunty, insouciant look, and failed.

'I assume,' I said, 'that this is something to do with Clifford Housley. Has he coughed?'

'Not yet, I was still—'

'There was no need to get ratty, just because—'

'OK, OK; keep it down. There's a gang of overgrown kids out there listening to every word.'

'George and Malc interviewed him.' Paula was determined to get her version straight. 'They showed him the anorak they found in that tatty wooden bungalow he calls a home. It's miles too small; he says it doesn't belong to him and he denies the lot. No visit to the pub, no following of Kevin, no GBH.'

'It's got blood on the sleeve. It's only a matter of time,' grumbled George.

'Then why not short-circuit the interview? Why not show him—'

'Because I'm building up to that. Start with the description, go on to him being identifiable from the pub and the fact that he's Jerry Blatt's mate – acquaintance, anyway. Then the anorak; the blood; then the money . . .'

'What money?' This I had definitely missed.

'When they searched him, they found two hundred pounds rolled up in his motorcycling boot.' Paula was still impatient, bouncing in. 'The way I see it—'

'Jeremy paid him to beat up his cousin; Jeremy gave him the burgundy anorak to put us off. That's why it doesn't even come down to his wrists. He's killing two birds with one stone; revenge on Kevin Cooke for opening his mouth too wide, and giving us the runaround about the description of his accomplice when he took the lorry.' George had no intention of seeing his moment spoiled.

'Speculative,' I said. 'We don't know for certain that he took it; we don't know the real accomplice, and your yobbo's not admitting a thing.'

'Dunno about that, boss. He did let one thing slip.' George gave hi immediate supervisor a smug, infinitely superior look. Enough to provoke another outburst if I didn't step in quick.

'And what's that?'

'He claims he's one of Jerry junior's mates. And' – voices were up again, despite all I'd said – 'he reckons he knows where Jerry is now.'

'Oh yes?'

'With Peggy, his girlfriend.'

Peggy; short for Margaret. Margaret Gilmour even. Something stirred.

'Where?'

'Scotland,' said George triumphantly. 'Gone to get married. There's nothing like romance.'

Nothing like the laws of evidence either, come to that. Restricts the legal process no end, the way they operate as between husband and wife.

19

'Bloody ridiculous!'

'Why on earth should we? Too preposterous for words!'

Derek Rodway and Christine Blatt. Tweedledum and Tweedledee, side by side on the drawing-room sofa, with her doing the haughtily indignant, and both looking as if butter wouldn't melt in their mouths.

'I knew something like this would happen.' The grieving widow applied the edge of a tiny, tiny handkerchief to the corner of one hard, dry eye. I tried not to smirk; she would not, I'm sure, have liked being compared to Kevin's mum. 'That's why I insisted on Derek being here.'

'And,' said her champion calmly, 'you'd never have agreed to see us together if you'd got one shred of evidence to link either Christine or myself to the crime. One scintilla of real suspicion, and you'd have arrested us both, and kept us well apart. I know I would, in your place.'

George, sunk into an overstuffed chintzy armchair, hands resting on the arms, stirred. His fingers flexed; I had the uneasy feeling that he wanted to wrap them around the throat of a colleague. He does not enjoy having the obvious thrown back in his face, and *scintilla* was not your usual Derek Rodway word. He'd probably picked that one up in the course of a pre-interview legal chat. All nicely prepared for our visit: complaint or no police complaint, we should have done this particular interview days before.

The odd couple: Christine Blatt, with her copper-gold hair, triple row of pearls, and her smooth, watchful, carefully made-up face; Derek, stocky, big hands sticking out of the sleeves of an off-the-peg suit; his East Coast accent, I noticed, carefully ironed out for the occasion.

A bit of a tough. Mind you, as a detective he had his points. I wasn't going to go right over the top; he's not exactly what you'd call rough trade. Besides, she could have done worse; her late lamented hadn't been anything to boast about socially, in his day. Blatant though, the occasional spot of hand-holding, with the inquest adjourned indefinitely, the Chief Chicken still unburied, and scarcely a fortnight dead.

'OK,' I said, conceding his point, 'so you've nothing to worry about, have you? Cards-on-the-table time. What about your statement, Lady Blatt?'

'What about it?'

'Is it true?'

Sharp intake of breath.

'So your husband got home just after seven o'clock that night?'

'Yes.'

'And had a meal?'

A nod.

'Who cooked it?'

'I beg your pardon?'

'Who cooked it? Surely that's simple enough.'

'I am not of the habit,' she snapped, 'of keeping staff and doing the cooking myself.' A touch of the Lady Bracknells; a strictly amateur production there, I thought.

'Your Filipino cook,' rumbled George. 'Sir Jeremy was expected, and the meal was prepared in advance?'

'Filipina. Filipinos are male, the word—'

'Thank you.' George positively beamed. 'Just like the police, you appreciate the importance of getting things right.'

From the look she gave him, not exactly, no. 'He rang me from the office just after five; he told me the approximate time he'd be home.'

'That's not in your statement.'

'It's not important. I didn't think you wanted every irrelevancy from my entire day.'

'Tell me . . .' It was my turn to beam. 'Was it usual, phoning to tell you what time he'd be home?'

'Not usual; he did it sometimes. Whenever he wanted to eat and then go out.'

'Ah.'

'Your next question,' she said calmly. 'Did I therefore know in advance that he would be going out? The answer, of course, is yes.'

'He told you he'd be going back to work?'

A nod.

'Did he say anything about, whatsisname?' I glanced across at George. 'The egg farmer man?'

'Paul Kinsley.' Helpful George.

'No. Why should he?'

'Oh,' I said, trying for vague, 'I just wondered, that's all. What did you do when he came home?'

'I dished up our meal in the kitchen, and we ate it.'

'But you've just said—'

'Staff,' she said coldly, 'are entitled to the occasional evening off. Rosa and her husband went to catch the cinema in Eddathorpe. I'm not entirely helpless, it's just that Jerry didn't like us keeping dogs and doing all the barking ourselves.'

'Dogs,' said my sergeant. Come the revolution, he wants to be Chief Commissioner for Public Safety with special responsibility for *ci-devant* aristos, does George. Then he added, a trifle over-promptly, 'It's all in their statement, boss. Rosa's the cook-housekeeper, Felipe the chauffeur-gardener-handyman, and anything else you'd like to mention. He drove Sir Jeremy home in the Roller; then he poddled off with his wife to see a film. One of their few chances to relax.'

Christine Blatt held her peace, but she awarded him the civilian version of the Glare. Derek Rodway, still in the role of Sir Galahad, flushed. Somehow, my sudden convert to Neo-Marxism had managed to express an opinion on the subject of servant exploitation, but nothing an irritated employer could pin down.

'And your husband,' I said quickly, papering over the cracks, 'told you why he was returning to work?'

'He told me that he suspected a substantial leakage of stock, yes.'

'In those words?'

'He said' – she paused deliberately – 'that some bastard was doing him over. Is that good enough?'

'So, you knew in advance that he was going out, and once he came home, he discussed what he was going to do. Had you, er, been in contact with Derek at all, prior to him coming in for his meal?'

'And what exactly are you implying by that?'

'Chris, we've already been through . . .' Derek Rodway let his voice trail away.

'Yes, yes, all right. Tell the truth and shame the devil; but why should I be humiliated like this? It's none of his bloody business what we do.'

George gave me a single self-satisfied glance. They'd had a rehearsal, then, well in advance of our visit. Nevertheless, Madam was far less inclined to open up than our suspended DI. *Tell the truth, and shame . . .* On second thoughts it sounded a bit contrived. Was this all part of a little comedy sketch, put together for the entertainment of passing cops?

She managed a contorted, glistening look. 'Very well,' she said. 'I telephoned Derek some time after six. He came over just before half past eight, and we both spent the evening here.'

Game, set and match to the home team. A mutual alibi; if they were together at Trippe Hall, neither of 'em could have been employed in a spot of skull-crushing at the premises of Daisy Dew. Unless . . .

'You didn't go out?' George, busy doing his dotting-and-crossing act, as usual.

'No.'

'Together all the time?'

'OK, that's enough.' Derek Rodway scowled. 'D'you want to get her to say it? Is that what's going to make you happy? We went to bed. We knew the cinema wouldn't be turning out till at least half past ten.'

'And Sir Jeremy?' My turn for a shot.

'We figured the same; he never came back till the pubs had shut, once he went out.' Not the country gentleman, then, confining his boozing to the cut-glass tumblers in his own home.

'Risky,' I said.

'Past experience.'

'I see.'

'We never used his . . . our bed, you know,' said Christine Blatt. 'We'd never do a thing like that.'

Women. Glad to hear it, I almost said. But not, I would have thought, part of an act. One of those stupid little irrelevancies that might just be ringing true.

'Derek,' I said, 'when did you leave here?'

'Just short of eleven, maybe a quarter to.' He stared at me boldly, looking for insults, ready to snarl.

'Cutting it a bit fine?'

He shrugged.

'And where did you go then?'

'Home.' Unmarried? No – divorced, I recalled. Bachelor flat; Aylfleet. I knew that.

'Can anybody vouch for you?'

'Met a neighbour walking his dog as I was putting my car away. That do?'

Name, street and house number. No extraneous information; he sounded as if he were practising to become a prisoner of war.

I turned to the woman. 'When did you begin to worry?' If worry was the right word.

'I didn't; I went to bed.'

It was written all over George's face. Again.

'Before or after your staff returned home?'

'After.'

'And the time?'

'Eleven-thirtyish.'

'And then?'

'I went to sleep.' That, I gathered, was her version of scoring a point. Not as bright, nor as mature, as I'd thought.

'Yes?'

'Oh . . .' Long pause. 'About Jerry, you mean. Well, I awoke about five. He still wasn't home; he wasn't exactly faithful himself, you know, but he'd never stayed out all night before.'

'What did you do?'

'I waited about an hour, an hour and a half perhaps. Then I rang Simon; I was very good, I didn't ask him if his wife was at home.'

She was disappointed; I didn't blink. 'I thought that was over a long time ago.'

She shrugged. 'Perhaps.'

'You don't think so?'

'Sorry, I was trying to shock you, Inspector. I don't know, and I don't really care. Jerry was Jerry, I knew that when I married him, and he usually had somebody in tow; that's all.'

'Names?'

She laughed: genuinely, I thought. 'I'd be the last to know.'

'But you wanted me to know about his fun and games, anyway? Sauce for the goose?'

'Something like that.'

'OK.'

Derek Rodway looked miffed. The bad news; it sounded almost as if he were being relegated to the role of the neglected wife's revenge.

'I knew Christine long before he did; years before,' he said, doing his best to establish his claims. 'How long is it now; ten years, twelve?'

'Of course.' She smiled at him brilliantly to cover her mistake. Male pride had taken something of a knock. 'I'm a local girl too; I was at art college, and Derek was a couple of years older. He'd just joined the Force.'

'What made you think of Simon Weatherby in particular? Apart,' I added dryly, 'from you knowing about Jerry's connection with his wife?' The pun was unintentional, but she took it as evidence of my general lack of tact.

'*Sir* Jeremy,' she enunciated clearly, 'always said Simon was an A-type person.'

Totally fascinating, but what had that got to do with early-morning telephone calls?

She waited, smiling superciliously, until I signalled my complete incomprehension, then she went on. 'Simon is get-up-and-go. First one into the premises of a morning, zooms through the admin and out on the road chasing business. A heart attack waiting to happen, according to Jerry.

'I thought that something similar could have happened to my husband. It was early morning by this time; I wanted Simon to go and check.'

'But,' objected George, 'there's security staff on duty at the factory all night. Why not ring them?'

'Or the office manager,' I said. 'Surely, he's the obvious choice?'

'Suppose he'd been out with some woman, after all?' Her voice rose in exasperation. 'I phone the security men first, then everything turns out OK apart from a night on the tiles. Inadvertently, I've fed some Tom, Dick or Harry with enough tittle-tattle to keep every mouth in the factory flapping for a week. He'd really thank me for that!'

'And that goes for Jack Causley, the office manager, too?'

'No!' Not quite so lovey-dovey, now; she detached herself from the Derek Rodway hand. She flapped one impatient wrist. 'But you're right, of course. Jack's a natural gofer, a sort of superior messenger boy, really, and loyal. But he's strictly nine-to-five. Simon's the early bird.'

'First in, last out?'

'Something like that.'

'Convenient,' I said.

She looked at me sharply. 'If that's supposed to make him a suspect, I think you're mad.'

A volatile, get-up-and-goer in a subordinate position? Plus alleged leakages on a grand scale? Plus the old, old tale of the boss and the lady wife? I might construct a few bricks on the basis of that. The trouble was, I hadn't got much in the way of evidential straw. Besides, the lady opposite was devious; cunning enough to plant an idea in the mind of a simple plod to protect . . .

Derek Rodway stirred. 'Personally—' he began. He wasn't allowed to finish.

'Derek, no! We agreed: it's best not to say anything about anybody else.'

'He's not just anybody, he's your stepson and he's a completely vicious bloody crook. He's got me suspended, he's suing the trustees, not to mention you in the High Court, and he's stirring everything up right and left.'

'Your favourite suspect, Jeremy junior?' I asked disingenuously, remembering what Pat Goodall had said.

'No,' he replied reluctantly. 'Not exactly; but if it hadn't been for that stupid old lesbian we'd probably have him locked up for the arson, at any rate.'

All out in the open. He hated Thea; Thea hated him. But there was no need for me to meddle in somebody else's nasty little feud.

'Slander,' I said, 'will get you nowhere; not unless you're looking for the sack.'

'About the arson?' Wilful misunderstanding; he grinned.

'About your superintendent, *Mister* Rodway; or have you forgotten that we're both still in the job?' I only had to pinch my own forearm and I could feel a pompous twit, but I'd never heard a breath of scandal about the sexual orientation of Dorothea Spinks, and I wasn't about to court cheap popularity with a very iffy DI. George looked sad; I think he thought I'd let him down.

Rodway bared his teeth in something like a grin. 'I'll say what I like; she's the least of my worries right now. Besides, she's the one who put the boot in for me; d'you really think they'd have suspended us for some half-arsed allegation, if it hadn't been for her?'

I had wondered; slightly marginal, I would have thought. An expensive business, suspension on full pay for as long as it took. The powers that be could have jumped either way; just as easy to remove him from the case and confine him to routine duties until such time as the assault investigation had been sorted out.

Perhaps Thea had played it nasty and given the Complaints and Discipline outfit a push, but I wasn't going to get myself called for the defence on this particular occasion, thanks. Derek Rodway had ended up in the mire, but he'd proved himself a willing volunteer, as well as leading an inexperienced DC into the swamp. Heads down, mouths shut for Derek, that was the style.

He watched me carefully; he knew the line I was taking, all right. Slowly, the grin faded, a calculating expression crossed his face.

'Know something, boss?'

'What's that?'

'People have been getting phone calls from that little twerp.'

'Jeremy junior? Yes, I'd heard.'

'Christine's been getting them too. He says he won't sue for her particular shares in the company, if she supports him against the trustees. He reckons he's due the return of his mother's twenty-five shares from the pot. Says he'd just as soon have theirs as hers.'

'Oh yes?'

'And that's not all; he's told her how he set me up. Says he'll withdraw the complaint if she supports him. Now don't forget, either of you.' He turned to George, a look of triumph on his face. 'In fact you'd better make a note, lads; you heard it from me first!'

Nice one, Derek. He was using us, but Christine Blatt, his main, his perhaps unwilling, witness, simply stared straight ahead.

20

Mrs Gilmour was in tears.

'Our Peggy's a good girl,' she said. And I wish I had a pound for every time I've heard a parent say that. She produced a handkerchief from a piece of designer crocodile with a gold clasp that must have cost Hubby a fair slice of the National Debt, and blew her nose.

Her husband wasn't quite so sure. Early fifties, I judged, around ten years older than his wife, with a thickening, expertly tailored body, and eyes like the bad news coming up on an electronic cash register. Tough.

Yorkshire, too. Had this inflexible desire to call a spade a spade; or a bloody shovel, if he liked. Everybody was a poofter or a snide bastard south of the Trent. Probably both.

'She's not so good now,' he rumbled, 'be'aving like a bloody little whore! Eleven and a half thousand a year for schooling, plus all the extras, and where does it get you in the end?'

As far as Aylfleet nick, I supposed, where the entire uniformed staff from Dorothea Spinks downwards had washed their hands of the problem, and landed him on me.

'Unlawful sexual intercourse,' he stated with something approaching masochistic self-satisfaction. Facing facts; telling it how it is. Mrs Gilmour continued to dampen the atmosphere. He was doing it on purpose, I suspected. Just to show that all women were soft.

'Oh, Albert, she's missing!' said his wife.

'She's gettin' irrigated silly,' replied Albert unfeelingly. That stopped us all in our tracks. 'And she's under-age!'

'She's well over sixteen,' I protested. She'd better be; apart from anything else, according to my information, she was driving a ruddy great caravette all over the shop.

'She's seventeen years and eight months. D'you have any idea of the law, young man?'

Do not let yourself be browbeaten by the peasantry. 'Yes.'

'Unlawful sexual intercourse: sexual relations outside the bounds of matrimony, right?'

'Well, technically speaking, yes; but that's only a legal definition of—'

'Removing a female under the age of twenty-one from the care, custody or control of her parent or lawful guardian for the purposes of unlawful sexual intercourse is a criminal offence under the Sexual Offences Act of 1956. I'm a taxpayer, and I want that little bastard arresting, tout bloody suite. Am I making myself clear?'

Somewhere, deep in the sludge at the back of my brain, something vaguely stirred. It is also an offence, if memory served me right, to fail to attend archery practice on Sundays, and to fail regularly to attend divine service in the established Church. There was also something, somewhere, designed to prevent young women being forced into prostitution; but not to provide a mechanism for revenge on the part of a rampant Yorkshire dad.

It, was a nightmare: the sort of thing they delighted in raking up in police promotion exams. Not exactly the forward-looking, on-to-the-next-millennium stuff. Still, Jeremy junior: arrest. Wholly impractical, but tempting all the same.

'No,' I said firmly, 'I can't arrest him for that.'

'Why not? Don't you mess with me, sonny, or you'll end up with your head in your hands!' Literally, I gathered. 'I know the law; I read it all up.'

'*Every Man His Own Lawyer*,' sniffled his wife, a note of asperity entering her voice. 'The 1967 edition.' Not so ineffectual after all; the lady could strike back.

Inspiration at last. 'I can't arrest him,' I said. 'Nothing unlawful, you see. They've gone off to Scotland to get married. according to what I've heard.'

'*Married? Oh, nooaw, not my Peggy!*'

Damn. Thou shalt take account of consequences when thou settest out to score points.

Albert Gilmour flushed a dull, aggressive red. 'Satisfied? Now see what you've gone and done. I suppose you know he's unstable? I'm not surprised he killed his own dad!'

Two good questions coming up. Not a totally profitless interview, after all.

'Unstable?' I said. 'Now what leads you to say that?'

'God almighty! You nicked him, didn't you? Five minutes' acquaintance, and I'da thought it would have been as plain as the nose on your face.'

Not entirely, no. Arrogant, devious, self-seeking and vengeful, OK. A happy, perfectly adjusted bad bastard, in my opinion; just like his old man.

'No thought for anybody, for a start. Self, self, self.'

He was describing two-thirds of the City of London there, not to mention ninety per cent of the membership of the Eddathorpe Chamber of Trade, poised, as ever, to make a grab. Albert, I was prepared to bet, had been raised in the same school. I remained unconvinced.

'Listen,' he said urgently. 'She met him while she was on a pony-trekking holiday in Wales in August last year, and afterwards she invited him up for Christmas.'

'*He was pony trekking?*' Not precisely the Jerry junior image I had in mind.

'Nah.' He raised one impatient hand. 'He was with some sort of hippie crowd. They met in a pub.'

Strictly no comment; pony trekking in a pub.

'Anyway . . .' his angry blue eyes were still patting me down for disapproval re the under-age booze. 'He came up to see us. Supposed to stay a week; I threw him out on the second night. Perverted little swine.'

'Oh yes?'

'Caught him padding into her room in the middle of the night. Not that I'm not broad-minded,' he added hastily. Then, 'D'you know what he told me? Told me I reminded him of the biggest bastard on the face of the earth, his dad.'

For the first and only time in my experience of Jeremy junior, the faintest traces of fellow feeling stirred.

'Is that it?'

'No. it is not! A couple of days later I got a parcel; gift-wrapped. He'd sent me an artificial turd, and a card. Know what it said? "Somebody, somewhere, thinks you're a shit!" Unstable, just like I said.'

'Signed it, did he; the card?'

''Course not; they're all cowards at heart.'

'Then how do you kn—' No, leave it, Robert. You could be getting yourself into deep, deep waters, lad.

'How do you know,' I amended, 'that he killed Sir Jeremy Blatt?'

He fixed me with a cold, contemptuous stare. 'Don't think you're going to settle me by flashing titles, son. I've met lords and ladies with the shirt tails hanging out of the holes in their pants.'

I took time to contemplate this interesting, not to say unusual, image. They obviously do these things differently in the wild and woolly North. He took my silence as a sign of precipitate retreat.

'As long as we understand one another,' he said, relenting. 'I went to that factory he owns, and asked around. I suppose he does own it now?' he added. 'He reckoned he was his father's heir: he wasn't lying about that?'

'He owns shares,' I replied ambiguously, 'and he benefits from the family trust.'

Slowly, Albert Gilmour's features relaxed. The potential son-in-law assumed some degree of acceptability. Who knows? Questions surrounding murder and mental instability apart, things might not be too bad.

'Gossip; probably idle gossip,' he said. 'You've not locked up the boy: that says something, I suppose.'

'Exactly.' Structured hypocrisy, as usual, was the name of the game. 'But who did you speak to at Daisy Dew?'

'The company secretary; I went right to the top. He was very helpful; put me on to his head of security, an ex-superintendent of police.' Gilmour gave me a sly look. Superintendents were usually better than chief inspectors; quite right. 'He told me all about it; seemed to have his finger on the pulse, but maybe he went too far?'

I could imagine.

'Ronald Hacker,' I said gloomily. 'You could say that; too far.'

'I took him out to lunch.' Gilmour appeared to be remembering something; probably the bill. Scrounging bugger, Silver. I could imagine that too.

'And Mr Hacker told you all about Jeremy junior killing, er, his dad?'

'Not in so many words, naturally. But a nod's as good as a wink to a blind 'oss.'

Mess Night came horribly to mind. Lots of cognac; Silver in

160

full spate; blind was probably the word. Blind drunk.

'Explained it all, huh?'

'Everything; the father's wicked ways, the divorce, the estrangement between the old man and his son.' He looked complacently at his wife, 'Mustn't be too hard on the lad, I suppose. Hell of a thing when the head of the household goes prancing off like that. A man has a duty to stay and exercise control.'

Do not, I advised myself, under any circumstances enter into an enquiry into what he might mean by that. The Gilmour domestic arrangements sounded depressing. Leave it at that.

'And Mr Hacker told you about—'

'The hole in the fence; the vandalism, and so on, yes. Well, I put two and two together; young bugger-lugs getting his own back, I thought.'

So now we had a pair of 'em; Silver, the ex-constabulary hack, followed by this unexpected Yorkshire nag. In my opinion, the second was not quite so well bred as the first.

'When did your daughter leave home, Mr Gilmour?'

'January the third.' Doreen Gilmour chipped in; a date obviously engraved upon her heart.

'Then why wait until—'

'We knew where she was: she kept in touch. Phoned me two or three times a week. She's a real good girl at heart.'

She stared stubbornly at her husband; it was obvious whom she was out to convince.

'She made her bed, let her lie on . . . Well, anyway,' he amended hastily, preempting the onset of more tears. 'She kept in touch with her mother, and I didn't object to the wife sending a bit of cash.' For a few seconds, I almost expected him to stick his fingers in the armholes of his waistcoat and say, 'Brass,' but the moment passed.

'And she's, ah, stopped phoning?'

'Not a word for the last ten days. Sh-she told me about the . . . accident to Jeremy's father, but now . . .'

'Accident?' I wasn't in the mood to let that one pass, tears or not.

'She said the police didn't know what to think.'

'Surely, Mrs Gilmour. you've seen the story in the press?'

'Oh, yes. I think our Peggy was just trying to let me down light.' She gave me a watery smile. 'She's such a—'

'Good girl. Quite.'

I drew the missing-from-home form towards me, and unscrewed the top of my pen. 'I think you ought to know, we've already started to try and trace your daughter. Only as a potential witness.' I said.

Albert Gilmour gave me a single look; the expression of a man about to consult his solicitor written all over his face.

'You circulating this, boss?' Detective Sergeant Prentice examined the completed form. He sounded doubtful. 'D'you think she's likely to come to harm?'

'You never can tell.'

'I see; belt and braces, huh?'

'Belt and braces and a piece of string. She's probably sloped off to marry that prat, but he *is* on police bail. Besides, her father and mother—'

'What does the old man do for a living, sir?'

'He's a wholesale butcher; it's on the form.'

Roger Prentice grinned. 'Yeah,' he said. 'Just testing, boss. Butchers and poulterers; meat empires meet. A marriage made in heaven, wouldn't you say?'

Coppers can be very childish at times.

21

George wore his cynical, world-weary copper look. I'd have worn one too, but he'd got his blow in first. I skimmed over the forensic report instead. Somebody had been having a lot of fun with Sir Jeremy's clothing, discussing the relative situation of the head wound and the flow of blood. No good to me, but no doubt he'd enjoyed discussing it with his fellow enthusiasts over lunch.

I don't altogether blame the Forensic Science Service for their new-found facility with weasel words. One mistake, a suspicion of misplaced enthusiasm, and their Home Office masters are more than inclined to throw them to the media wolves. Retiring the unfortunate scientist on the grounds of limited efficiency, I think they call it. Saving the Westminster politicos from embarrassment, if the truth be told.

'Well,' said George, 'what's it supposed to mean?'

'Provisionally,' I parroted, skipping to the next section, 'the evidence is not altogether inconsistent with the wire surrounding the Daisy Dew compound having been severed from the inside. Perhaps.'

'Always taking into account that Pancake Tuesday falls late this year, an' we never sent the Home Secretary a Christmas card,' muttered George.

'Never mind; it's a fair bet we've got an inside job.'

'We knew that already, pretty well. All part of the grand persecution of Sir Jeremy Blatt.'

'Persecution? Culminating in a blunt instrument and a fractured skull? Going a bit far with persecution, wouldn't you think?'

'Persecution with extreme prejudice,' amended George. He's always fancied a touch of the CIAs. 'So, we've got the entire evening shift at the factory to choose from,' he moaned.

'Plus Jeremy junior, the kid who hates him most. Although we don't know how, or even whether, he managed to get in.'

'And *all* the management team; Lang, Weatherby, the factory manager, the shift foreman, Causley, that crummy little company secretary, or whatever he is. Even Kinsley, the egg man, could be in the frame. No solid suspect, and we can't absolutely eliminate anybody either. Great!'

'We can't be sure about the timing of their movements, and Blatt's time of death tells us nothing about the time of the attack. Thanks to their stupid system, and their dopey security staff, we don't know anything definite.

'All we can say is that whoever it was wanted to give the impression that it was a burglary.'

'And there they came unstuck.'

'Perhaps.' Open sarcasm; unforgiving of other people's shortcomings is George.

'Of course,' I said cunningly, 'we could always blame the two guys we've overlooked.'

'The evening security man and the night security man,' he replied promptly. 'And a right pair of semi-geriatric thickos they are.'

'Yeah,' I said absently, continuing to skim the report. Not altogether fair to dump the blame, but they'd do. The security staff were there to record movements of vehicles; to control the gate. Was it their fault if they'd confined their activities to *goods* vehicles, and left the staff, particularly the management movements, severely alone?

The fact that the one ex-copper on the gate was inclined to record the movements of anything larger than a passing mouse was irrelevant. He hadn't started work until 6 a.m. The lorry containing the dead or dying victim had been well on its way to the ferry by then.

'The two-till-ten man doesn't fill in his records of comings and goings, an' he's got a memory like a sieve, or so he says. While the night man—'

I stopped. Serves me right, I suppose; I was so interested in having a good depressive moan that I'd neglected the final three paragraphs of the report. Scenes of Crime had been busy; they'd cut out a section of the frame of the jemmied side door and submitted it to the Home Office scientists, along with the jemmy, the wire-cutters and the rest of the stuff.

No ifs or buts or face-saving ambiguities this time; in the depressions in the jemmied door frame, forensic had found human blood. Minute traces; insufficient to group; insufficient for DNA; human all the same. DNA match on the blood on the case-opener, though. His bodily fluids reduced to being a subject for forensic analysis; poor old Jeremy Blatt.

'Apologies to the back-room boys at Huntingdon,' I said, handing over the report. *'Definitely* an inside job. Somebody trying to be clever, and failing miserably.'

'Attacked the old man with the case-opener, stuck him in the loaded articulated lorry, vandalised the premises, faked a burglary, made sure there were no prints on the murder weapon and finally made his escape by clipping the wire fence.'

'Whooa!' Still speculative, the exact sequence of events. A strange mix of calculation and panic on the part of the killer, if George was right. The pathologist had settled for the case-opener as the likely weapon, but it was distinctly odd, that almost Levitical cleaning apart from the very tip, followed by the deliberate dumping of the weapon outside the perimeter fence . . .

'Let's stick with what we know; you're taking things too fast, too far.'

'Not as far as some murderous bastard took the Chief Chicken,' said George.

Dorothea Spinks in full spate; a lady with blood in her eye. She sat behind her slightly shabby, overloaded desk, ramrod straight and with her bosoms thrusting against her visibly straining tunic like infernal devices about to explode.

Even her necktie, black-and-white check, usually worn floppy, police-women for the use of, looked less than feminine. Starched in her case, aggressive, it looked more like the black-and-white war banner of the Knights Templar floating stiffly in the breeze; the one they carried when they were offering no quarter, determined to grind their enemies into the dust.

The latest phase of the Holy War had been turned in my direction; Robert Graham, enemy and infidel, could very easily become her next candidate for the chop.

'Three weeks,' she said, tapping the untidy pile of post-mortem photographs in front of her, 'three solid weeks. And you're no further forward, are you? Statements, photographs, reports; enough to stack a shop, and young Blatt is still sneering at us, smirking all over his face.'

Was he, now? Personally, I'd have liked him to have been around so I could get to see him doing it. Chance would be a fine thing.

'We had him in custody,' I said reasonably, holding fire for the moment, 'and you decided—'

'Damn it, you hadn't got a shred of evidence then. You were supposed to bail him for six weeks while you constructed a case against him, and what did you do?

'You let loose a pack of overtime-hungry detectives, chasing God knows how many half-arsed ideas they've dreamed up merely to keep their mortgage payments afloat!'

Roughie-toughie female superintendent imitating what she'd overheard while playing with the boys. Sod that for a comic song; I wasn't putting up with that.

'Jeremy whatever-you-like-to-call-him,' I said coldly, going for the nasty, ironic bit, 'isn't the only suspect. The enquiry team are going where the evidence leads. It's all in the policy file for you to see whenever you like.'

'Thank you, Chief Inspector, I did like, and I do know my job. I've seen your file, and your enquiry seems to include most of the adult population of two police divisions. What are you doing, recording the contents of the voters' register or something?'

'That's an absurd remark.'

'What?'

'It's hardly my fault that Aylfleet's been landed with this enquiry, and I resent you turning your disappointment in my direction.' Pause to emphasise the timing. 'Ma'am.'

I watched with interest while she reddened, then swelled. Perhaps, after they'd scraped the bits of her off the ceiling, I'd become the second CID man she'd managed to get suspended inside a month.

The same thought, I'm pretty sure, suddenly pushed its way to the forefront of Madam's mind. The reddening, the swelling, the fine display of indignation, went into instant suspense. Not, after all, the wisest of moves for a divisional commander to make. One suspension, unfortunate; inevitable, considering all the circs. Two, however . . . and where, as they'd say at Headquarters, was Boudicca going to stop?

'Tell me,' she said, struggling for icy, objective calm, 'why does your interview policy include the tenants of the houses in some grubby Eddathorpe back street?'

'The houses are slums; they were owned by the victim, and one way or another the people who live there have good reason to hate his guts, according to his nephew, Kevin Cooke.'

'I see; and that goes for his entire workforce, too?'

'The twilight shift had to be checked and eliminated; as for the rest—'

'Showing how thorough you are; something for HM Inspector of Constabulary to admire on a wet afternoon?'

'Serious enquiries are audited for the annual inspection, and nobody,' I added meanly, 'would thank me for putting all my eggs in one basket.'

Thea was not in the mood for humour. She didn't like puns either, but she'd managed to rise above that sort of thing by now.

'And where has all this got you, so far?'

'Routine elimination.' I shrugged. 'It had to be done; one of the Eddathorpe tenants turned out to work on the twilight shift. Low paid, badly housed, good reason for—'

'Murder? You are clutching at straws!'

'Good reason for a man to lose his temper, if he was confronting somebody as selfish and bloody-minded as Jeremy Blatt. We took statements, and we can account for his movements, as it happens.'

'And does your policy include the active elimination of *everybody* who may have had some cause to dislike Jeremy Blatt?'

Well, no, not absolutely everybody... Mess Nights, drunkenness, presidential embarrassment and silly jokes could be safely excepted, perhaps. Mum was the word; you can, after all, take these things just that bit too far. I still had to work with the woman, totally unreasonable and bloody-minded though she was. But she wasn't stupid; she saw temptation written all the way across my face.

'If you want a statement covering my movements, you only have to ask.' Bad-tempered and psychic too.

'No, ma'am.'

'Oh, good; that might save us a little public expense.' Having got that one over, she seemed to relax. 'My point, Bob, is simple enough. We can't afford to deploy unlimited resources, and you can't afford to fart around for ever, that's all.' I felt a twinge of sympathy; one of those occasions, in her own eyes at least, when rank wasn't quite enough. Thea, striving unsuccessfully to become as foul-mouthed as one of the lads.

'Jeremy junior,' I said, 'is still very much in the frame. It's all the to-ing and fro-ing at the factory that's the problem.'

'And?'

'Simon Weatherby strikes me as a pretty ruthless character, and Blatt had an affair with his wife; she's the one who claims he was home all night when it happened.

'Kinsley, the manager of Lowbarrack egg farm, is in roughly the same position. He admits that Blatt visited him that night, and his wife left him at Christmas, after he found out she was another of the old man's darlings. Lang, his other general manager, didn't exactly love him, either, and his wife alibis him, too. Christine Blatt and Derek Rodway—'

For a moment her eyes lifted, glittered vengefully in the neon strip above her head, 'You've interviewed him?'

'Yes, and his girlfriend. They're possibilities, I suppose, but they support each other, and he's got a partial alibi, at least. Jeremy junior seems to be gunning for him. Vicious, as well as devious, that youngster. He's made a couple of nasty phone calls to Weatherby's missis, come to that.'

'What about the nephew, Cooke?'

'Very unlikely; although Jeremy took the trouble to have him beaten up.'

'Oh, yes. Anorak man; how's he doing, by the way?'

'Clifford Housley? Remanded in custody for GBH. Another of Jeremy's dirty tricks.'

'And now he's away to Scotland with this girl. Being devious again?'

'Probably, yes.'

'Vandalism, arson, theft,' she murmured. 'Murder, perverting the course of justice, and GBH. You'd better get your finger out, Robert. It all comes back to the junior Blatt.'

Absolutely terrific, especially coming from her; and what about finding the evidence she'd been so fond of the day she'd kicked him out? And as for perverting the course of justice, that was really rich! Since when has marriage, even Jeremy's marriage, and whatever his reasons, become a criminal offence?

Totally bloody illogical.

Male chauvinists are finished; definitely a woman's world. I sighed.

———◆———

Pat's voice on the telephone was cautious, subdued. 'Everything's OK; there's a Headquarters memo, boss.'

There were always memos, and Home Office circulars, and crime bulletins, demands for statistics, amendments to Force orders, personnel assessments and anything else you cared to mention. All in my filing basket at Eddathorpe, and all forming a lonely, neglected wadge of paper about four inches thick. I was busy, and I've only got one pair of hands.

'Detective Inspector Baily knows.' Not Paula, not the DI on this occasion; so he was doing the formal now, as well as being cautious and subdued. I could practically hear the rustle of new leaves being turned over. I was tempted to rummage madly through my untidy pile of paper in search of Detective Constable Patrick Goodall's good news.

'Welcome back; tell me about it,' I said, instead.

'I'm reinstated to duty, as from today. They got fed up with paying my salary for nothing, I suppose.' Not entirely crushed by adversity, then. Still capable of sarcasm, my most thoughtless, tactless and bumptious DC, but I was unaccountably pleased.

'They've withdrawn the disciplinary notices for assault?'

'No, sir. Mr Baring says they can't; the complaint against me and DI Rodway still stands, and nobody can resolve it until the Blatt bastard turns up.'

'I see.'

'That's what I've rung you about. I've got to confine myself to local enquiries at Retton, and keep about a million miles away from your murder enquiry; that's what the memo says.' Not, I was prepared to bet, in so many words. Irritating, but that's something else he does; he's got

169

a talent for the slightly subversive reinterpretation of officialese, has Pat.

'Yes?' My turn for the note of caution. Just the tiniest whiff of gunpowder in the air.

'I met this woman in the pub last night.' Heigh-ho: sex and the single man.

'She knows I'm a cop.'

Definitely nothing to do with me, Patrick, me boy. You should have told the lady you sold insurance, or worked on an oil rig, and that you were only passing through. If you charm 'em out of their knickers in your role as the big, bold, glamorous detective, it's no affair of mine. Not until they create a stink down at the police station, anyway, pushing the pram.

'I thought I'd better tell you; I don't want to tread on anybody's toes.'

Cross-purposes, obviously. Nasty, dirty-minded boss.

'In what way?'

'Getting involved in the murder; none of my business any more, they've made that clear. But she knew I was with the CID and she said we were all the same, a lazy, idle lot, and the higher people got the worse they became.'

'And?'

'She said this detective inspector had promised to come and see her about her information weeks ago, and he'd never turned up. Sounds very much like Mr Rodway from what she says.'

'What's her name?'

'Ruth Kinsley. She reckons she's fed up with waiting; she's going to contact somebody big at Headquarters soon, and play hell.'

Somebody big. True enough, Peter Fairfield, about sixteen stone. My second run-in with a senior officer within twenty-four hours. *Trace Ruth Kinsley*; actioned on the computer, but still outstanding. No indication from Derek that she'd been due for a visit, or even that she'd been found.

'She's got a suggestion,' crackled Fairfield down the phone less than twenty minutes later. 'So have I.'

'Yes, sir?'

'She says her husband is cunning as well as violent. Makes him a candidate, right?'

Hell hath no fury etc., but I had to agree.

'Now for my suggestion: *get your bloody finger out. Now!*'

No doubt about it, a clear majority of senior officers borrow their management style from the same out-of-date book.

'Come with me,' I pleaded. 'It's a woman, and she's none too chuffed.'

'OK,' said Paula helpfully. Nevertheless, she grinned. Men in trouble again; nothing but a load of big kids, her expression said.

She drove, I brooded; nobody to blame but myself. I should have audited the outstanding actions in the murder room. Maybe Paul Kinsley was a killer. What would have happened if he'd lied about his wife leaving him, and chopped her instead? One, probably two idiots less in the police force, that's what. Paranoia ruled.

And that was putting it mildly, so far as the informally separated Mrs Kinsley was concerned. Two-roomed flat above the newsagent's shop in the Retton High Street, job in the supermarket stacking shelves, and a twist to her mouth as though she were sucking a lemon at a marital half-time. Marriage, to Ruth, was a tough, rough-and-tumble game.

'You're lucky to catch me in,' she said. 'I'm working a twelve-till-eight today.' Then, 'Amazing how quickly you lot can come, once a party finds the right person to kick 'em up the arse.'

Not my type, short, top-heavy, adulterous brunettes with deep scoop-necked blouses, and a lot of melon on display. Only grovel when grovelling's worth while. Otherwise, start as you mean to go on.

'A party might have managed to pick up a phone and speak to a person, long before this.'

'One of those, huh?'

I nodded cheerfully. 'One of those. Does Paul, your husband, know where you are?'

'No; is that some sort of threat?'

'Not at all. We've seen him once or twice; he's less than twenty miles away, and yet he reckons he's got no idea where you've gone, that's all.'

'He won't have, with a bit of luck; 'less you tell him, of course.'

'Isn't your solicitor going to get in touch?' asked Paula. 'Maintenance, and so on?'

'Firstly, he earns about enough to keep a mouse alive, and secondly, if he finds out where I live, he'll probably chuck a petrol bomb up the stairs.'

'That bad?'

'Think he's a harmless dumbo, don'tcha? You ought to have been around at Christmas; he beat me black and blue. Then he threatened to tip me head down in a tank of liquid chicken gunge, and leave me there for good. That's when I buggered off.'

'Because, er . . . ?' said Paula.

''Cause, er,' replied Ruth Kinsley mockingly. 'That's right; I'd been playing Doctors and Nurses with Jeremy Blatt. Gettin' past it, maybe, poor old sod; but at least he doesn't smell as if you ought to be spreading him across a farmer's field!'

'Didn't smell; past tense,' I said. 'That's why we're here.'

She looked at me slyly from under her heavily mascara'd eyelids for a moment; then she tried a quick burst of the sincere, sorrowing friend. Paula stared neutrally ahead; she was getting the message too.

'Sorry; get sort of tied up in your own affairs, don't ya?' No handkerchief, but the forefinger to a lower eyelid reminded me of at least two other devious females I'd recently met. 'Gave me this, y'know; he wasn't a bad old stick.'

She held out her left arm; a broad, elaborately moulded bracelet set with three small turquoises. Nine-carat gold; retail, two hundred to two hundred and fifty quid. Not for nothing have I been attending burglary scenes for close on twenty years.

'Very nice, and, er, how long were you friendly with Sir Jeremy?'

'A year,' she said, 'on and off. Christmas party to Christmas party, as a matter of fact.'

Twelve months' nookie for what one multiple jeweller, in an unfortunate and commercially fatal outburst of honesty, once described as a load of absolute crap. Impossible to tot up the hourly rate, but she'd probably been on something between the shit scrubbers' two ninety-two, and the security men's four quid an hour. Generous Jeremy rides again. Still, she seemed to be satisfied with the rate; what you might even call a happy lass.

'This year's company party?' Paula dropped her neutral, disinterested stare. 'Did you fall out?'

'Not with Jerry; it was all that bastard Weatherby's fault. Him and creepy Causley, I suppose. They were on the same table as us at the Daisy Dew bash.'

'Oh yes?'

'Weatherby and Causley were sitting next to each other, a bit rat-arsed, I suppose. And Weatherby started getting on at the miserable waste of space. Y'know, calling him a bachelor gay. *Gay*, you see. That kind of thing.'

'And is he?'

'Don't know; shouldn't think so. Don't care; probably hasn't got the guts to be anything in particular, him.'

A truly happy band of pilgrims, the Daisy Dew management team. The executives from hell.

'And?'

'Causley said something about wives being too much trouble; Simon Weatherby ought to know, nudge, nudge. Then Mrs Weatherby tried to slap his face. She couldn't quite reach across the table, and Weatherby said that Jack had better be careful or he'd get Paul, a fellow member of the cuckolds' club, to take him outside. He couldn't be bothered himself.'

'I bet that cheered Mrs Weatherby up!'

'It got lively,' admitted Ruth Kinsley. 'Paul went absolutely spare. It was a fair old scrap.' She sounded almost pleased; one of the females over whom the bulls battled, apparently.

'Did Sir Jeremy get involved?'

'Nah; too fond of their jobs to involve the boss. He who pays the piper calls the tune, but he dropped me after that. Gave me the bracelet, though.' Once again she flashed the major prize.

'So that was the first your husband—'

'Knew. Happy Christmas, everybody! He beat me up, and he said he was going to sort out Jerry in his own good time, and now he has.'

'And that's it?'

'You looking for jam on it, or something? Paul hated Jerry after that. Said he was going to screw his nuts off and make him pay.'

'In so many words?'

'Yes.'

I looked at my watch; another hour before she had to go to work. Take the statement, chase it up, but looking at it realistically, she'd hardly told us anything we didn't already know. Nothing crucial; no hows and wheres. Motive, yes, but practically everybody, with the possible exception of the Lord Chancellor and the Archbishop of Canterbury, was a highly motivated contender for the former Chief Chicken's scalp.

'It's still a whodunnit,' said Paula afterwards, with what I chose to regard as unnecessary relish.

'Just concentrate on the driving,' I grunted.

'A locked-factory mystery, eh?'

'If there is one thing it isn't,' I grumbled, 'it's locked. Apart from the stupid hole in the fence, practically anybody could have got in and out whenever they liked. Security was a joke.'

'What about Ruth Kinsley's information?'

'Getting her own back; a racing certainty there.'

'Male chauvinist pig,' she said. You never know with Paula; ambiguous, to say the least.

'Male chauvinist pig, sir,' I corrected, just in case.

We both laughed.

That's when the van came whistling out of a side turning to our right; the driver slammed on his anchors too late, and executed a perfect one-hundred-and-eighty-degree turn, broadside across the main road. Paula's good, but not that good. She managed to stop, but not before clipping the rear offside of the unexpected obstacle in her path. Crunch, bang, a tinkle of glass, silence and a touch of shock.

Seconds passed before we took it all in: white van, red lettering, Daisy Dew, and just our luck. We unclipped our seat belts. Providence, as Teddy might say, had obviously been working overtime, not necessarily on our behalf.

But that was before we stepped out to meet Frank Pollard, driver, reinstated in the face of the loudly expressed wishes of the late Sir Jeremy Blatt.

———◆———

Joe stirred, growled, his head against my foot, the voices in the hall disturbing his aggressive terrier dreams.

'Careful.' I could hear Angie's dulcet tones through the closed sitting-room door. 'The doctor says he won't be going back until Monday, and he's mooching about like a bear with a sore head.'

A fat chance I had of mooching. Dressing gown, slippers, propped up by cushions, immobilised by a snoring Lakeland at one end, and bruising and swelling at the other. Tenderly, I placed right hand under left elbow and changed position, preparing to greet my guests. Not even as if I'd fallen victim to honourable wounds. Ruddy seat belt injuries; my shoulder and the left side of my chest *hurt*.

Paula and George appeared, full of the joys of spring, doing their Christian duty by visiting the poor sick boss.

'G'morning,' said George.

'Feeling better?' asked Paula.

'No.'

'Told you so,' said Angie with the air of a zoo-keeper exhibiting a vaguely unpleasant, none-too-important specimen. 'Coffee, I think.'

She departed, just a smidgen too promptly for my taste. Twenty-four hours of my exclusive company on a bed (or chair) of pain might, she could be implying, be more than enough.

Paula, a totally fit, healthy, uninjured Paula, smiled and sat down. 'We didn't think flowers were appropriate,' she said.

'And I ate all the grapes on the way,' lied George, earning himself an unappreciative invalid grunt.

Joe awoke with a start; unable to forgive himself for missing something, he leapt to his feet and snarled. Perhaps he was looking for somebody to blame for my injuries. Unfortunately, it's not entirely sensible to impute altruistic, or even halfway decent motives, to that dog.

'You're a right little ray of sunshine, aren't you?' Eyes fixed firmly on Joe as he spoke, and only a twitch of the lips to betray his meaning; sly, ambiguous George.

Wandering over to the door, Joe watched the handle with anxious, beady eyes. Visitors, hospitality, biscuits, ambush; for an experienced detective it wasn't too difficult to follow the processes of the criminal mind at work.

'Grab him, will you?'

'Not ruddy likely!'

Paula, delighted to show off her superior prowess over the mere cowardly male, unfolded herself gracefully, took firm hold of my bandit and placed him on my lap. He licked her gratefully, as if he'd wanted her to do that all the time.

'Just your plain old-fashioned psychopath,' said George.

'I hope you didn't come here just to be nice about my dog.'

'There's news,' said Paula, resuming her seat with a tiny wince. Not totally uninjured, after all. Join the club.

'Aches and pains this morning?' I asked.

'Nothing like yours,' she said comfortingly. 'My feet were braced against the brake and clutch at the time, and I had a grip on the steering wheel too.'

'What's the news?'

'The coroner's releasing the body for burial; the funeral's on Tuesday.'

'I'll root out my black tie.' Traditional, sometimes professionally rewarding to join the mourners. Murderers occasionally took care to attend, or even more significantly, to fail to attend last rites. It had happened to me once before; a close associate of a victim had failed to turn up.

'That's not all. Jeremy junior is on his way back.'

'What?'

'He rang up Teddy first thing. You'll be pleased to know he's bringing his new wife; they're both attending the funeral of his dear old dad. He's coming in to see the boss afterwards.'

'Not,' I said vengefully, 'if I catch him first. And this time I'm going to lock him up for ever at Eddathorpe, not Aylfleet nick.'

'Not a lot of point, boss.' Paula looked prim. 'Besides, Mr Baring feels we ought to let him attend the funeral, at least.'

Good old Teddy; as straight-laced as ever, doing the decent thing. Another grand example of the puritan conscience at work. Personally, I'd have happily chained Jeremy to a passing gravestone, any day of the week.

'OK; but it's no coincidence, is it? Somebody's been in touch with him about the funeral. They must have known where he was all the time. Who's his mole?'

'Derek Rodway? Lady Blatt?'

'*Lady* Blatt,' I said disgustedly. 'Derek's bit of stuff.' Then I pulled myself up short; none of my business what they did. My own emotional slip was showing yet again. Neither George nor Paula seemed to notice, or maybe they were tactfully passing over what they might have put together about the private life of the boss and, more specifically, about the boss's wife.

Angie, Clive Jones, the state of my patched-up marriage . . . Had the story travelled across Force boundaries? I'd be crazy to think it had not. And there were times when the scar still itched, and I had this almost uncontrollable, foolishly ruinous, desire to scratch.

The door opened; a tray of coffee and biscuits. Keeping a firm hold of Greedy Guts, restored to my knee, I glowered. Angie must have thought it was a combination of dog-restraining measures and enforced inactivity which had put the scowl on my face. Silly. I had what I wanted – almost. Unexpected twinges of jealousy and fruitless postmortems weren't going to do me the slightest bit of good.

George, a soft spot for every woman under the age of eighty, helped her with the tray and thanked her nicely, underpinning my role as the local grouch. Angie treated him to a brilliant smile, and departed with the air of a woman with a terminally ungrateful spouse. Paula, twiddling with the engagement ring on her left hand, obviously agreed. Maybe she was signalling second thoughts herself; never marry a cop.

There was a bit of a hiatus, a silence. People, two people, anyway, reached for cups. I kept my poor bruised body to myself, until, taking pity, Paula handed over my drink. George harrumphed, staring fixedly at the pattern on the china. I'd never seen him display such an interest before.

'So, you don't think it was either Derek or Christine Blatt?' he said at last.

'Kevin Cooke's out of hospital,' said Paula helpfully. That I already knew.

'Not Kevin, definitely not the mole; he doesn't like his cousin any more.'

'Somebody at the factory?'

'Weatherby?'

'He doesn't like Jeremy junior either, or so he says. Remember, he made the nasty phone call to Weatherby's wife.'

'Weatherby doesn't care a damn about his wife; he's as good as said so. Weatherby cares about Weatherby, and his own career. Full stop.'

'Could be.' Paula looked thoughtful. 'Planning a future which is probably going to include Jeremy Blatt as an active member of the board. I suppose,' she added slowly, 'he's the man that hires and fires at Daisy Dew right now?'

'So far as frozen foods are concerned,' I said. 'Yes.'

'So he's the guy you have to thank for rehiring Frank Pollard, the demon driver, eh?'

I shifted uncomfortably; biscuitless, Joe growled and launched himself off my knee. My cup and saucer went flying; not the benefit I expected from a nice warm drink. I achieved immediate vertical take-off combined with an instant disregard, if not a cure, for the pain in my chest and shoulder as the hot coffee soaked into my lap.

'You little bastard!'

The immediate cause of all the trouble retreated behind the sofa, very hard done by, and moaned.

I refrained from screaming, ripping off my dressing gown and pyjamas, doing a striptease, going in for indecent exposure; anything vulgar like that. Grahams are capable of good manners and self-restraint whatever the circumstances. Grahams are tough.

'Bugger Pollard!' I howled unreasonably, making for the door. 'Look what he's made me do now. It's all his fault!'

He sat on the other side of the desk, elbows resting on the surface, his fingers poised in a carefully posed judicial pyramid as he smiled his thin-lipped smile. The Chief Nerd – sorry, the company secretary of the Daisy Dew Group – was enjoying this.

'I can quite see how unfortunate it is,' said Jack Causley, 'from a police point of view, but I am authorised by the company to tell you that we do not intend to pursue these complaints.'

'This is a murder enquiry, and the company will pursue anything I damn well say.' The age of diplomacy had passed. 'And if it doesn't its officers will find themselves with witness summonses in their grubby little fists.'

Monday morning and in more ways than one I was sore. He didn't even blink.

'Ah, I think you misunderstand me, Chief Inspector.' Like hell I did. 'Everyone is anxious to assist as much as they can, I'm sure. The death of Sir Jeremy is at the forefront of all our minds; the, er, cases of damage and the taking of the lorry are separate issues.'

'Let's get this straight; the board wants to withdraw the complaints of paint damage to the battery house, the arson, the taking of your lorry without consent, and the damage to its load. No further enquiries; no prosecution, right?'

'Precisely.'

'We've got signed statements; you realise that the police can still prosecute? If you fail to co-operate, we can enforce your attendance at court.'

A hole in my argument; the Crown Prosecution Service had the last word, and they were notoriously windy on these occasions, but I wasn't going to tell him that.

Causley took another line altogether; somebody had been thinking this one out. 'Forgive me if I'm wrong' – his smile remained firmly in place – 'but wasn't your original statement signed by Sir Jeremy Blatt?'

And Sir Jeremy was now somewhat beyond the range of a witness summons. Thanks a bunch.

'That doesn't alter the situation.'

'My dear Mr Graham . . .' The fingers were still poised. 'It does from our point of view.'

I wasn't pleased, but a second homicide in the same factory was quite out of the question, while Jeremy junior, arsonist and thief, had definitely stitched me up.

'Explain.'

'Well, yes; I do think we owe you that.' The smile faded. 'First of all, we can't change the facts, can we? Therefore the events leading up to the murder remain. In other words, if a certain person were to turn out to be responsible for the killing, then our current attitude would not ultimately embarrass you, eh?'

Gobbledegook now, but, once it was stripped of the verbiage, I thought I understood. Jeremy junior was their favourite arson, theft and damage suspect. He was also in the front row of the stalls for terminating Dad. He was, however, Papa's heir and they were going to have to see his smiling face across the width of the boardroom table, any moment now. Therefore, I was being blown out.

If, however, he turned out to have chopped his dad, they had no alternative but to weigh in with the evidence of what happened prior to the big event. In the meantime, they'd done a limited deal.

'Supposing' – the slightly high-pitched voice softened – 'just supposing that someone closely associated with our organisation was only responsible for the, ah, lesser unfortunate incidents.'

'The minor ones,' I said. Sarcasm is the lowest form of wit; I was in no mood to be nice.

'The *comparatively* minor ones,' he conceded. 'And supposing that person was in possession of documentary evidence that a close relative, a deceased relative, had been cheated out of a substantial asset by another relative who is now also dead.'

'If that certain person owns shares in the company, and now looks like recovering a further twenty-five, that would make him the major share-holder in this outfit, apart from the trustees?'

'You seem to be ahead of me, rather.' He rewarded me with a humour-less, thin-lipped smile.

'And if we assume that the shares he recovers come from the trustees, and not from a grieving widow, then the trustees' position is weakened. Not only that, they have to act in the interests of the beneficiaries of the trust, of which this other certain person is one?'

'You appear to have grasped the point admirably.' Not as much as I would have liked to have grasped the board by its collective throat, but business was business, especially in this neck of the woods.

'What about the vandalism claims? No insurance company in the world is going to stand for this.'

'No-o . . .' The fingertips parted, the hands spread in what might have been an apology. 'Quite true, I suppose. But what with one thing and another, the insurers haven't been notified about the losses. And after all, the battery house was very old. It was probably grossly overinsured.'

Then it hit me.

What with one thing and another; it didn't take a genius to figure out which company secretary, which office manager, which dogsbody, which nerd. exactly, had deliberately failed in his duty on this occasion.

No prizes, then, for guessing the name of the old family retainer who'd been keeping in touch with that all-round good fellow and potential majority shareholder, Jeremy Blatt.

24

---•---

The morning of the funeral was bright and clear; a deceptive day of pale
sunlight with a breeze coming in off the sea. A downright devious day,
thin with frost. I climbed into an old sweater and a pair of cords at a
quarter past seven, and took the dog for a trot.

A stroll along the beach, a few lungfuls of fresh air followed by a
good cough, and I was ready to smile weakly and face the world. Despite
all my good intentions, however, by ten to eight I was embroiled in an
Angie-being-bossy scrap. It started innocently enough.

'What are you wearing?' she said.

'For the funeral? The navy blue suit, I think. And my proper police tie.'
By 'proper' I meant the old black, silky specimen from my uniform days.
The one that really tied, as opposed to the knitted, clip-on version the wooden-
tops wear these days to prevent themselves getting throttled in a fight.

'And your sheepskin,' she said. 'It's cold out.'

'Er, well—'

'Never mind the excuses, Rob. It was a Christmas present. I don't
know what's the matter with you, it looks very smart.'

'Yes, but . . .'

'You are not taking that filthy old Barbour; it makes you look like a
tramp, and you need something windproof on a day like this.'

'I know, but that thing makes me look like one of them.'

'One of what?'

'Like a second-hand car sales—' I began unwisely. The eye of
the donor glinted. Hastily, I changed horses in midstream. 'Like one
of the businessmen around here,' I amended. 'Half his associates will
be wearing one. Makes me look like one of his mates.'

Angie boiled; abandoning her usually carefully concealed anti-copper stance.

'I could wish, sometimes I could sincerely wish,' she said, and we were off . . .

I mulled over some of the things I *ought* to have said all the way to Eddathorpe nick; I picked up George, and drove over to Aylfleet in time for the morning briefing. Trouble. Detective Chief Superintendent Peter Fairfield had turned up unannounced. He stood in the doorway, accompanied by Thea, wearing his big ploughboy grin.

The majority of the troops in the murder room looked uneasy; they shuffled, sneaked glances over their shoulders at the visiting brass. A small mercy, but I was thankful; Fairfield declined the opportunity to make a speech.

I went through the current state of play, concentrating on movements in and out of the factory on the night of the killing, backtracking on times, looking for corroboration of each and every story, throwing in the key names: Lang, Weatherby, Kinsley, Causley and Jeremy Blatt. It wasn't my best-ever performance. Fairfield and Thea lurked; a hint of depression, of winding down.

It didn't last long; fifteen minutes at the most. The occasional pillock went for the over-rehearsed, carefully constructed question as usual, and took what they fondly thought was their chance to shine. The rest sat around, rustling action forms, and anxious to get out from under, p.d.q. Once this was over, people who stood around blocking doorways were likely to get killed in the rush.

'I suppose,' said Thea afterwards, trailing one hand along the piles of statements set out on the trestle beside my office desk, 'that it couldn't possibly be . . .' I didn't understand immediately, and wisely, she left the name of her favourite candidate unsaid.

'Don't let's be ridiculous, eh?' Fairfield was way ahead of her: Chief Superintendents get paid for that. I was expecting fireworks, a genuine explosion of feminist rage, but I swear she blushed.

It had never occurred to me before; was that why Fairfield usually kept far, far away from Aylfleet, and all that was hers? That's the trouble with not being a home-grown lad; you have to pick up all the ancient scandals from scratch.

'Couldn't possibly be what, ma'am?'

All suggestions gratefully received; but it was a bad move. This was a

184

private fight, and Peter Fairfield stared at me as if I were irredeemably thick.

'Rodway and that woman,' she said.

'No,' said Fairfield coldly.

I wished I'd never asked.

'Who, then?'

'Maybe, Thea' – the voice was a cocktail of acid and gall – 'we might have been a bit further forrad in the first place if you hadn't released young Blatt.'

'Typical CID man,' she snapped. 'Unreasonably detaining a suspect. Rules there to be broken, every time!' I twitched. 'And you stay where you are, Mr Graham. No need to be so sensitive on my account!'

I'd no real intention of moving. Round one of the heavyweight contest: this was too good to miss.

She gave the male animal a dose of her Rommel look, and treated him to two or three pithy sentences on the shortcomings of his protégé, Derek Rodway, and why she would not personally have promoted him to the rank of lavatory attendant, second class.

'He drinks,' she concluded, 'he womanises, and he's absolutely tactless; then you go and foist him off on me.'

It might have been my imagination, but she seemed to dwell on the womanising slightly; I had the feeling that she might have been dropping her shells a bit too close to home.

Her adversary was unperturbed. 'He's a single man, and he's a good copper on his day,' said Fairfield. 'The fact that he don't get on with you doesn't make him a suspect for anything. And as for his drinking; you could drive the Band of Hope to drink at times.'

She flushed again, but she didn't rise to that.

'When all this is over, Peter, I want him moved to the other side of the county. Quick as you like.'

'Reckon he's away with it, then?'

'Away with what?'

'The assault.'

He sounded unexpectedly jocular, and, half turned towards me, for an instant his left eyelid drooped. This was definitely not your usual senior officer versus senior officer match.

'You've been speaking to Baring, haven't you? You know bloody well he's off the hook.'

Coming down from her high horse; more news. Teddy obviously had his own special reasons for allowing Jeremy junior to make an appointment and play the volunteer, prior to my getting my hands on him for a chat.

'OK,' said Fairfield amiably. 'I'll move him after this; mebbe he's made Aylfleet a bit too hot for his own good. Can we get on now? Can't stand around enjoying meself all day.'

Casually, he picked up one of the files. 'This your enquiry about the leakages of Daisy Dew stock?'

'That's right.'

'Anything worthwhile?'

'Ron Hacker seemed satisfied, for what it's worth. Paula's had another go, just in case. The stores records reconcile with the deliveries; payments reconcile with—'

'I don't need chapter and verse, Bob. I suggest you take another look.' Abruptly, he turned on me. 'Take another look at everything. It's somebody in the factory; somebody close to him, anyway. Right?'

The proper business of today's meeting: the life and times of the late Sir Jeremy Blatt. I had a fair notion of what was coming next.

'Probably.'

'No probably about it; fifty to one your killer's already in our system. Time to draw in our horns, Bob; no more gadding about.'

Not a word about funerals; subsequent interviews; arrests. Budgets and money; that was the name of his game.

'Sir?'

'I'll continue to authorise the manning of the incident room, but I'm reducing the scale. Apart from that, you can keep four enquiry teams, and anybody else you want will have to come from divisional resources. Got it?'

Thea promptly went ballistic. 'Now just a ruddy minute, Peter. You can't expect me to run a murder enquiry from divisional strength! We're already—'

'Sorry; the gravy train just got derailed. Overtime throughout the Force has gone through the roof. There's a budget for major enquiries, just the same as anything else.'

'Sir Jeremy was—'

'A very important man locally, huh? Don't care if he was the king of the Cannibal Islands, ducks. It's the end of the financial year and the budget's on the point of collapse.

'Besides . . .' He gave her another sample of his unscrupulous grin. 'You just heard the man: a policy decision. Enquiries to be concentrated on the activities of existing suspects, right?'

Neat, I had to admit. My signature on the decision in the policy file, and, if it all turned sour, one name on the death warrant. Mine.

Thea thought about it for all of two seconds. A new expression crossed her face; for the first time since Peter Fairfield's arrival, she looked pleased.

Built by the Normans, buggered up by the Victorians – St Edmund's church, Trippe. By the time George and I arrived, a line of vehicles was already blocking the country lane for nearly a hundred yards on either side of the church, leaving only a short, traffic-coned strip outside the entrance for the principal mourners and the hearse.

A brace of special constables spotted us straight away, and, determined to defend the only unoccupied stretch of kerb in the village, they flapped their arms like a pair of demented Boy Scouts, semaphoring us beyond their jealously guarded patch. All they needed were the hats, shorts, a set of sticks and the silly flags to make the image complete. We parked eventually; the lane was muddy and it was a long way back.

'Bloody hobby-bobbies,' grumbled George. He said more than that, but who am I to discourage recruitment among those stout defenders of law and order, our brave citizen volunteers?

Ungreeted, and failing to recognise real ones when they saw them, they watched us swing past a hopeful TV camera crew and a couple of terminally bored members of the press, and pass through the lychgate into the churchyard. Job well done; they both smirked.

Inside, the church, elaborately chancelled, the nave laterally extended by some mad nineteenth-century philanthropist beyond the wildest possibilities of village expansion, was already three-quarters full. The first time for years, I guessed. I'm not being nasty; you don't have much call for a mini-cathedral in a village of eight hundred souls.

The Daisy Dew feudatories and the minor hangers-on, had, as is usual at funerals, chosen to huddle at the back. Kinsley, in particular, appeared to have found a comfortable position behind a pillar, half out of sight. A glint of gold chain over black velvet in the front left-hand pew signalled the presence of the chairman of the county council and his lady wife paying tribute to a departed opponent. He was accompanied by a scattering of officers and elected members, ex-colleagues of Sir Jeremy, either paying their respects, or making absolutely sure he was gone.

Instinctively, George made for a solid phalanx of sheepskin, pin-stripe and British warm, interspersed with sombrely coated, chicly hatted women occupying the centre ground. He genuflected in the aisle, drawing the attention of every hard-nosed Prod in the place, devoted a moment to a half-concealed grin in the direction of my Christmas present, and took his place in one of the pews to the right, forcing two sets of sheepskins and their adjunctives to shuffle up.

George being Catholic; George pushing the merest *soupçon* of irony in the general direction of his boss. I unfastened the three leather buttons, pulled out a hassock and knelt to observe the decencies for a few moments. My new coat was an embarrassment; a mistake. Suddenly it felt hot, unyielding, far too tight. Angie had a lot to answer for today.

Once settled, we went into the ritual of checking faces, counting heads; it wasn't easy. For one thing it made us look like a pair of callous rubber-neckers, fidgeting, craning around and otherwise misconducting ourselves on a solemn occasion. We became the subject of disapproving glares from complete strangers, puzzled as to the identity of the pair of mannerless yobs, each with St Vitus's dance. Having spotted Simon Weatherby and his wife two rows in front of us, I gave up; congregation-clocking was something best done afterwards, and outside.

The service brought only one minor surprise; coffin, rector, Christine Blatt, followed closely by Jeremy junior and the new Mrs Blatt, processed slowly down the aisle, trailed by an elderly man and woman whom I took to be the widow's parents. Jeremy, for once, looked chastened; the widow pale, dry-eyed. At least she had spared him that.

'We brought nothing into the world, and we take nothing out. The Lord gives, and the Lord takes away; blessed be the name of the Lord . . .'

I hate funerals: now there's a silly, egotistical remark. They're hardly designed to entertain Detective Chief Inspector Robert Graham, or to cheer him up. Morbid, irrelevant, profitless thought; and in any case I'd never know, but, whatever they did on my behalf and whenever they did it, I hoped the quality of both service and turn out would be an improvement on this. He was even being buried by committee: the Alternative Service Book, I noticed.

Poor old Jeremy; he wasn't taking anything along with him; not much in the way of family to follow him, anyway. A widow playing a part, a son who disliked him, certainly to the point of persecution, if not beyond, accompanied by a daughter-in-law who never knew him, followed by the in-laws . . . A significant gap, and then Kevin and Kevin's mum in the rear.

Kevin in a black tie, not exactly blending with his bright blue suit; Mum in a navy winter coat, with a gauzy black scarf; too much lipstick, nevertheless. He looked very uncomfortable; Mum looked grim, and the gap between them and the rest of the family mourners was definitely her choice rather than theirs. Still, she was there, and choosers can't be beggars on these occasions; something like that.

A sorrowful, faintly tacky event: the late tycoon, one or two local politicians, a congregation of creditors and debtors, two semi-detached policemen; a murderer, probably, and all the so-called relatives they could manage to scrape up.

George shuffled beside me; the coffin reached the chancel steps as we spared each other a glance. Just because you're there professionally, doing the job, doesn't mean you can't have feelings. Hardly knew him, never liked him, but I felt unaccountably sorry, slightly ashamed.

Just for the record, though; everybody we expected, including Ronald Hacker dressed in a new three-piece black worsted, turned out.

The money that man must spend on clothes.

25

———◆———

'Surely,' said Jeremy Blatt, 'it's of purely historical interest now they've withdrawn the complaints?' He was smiling at Paula, but he was addressing me. 'Complaints of vandalism et cetera withdrawn by the company; no more complaint against the police from me. Everybody back to square one.'

He leaned back, balancing on two legs of the interview room chair, and smiled disingenuously. We both hoped he'd fall flat on his back. For a man fresh from what should have been a bruising encounter with Teddy Baring, he was far too full of pep. A potential perjurer, a proven liar, he didn't seem to care that the statement of the police surgeon, combined with the expert's report on Derek Rodway's interview tape, had torn his allegations apart.

I ignored him for the moment; she stuck to her guns. 'You do not have to say anything, but it may harm your defence if you do not mention when questioned something which you later rely on in court. Anything you say may be given in evidence.' Being interviewed, not, for the moment, under arrest.

'You people enjoy these little mantras, eh? Positively quaint.' He swayed backwards and forwards gently; this was his idea of fun.

Paula shot me a glance; time I opened the batting for the home team. The democratic process, the rule of law, silly things like prisoner's rights, have a strictly limited appeal at times like these. Still, as he'd so rightly said, we'd only just got over one complaint of assault.

'Purely as a matter of historical interest,' I said sarcastically, 'tell me again about the childish graffiti you scrawled on the battery house at Lowbarrack farm.'

'What's the point? You no longer have a complaint.'

'Nevertheless, you sent your girlfriend to spy out the land by working there, and afterwards you went in for a spot of vandalism. Peggy the poultry worker equals Margaret the girlfriend, right?'

'If you say so, but you surely know you're wasting your time – sorry, taxpayers' time – on this.'

'And your nasty little games were nothing to do with animal rights,' I persisted. 'They were all part of your campaign against your dad. I bet your pals at the New Age travellers' camp are going to love you for that, especially if they're nicked as accomplices, or have you done a deal on their behalf too?'

'Tough titty, my old gendarme mate. Firstly, you're bluffing; secondly, it's hardly going to stop me sleeping at night. If I don't use 'em, somebody else will; they're the poor bloody infantry of life.'

He was childishly proud of that one, but I wasn't inclined to wipe the floor with him; not just yet. Besides, he was right about the bluff; if he was out of it, the small fry were bound to be off the hook. He was, however, the second member of his family to labour under the same delusion; I was not, and I never would be, his mate.

'As I said; all part of your campaign to put pressure on your father; to get him to hand over your late mother's twenty-five shares.'

'And why shouldn't I, eh? He forged those share transfers. He cheated her, and then he gave her a pittance after the divorce. I can prove it; even the trustees agree with me, and once the estate's settled, they're very, very likely to cough up.'

'You're not going after your stepmother's shares?'

'Why should I? She'd fight; it's of no interest to me which *particular* twenty-five I get back.'

'So, she keeps twenty-five, you get another twenty-five making your total thirty-four. There's three with the company secretary, and three with Weatherby; that leaves the trustees with—'

'Thirty-five. Britain's modern police force; they can even add up.'

I smiled; perhaps I could elevate keeping my temper to the status of an Olympic sport.

'That leave the trustees in a minority,' I said.

'Better than that; they have to vote their shares in accordance with the best interests of the beneficiaries of the trust.'

'Effectively, you.'

'Effectively, me; and, naturally, Christine. Hers is only a life interest, of course.'

'Oh, yes; a trust which will ultimately benefit the children – she hasn't got any, so that means you.'

He shrugged.

'Not a bad motive for murder, is it; the chance of becoming the largest independent shareholder in a substantial private concern? What's the whole outfit worth; three million, four?'

The chair swung forward with a smash, and I thought he was coming up and over the desk. No pretence, no cool supercilious smile; just raw, red rage.

'You slimy bastard! You're getting nowhere, so you're trying to set me up. I loved him, you shit!'

It's a bit like lion-taming sometimes; you have to keep your eye on the beast. Rely on the odds of two against one; no circus roustabouts, no whip, and you can't keep 'em off with a chair.

'Sit down, Jeremy. Tell me about love, instead.'

Slowly, infinitely slowly, he sat back, both hands gripping the arms of the chair, his face thrust forward, cheek muscles tense. He was still undecided; still considering the sheer pleasure he'd get from hammering me.

'You wouldn't understand.'

'No?'

'No. Not losers; not third-rate people like you. Never had anything, never want anything. Never going anywhere in life.'

'Not like your dad?'

'Not within a thousand miles of my dad. He started from nothing, and he made it, mate! He could buy and sell every one of you. He only had to snap his fingers and you'd all come running, OK?'

'So why—'

'God; you're so stupid! You don't understand people like us. If you want it, you've got to fight for it in this world. He understood that, and I'm like him; I'm the same.'

'Ruthless?'

'In business, yes.'

'Do anything?'

'Up to a point.'

'That's the trouble, isn't it, Jeremy? I've no idea what that point is.

How far would you go? Take your dad now; he womanised?'

'Sure.'

'Used people, then he dumped 'em?'

'Yep.'

'He screwed his business associates down to the last penny?'

'Right.'

'A slum landlord?'

'You get what you pay for, OK?'

'He cheated on your mother, he eventually dumped her, and then he made sure she had no part in his business by forging the transfers on the shares he'd put in her name. She must have been pretty third-rate too, to stand for that.'

He hesitated for a moment; torn, perhaps. Then he chose his side. 'She was promiscuous, and when you come down to it she was just another drunk in the end,' he said.

'And he took advantage. He was ruthless; you're telling me you're the same; so how far does ruthless go?'

'Him; me; we were both the same, that's all.'

Evasive; halfway there, but still failing entirely to convince.

'So why didn't you show him that by working with him? You fought like hell, and despite taking the director's fees, you only attended a couple of board meetings in your life.'

'You still don't get it, do you? At any one time there can only be one top dog.'

'You wanted to beat him, but at the same time you wanted to earn his respect?'

He flushed, he glowered; he wasn't prepared to go so far as to admit it but it was there. Anything, anything short of murder apparently, was OK. Merely part of beating Daddy at his own game. It was the proper way to seek approval; a chip off the old block doing something worthwhile with his life.

He watched me; his hands left the arms of the chair, inch by inch he relaxed; the same supercilious smirk spread slowly across his face. 'D'you believe me now?'

'Should I?'

'It's a bloody good job you people don't have any money,' he snapped impatiently. 'Gone in five minutes, if ever you had.'

'Really, and what's that got to do with whether you committed parricide, sonny?' Tit for tat: *you people.* Finally, he was getting under my skin.

'God, you're thick. I don't suppose you ever gave a thought to death duties – capital transfer tax?'

'I know; us poverty-stricken peasants,' I said.

'Look.' He leaned forward. 'Supposing, just supposing, I'm one of the biggest bastards under the sun.'

Our turn to smile; we could certainly live with that.

'But a self-interested bastard, OK?'

He was definitely singing our song.

He let his breath out in a sharp hiss of contempt. 'You still don't get it, do you?'

'Not entirely, no.'

'If he hands over the shares quietly as a gift, the Inland Revenue eventually loses any right to their pound of flesh, so long as he lives seven years.'

'If you say so.'

'Alternatively,' he was being patient with us. 'We all go to court, and bingo! I'd have probably have had to pay up.'

'Why?'

'Because the bloodsuckers would have cottoned on. They were her shares originally, and they become a tax liability on her estate now she's gone. So going to court, or even killing the old man would have given me an unnecessary tax problem.'

He stared at us complacently: the logic was incontrovertible, at least from a Blatt point of view.

'How nice,' said Paula, 'the dutiful, loving son. Your father wouldn't play ball, so you tried plan B. All the same, he was pretty mad, I'm surprised he didn't report you to the police.'

'Blood thicker than water, and anyway, he didn't even catch on at first.' He was openly smiling now, adopting a comfortable, slightly patronising tone. 'By the time he did, I think he was probably coming round to my point of view. Pity, huh?'

'Anyway, no complainant, so there's no case any more. And for the last time, I wouldn't have been stupid enough to kill him. Surely, even you can see that.'

I said nothing, but I was prepared to buy the package. It was an Eddathorpe matter now. Paula arrested him for conspiracy to cause GBH on Kevin Cooke; she went on to dwell lovingly on questions of wasting police time, and making false reports. Something, at least, to knock him back, but not for long.

'Look,' he said, 'I can't help what Cliff Housley might have thought, can I? It was all a mistake.'

'A mistake?'

'Sure.' He was gaining confidence again. 'I must have said something to Cliff about Kev, and he thought he was doing me a favour. Simply got hold of the wrong end of the stick, OK?'

'Cliff's pretty thick, eh?'

'That's right.'

'Got it all round his neck; you never wanted him to thump your cousin at all?'

'Correct.'

'And what about the two hundred quid we found in Clifford Housley's boot?'

Oh dear.

He turned red, white and blue when she produced the burgundy anorak; the one he'd deliberately donated to Housley, the former property of motorcycling, van-stealing Peggy, to put us off the scent over frozen chickens and stolen vans. Too clever, said Paula, going viciously for his ego, by half.

She even suggested, in a subtle sort of way, that his machinations had landed him with a fairly unnecessary wife. After all, his deal with the company, the withdrawal of their complaints against him meant that he didn't need the evidential immunity between married couples.

What was he going to do with Peggy now? He loved her too, perhaps.

It was never going to be what you might call a friendly interview right from the start. There were no more police complaints, but it was all downhill after a remark like that.

'Congratulations,' said Dorothea Spinks, 'for clearing up another Eddathorpe crime.' A touch of bitterness; a far-from-gentle reproach. I could tell straight away, she'd been saving that one up.

'Nothing to do with me,' I replied evasively. 'Paula Baily's patch.'

'Really?'

'Really,' I said. All girls together; the atmosphere lightened a touch

196

'But you've eliminated him from the murder – Jeremy Peters, or is it Blatt?'

'Blatt; he's back to Blatt. He's a big wheel in his father's company now. He loved his dad, after all; just a little local difficulty on the domestic front.' She caught the laboured irony, just a bit.

'What makes you think he's telling the truth?'

'Self-interest; he's about as sentimental and family-orientated as the great white shark, but he can tell you to the last penny where his own best interests lie.'

Thea got up, wandered over to her office window, and stared moodily out.

'Baring's got Derek Rodway reinstated.' No mention of Patrick Goodall, a mere detective constable, I noticed. Thea riding down the peasantry, and then discarding her victims without a second thought.

'Well, no, not exactly; the expert examination of the interview tape—'

'He bullied 'em into it,' she said stubbornly. 'All part of the big boys' club. Typical police force; the canteen culture at its worst.' I experienced a twinge of irritation; I'd just been thinking something similar, the other way round.

She kept her face to the window; I watched her back. I was going to have to watch *my* back too, if that was what she really believed. She wanted rid of Derek at any price, and now paranoia was setting in.

Suddenly, she swung round to face me; not just moody, she was enraged. 'When I joined this job you had to watch your p's and q's. One sniff of immorality, and you were out. Nowadays, you can get away with murder!'

I didn't quite remember this version of the New Model Army myself, and I only had eight years' service less than her. Ageist rather than sexist, I reflected comfortably on how much older than me she'd been when she joined. As I recalled it, however, the service had always had one contingent with permanently bent elbows, and another lot who managed to get their end away on a regular basis, married or not. Thea in combination with Peter Fairfield came to mind; people who live in glass houses shouldn't throw bricks.

'Murder?' I said.

'You know very well what I mean.'

Oh good. I wasn't expected to go out and arrest Derek Rodway for something serious, just to make her happy again.

Recklessly, she hammered on. 'Talking of murder, I don't suppose for a moment,' she said, 'that anybody at Eddathorpe cares one solitary damn about the undetected crime they've managed to foist on my division.

'My first instinct was entirely correct, despite the pressure you tried to apply, Chief Inspector; I was absolutely right to let that young man go!'

'Jeremy Blatt?' The sheer effrontery of it almost took my breath away. Not exactly as I remembered it; words and phrases like 'parricide' and 'get your finger out' came to mind.

I watched her carefully; the heavy features were set in a discontented scowl. I'd seen it all before; a disgruntled senior officer hiding behind rank, once things started to go wrong.

Absolutely no point in shoving the blame, if blame there were, right back where it belonged: if you, madam, had not interfered, the young man in question might have told us the truth earlier. Well, his version of it, anyway.

'Have you thought any more,' I asked instead, 'about the number of Aylfleet officers you're going to deploy, once Mr Fairfield withdraws—'

'To what end?' The voice, the phraseology were grand enough; the sentiment was pretty damn silly, though. Whichever way you looked at it, she was still the proud possessor of an undetected murder. Well, *we* were, come to that.

'The enquiry isn't dead, you know.' The softish rejoinder, designed to turn away wrath. 'There're still plenty of lines of enquiry to pursue.'

'Then pursue them; just don't go around expecting any favours from me, that's all!'

OK, fine by me. Time to remove the gloves.

'That was a formal request.'

'And that was my formal response.'

'I'll record it, then.' Not exactly a worthwhile remark; nothing to make me proud.

We exchanged a high-octane version of the Glare. Time to go, but go with dignity, whenever you can.

'One thing,' I said. Inspiration struck as I reached the door, 'I take it can have Detective Inspector Rodway back, now he's being reinstated, eh?'

And without waiting for an answer, I closed the door gently on an unexploded nuclear device.

26

'Security,' said Ronald Hacker contemptuously. 'It was just like trying to keep a fart in a colander around here. Please, Bob, don't make me laugh.' He smiled his supercilious smile, and fingered the edge of the file of computer print-outs, orders and invoices I was returning, which Paula had examined with such disappointing results.

We were back to Bob and Ron, the most unlikely double act in the history of the stage. I'd heard about Laurel and Hardy, two men who couldn't stand the sight of each other when they weren't working, but this was ridiculous. A few scant months before, Hacker and Graham had hated one another's guts; *especially* at work.

Besides, I was wary; Hacker the hearty good fellow was probably after something. He'd not, so far as I knew, undergone any sudden spiritual enlightenment, and leopards do not change their spots.

'I sacked a couple of 'em, of course. Just to encourage the others,' he leered. That was better; it restored my faith in human nature. Sacking security men; he was running true to form after all. Hacker the bully, Hacker the total creep.

'I soon caught on to their little games; skiving off in the evenings for a cuppa; sleeping half the night; sneaking away with the canteen keys for a midnight fry-up, and stealing bacon and eggs.'

'So,' I said, 'it was even worse than we thought. Nobody reliable on the gate, anybody could have sneaked in?'

'Right.' He bared his teeth at me happily; he was always at his best when he was delivering bad news.

'Except' – I paused for maximum effect – 'that the case-opener, the wire clippers, almost certainly came from the loading dock. Forensic are prepared to say that the fence was cut from the inside.' Overstating it slightly, but never give a sucker an even break.

'Oh.'

'Talking of theft,' I said smoothly, 'have you thought any more about—'

'Nothing there,' he interrupted briskly, 'believe me, old son. I've been through it all with a fine-tooth comb. Even that bugger Weatherby admits it; nothing passes me by.'

And this from the ex-CID man whose juniors had changed his nickname from the Lone Ranger to Silver; the solitary credit-snatcher, selfish towards his colleagues, stealing any kudos going, but only as bright as a fictional cowboy's horse.

'Weatherby?'

'Yeah; none too keen on me looking for the stock leaks in the first place, you know that? If there had been anything, I'd have definitely put him on the front row.'

'Is that right?'

'There's something about him, Bob. Always trying to set himself up as a bad imitation of poor old Jeremy.'

Poor old Jeremy, indeed: undoubtedly one of Ronald's oldest, closest, most socially acceptable friends. According to my information, he'd known *Jeremy* for all of six weeks.

'Personally,' he continued, riding high on his own prejudices, as usual, 'I think that overbearing bastard's as good a suspect as you'll find anywhere. I'd get him down the cells, and give him a right seeing to, if I was you.'

'Why, exactly?'

'Well, there's that wife of his for a start. Can't blame a man for committing murder, I suppose, when people go around screwing his wife.'

Nothing obvious, but for a flicker of an instant it was definitely there. An eye movement; the tiniest knowing hint in the voice. Ronald Hacker, my new friend Ron, the man who'd once been to a conference in London and met Superintendent Clive Jones, Angie's former light o'love.

I did not react; short of thumping the man there was nothing effective I could do. Besides, I was older, wiser, happier, more able to cope these days; reasonably good at the polite, slightly quizzical look. Disappoint Ronald day. He studied me for a moment; a look of uncertainty passed over his face.

'Tell me about the stock leak situation,' I said.

'I've already told you; nothing. It's a myth.'

'I mean about Weatherby, and his reluctance to help.'

'Oh, you know, I got the runaround when I first came here.' He made it sound as if he'd slaved away in the interests of Daisy Dew, man and boy, for forty years. 'Too busy to show me how to do it; the usual stuff.'

'Too busy to show you how to use the computer?'

'That's right.'

Teaching Ronald to use a computer; teaching Ronald to cast accounts. Simon Weatherby could well have had something better to do.

'Hardly decisive, is it?'

Ronald Hacker glowered. 'Think about it, old son. There he is, the director of frozen products. Trying to maximise profitability, eh? The old man dead, serious discrepancies on the cards, and him trying to leave an experienced investigator high and dry; behaving as if he couldn't care less.'

I let that one ride: serious investigator. Hacker of the Yard.

'What happened?' Reluctant though I was to admit it, Silver had a point.

'In the end he foisted me off on to David Lang.'

'Ah, good; and he was able to help?'

'No. He gave the job to poor old Jack; nice bloke, but he's the usual management dogsbody around here.'

Weatherby and Lang: great minds think alike? I was tempted, but discretion, and just a smidgen of sympathy, was the name of the game, 'Well,' I said, 'it's irritating, but he is the office manager, after all.'

'Yeah.' Slowly, reluctantly. 'Yeah, I suppose so.'

'And you found nothing, anyway.'

'That's because there was nothing to find!' Hacker sniffing criticism, and reacting like a bear with a sore head.

'You checked all the production records, right?'

'That's right; once I got the hang of it, I went through them like a dose of salts.'

'Er, Jack Causley helped?'

'Come off it; I wasn't born yesterday, Bob. Once he taught me the system, I did it all myself. Nobody pulls the wool over my eyes; I thought you knew me better than that.'

'Of course.' Absolutely no further criticism intended; I looked at him with the innocence of a newborn babe. He was not, however, wholly convinced.

He began to chant out the system with the fervour of a convert to some exotic Eastern cult. 'Four copies of the order raised; a confirmation by post to the customer, and one for accounts; one for stores records and another to accompany the load. That's signed for at the other end.

'Invoices raised in triplicate within thirty days. One for the customer, one for accounts, one married up with the signed delivery on the office file. Everything recorded on the computer and cleared on the monthly reconciliation after payments made. Stores' copies of orders to the accounts department after the stocktaking at the end of each month, too.'

'That's good.'

Not exactly mollified; not yet.

'I even checked the accounts copies of orders against the signed delivery notes to make sure they were delivering the same amount of stuff.'

'Fine, fine.'

'And also, for your information' – his voice rose, hitting the top note in an authentic maniacal scream – 'I reconciled the invoices and the actual bankings against the flaming lot!'

He sat back in a kind of sweaty triumph; he'd gone a slightly worrying shade of puce. Short of fiddling him a fellowship of the Institute of Chartered Accountants of England and Wales, not to mention the OBE, I didn't quite see my way back into his heart. Somehow, I suspected, we were no longer on the old, easy terms of Ron and Bob.

'Paula had a look,' I conceded. 'She said something similar herself.' She had not, however, managed to work herself up to the verge of a stroke on the basis of a little healthy scepticism from the boss. Silver, unless he began taking things easy, didn't look as if he was long for this wicked world.

He fixed me with a bulging, marginally red-rimmed eye. 'You're none too popular around here; you know that?'

'I do my best.' Modest ambiguity, and hold your fire until the sights come on.

'Poor old Frank Pollard,' he said unexpectedly. 'You and that woman almost got him the sack.'

'He must be getting used to it by now.' Frank, van-loser, demon driver and accident-prone moron, did not feature prominently on my Christmas card list for the coming year.

'She must have been driving like a maniac, and then you both go whining to Simon Weatherby, saying it was all that poor bastard's fault. He can't afford to lose his job; he's got a wife and three kids.'

Silver exercising a selfless concern for others; I could hardly believe I was hearing this. Mistaken, of course, but still . . .

'He came whistling out of a side turning,' I said mildly. 'We're all lucky to be alive.'

'Aw, come off it.' He was determined to get his own back somehow. Nobody, but nobody, questioned the abilities of Detective Superintendent Ronald Hacker (retired) and got away unscathed. 'You're just standing up for your precious Paula. Think I don't know? One glimpse of a pair of bouncing tits and you're anybody's, you'll say anything; you're well away.'

'Now just a minute—' The injustice, his sheer bloody-minded malice, had me up and running before I'd gathered my thoughts. Leave the silly old sod to his fantasies; a much better way. The attack, however, was so unexpected, so unfair that I couldn't possibly leave ill alone. Preparing for battle, I drew a deep, angry breath. Too late.

'It wasn't an easy decision, you know; reinstating Frank.' He was unstoppable now. 'One of the last decisions Sir Jeremy made, and it wasn't at all easy for Simon to overturn it. Then you go and try to get him the push again, just like that!' He snapped his fingers and snorted. 'Talk about callous coppers!'

It was the 'Simon' that did it; common sense reasserted itself; a degree of sanity returned. One minute Simon Weatherby was a prime suspect; the next he was Hacker's compassionate colleague, and probably his closest living friend. I ought to have known better by now; Silver would say anything, however stupid, defamatory or downright inconsistent, just to score a point.

I eyed him coldly across the expanse of his brand-new desk, and it was then, totally illogically, that it came. A reminder of the one fixed, shining star in the midst of an appalling professional relationship. Something to cling to in a callous, naughty, uncaring world. It was a law of nature, almost: Hacker possessed a single talent; he was never, ever right.

I gathered up the all-too-recently returned files and rose abruptly to my feet. 'I've changed my mind,' I said, seizing the opportunity to have the final word. 'I want those papers back.'

Paula stared at the untidy bundle of computer print-out, orders, invoices and her own scribbled notes. She was not, I realised, pleased. 'I thought I'd seen the last of this.' George, the other occupant of the glass-and-plywood box beyond the CID room, traditionally occupied by the Eddathorpe detective inspector, loomed over her left shoulder and grinned.

They appeared to have stopped resenting each other in their newly adjusted roles; their row had probably done them both good. Clearer air: something, at least, was in the course of being resolved. Maybe I could quietly allow George's request for a transfer to slide quietly into the background, after all.

I stirred uneasily; suddenly, the reappropriation of the Daisy Dew paperwork didn't seem to feature as one of my better ideas. Paula was busy; short-staffed because of my murder enquiry, she still had her own divisional CID to run. I found myself needing a better excuse than Hacker's previous track record to inflict another dose of documentary pain.

'I just wondered . . .' I said.

'I just went on a computer course, boss. I don't work miracles, you know.'

'Why not try one of the county council accountants?' suggested George.

'Or someone in private practice.' I was into a concessionary mood.

'At sixty quid an hour!' Busy with her own affairs or not, Paula was stung. 'You two might not know it, but I'm quite capable of adding up.'

'It's not the adding up that worries me,' I admitted.

'The system? Somebody's done something childishly simple, and left us all with egg on our face?'

'Something like that.'

'It's unlikely that any outside number-cruncher can help you there.'

'Short-circuit the ruddy system, then. If old man Blatt was right about the thefts, it's got to be down to Weatherby,' suggested George.

Suspicion or no reasonable suspicion, I supposed that if push came to shove I could just about stretch it out. Nick Weatherby; screw him down; lock him up. A touch of the olden days, and the roughie-toughie rednecks of the old-time CID.

I hated the whole idea, not least because I knew a man who'd love it to bits. Sod the Home Office *Codes of Practice*, and to hell with finesse. Follow in the footsteps of Ronald Hacker, the man who'd built an entire police career on loudmouthed ignorance, and a game of kick and rush.

27

'You do not have to say anything,' I said. 'But it may harm your defence if you do not mention when questioned something you may rely on in court.

'Anything you do say may be given in evidence.'

Tape rolling, word perfect; I'd actually got it right. So I should, mind you, after all this time. The 'new' caution is no longer new, and however old-fashioned I am, however resistant to change, I don't suppose it's too much to ask to get me to stop fiddling with the little printed white card, and learn thirty-six words by heart.

Nobody applauded; George stared stolidly ahead. Thomas Munton, solicitor of Eddathorpe rather than Aylfleet parish, and specially imported for the occasion, looked his usual worldly-wise, lugubrious self. Pale, with crumpled features, thin, with lines like razor slashes at either side of his mouth, he's perfectly suited to his professional role. The clients love it; his very expression must be worth an extra few thousand a year.

'I'm entirely innocent of any of this.'

Simon Weatherby being chippy, and that was definitely agin the rules. My rules, that is. I'd given him the reasons for his arrest on his front doorstep prior to dragging him down to Aylfleet nick, and now, for the sake of the tape machine, I'd wanted to do it again. He'd spoiled my big moment; he'd got in first.

'Perhaps,' said Thomas Munton gently, 'you ought to listen to what Chief Inspector Graham has got to say.' Not, his tone seemed to be implying, that it would do me the slightest bit of good.

'You have been arrested,' I said flatly, 'for theft from your employers, Daisy Dew Products, and on suspicion of the murder of Sir Jeremy Blatt.'

'I've told you before, I'm a director of the company, not an employee. Can't you get anything right?'

Still short, still squat, still aggressive, and wearing a double-breasted pin-stripe suit. It made him look a bit like the late Nikita Krushchev, plus hair; and he'd set the tone of the interview for the next three and a half hours.

Munton entered my temporary office, and, adjusting the creases of his old-fashioned, not to say ancient, striped trousers, he seated himself neatly in my only other chair. He appeared to be entirely taken up with the coffee set, cups and saucers on my desk. He even smiled in an anticipatory sort of way. I poured; he reached forward, stirred without helping himself to sugar, and took a single sip.

'Most welcome; which is more than you can say for Mr Weatherby's opinion of the meal downstairs.'

Not my problem. I smiled back politely: tough.

Staring deliberately around the room, he went on to examine the ragbag of battered Aylfleet police station furniture with the air of a superior house-clearer who'd just been invited to make an excessive offer for junk.

'Not exactly what you're used to, is it?' he said. This remark, I gathered, was only marginally relevant to his examination of the desk, blotter, filing cabinet, cupboard, strip of carpet and two chairs.

'No.'

'My client has been exercising his right to silence; it does not necessarily imply guilt.'

'On the other hand,' I said, with totally unjustified bravado, 'it won't exactly help his cause in court.'

Thomas Munton took a second judicious sip. 'Always assuming that this is going to court, which, unless he was fool enough to convict himself out of his own mouth, I very much doubt.'

So did I.

From the expression on his face the joint Weatherby – Munton trials of Aylfleet hospitality were now concluded; the vote was unanimous. He leaned forward once again and deliberately returned his unemptied cup.

'Mr Munton,' I said warningly, 'this isn't over yet.'

'You misunderstand me, Chief Inspector; my client is not stupid, nor is he being deliberately obstructive. He may not have said much, but he

208

did listen. He knows that you have little or nothing against him, and my, er, instructions have therefore changed.'

'Meaning?'

'There are some aspects of your interview which interest him. He feels that he may well be able to help.'

Simon Weatherby; he'd engaged a man with a black jacket, pin-stripe trousers and comic-lawyer diction to look after his interests, while he sat down there in the cells consuming microwaved pap. A company director being questioned for theft and murder; precisely how interested could he get?

'You believe, Robert, that the death of Sir Jeremy was associated with a large-scale and well-organised theft?'

Gee whiz! I was on first-name terms with a solicitor; things were looking up. What next, I wondered; an invitation to join the golf club, the Rotarians, the Masonic Lodge?

'It seems likely.'

'But you don't have chapter and verse?'

'Jeremy Blatt found significant stock discrepancies,' I said.

'And that's as far as it went.' Not a question; true.

'And you have, ah, decided on Simon Weatherby on the basis of his refusal to aid the Hacker man with his research on the company computer?'

'Your client,' I replied, 'is ultimately responsible for everything to do with frozen products. He's faced with a series of thefts, and he doesn't seem to give a damn.'

'Two points.' Thomas Munton sat back comfortably. 'Firstly, there are *apparent* discrepancies; nobody has proved a theft, let alone pointed a convincing finger at the thief. Not yet.'

'And secondly?'

'He tells me that he doesn't believe in keeping a dog and doing the barking himself.'

I'd heard that one before; another well-used cliché, I suspected, from the mouth of the late Sir Jeremy Blatt.

'So Ronald Hacker is supposed to struggle on alone?'

'Not at all.' Munton shook his head and smiled.

It was there, I have to admit, that I missed a trick. Too busy plugging away, the bit firmly between my teeth.

'Let's go back to an older, nastier matter,' I said. 'Revenge: what about your client, Sir Jeremy, and the affair with his wife?'

'Mr Weatherby still finds the whole episode, er, distasteful, but he says that life is a compromise; things happen, then you have to decide what you want.'

I stared silently at Munton. Obscure cracker-barrel philosophy now, and from a small-town lawyer at that, but he was definitely striking a chord; it was uncomfortably close to home. Never mind, time to press on.

'What he wanted was a spot of revenge combined with financial compensation from Jeremy Blatt, and so he worked out some sort of scam. And when Blatt found out he shut him up for good.'

'You're quite wrong; in his case, at least.'

'So once I've finished my coffee' – I stared pointedly at his neglected cup – 'I can expect a series of denials from him, then?'

'Not entirely.' His eyes went from me to his cup of dark brown, stagnant liquid and back. Unused, obviously, to supermarket instant, he gave it a tiny grimace of disgust.

'What else does he want to say?' Nothing to help me nail him; by this time I was pretty sure.

'I'd much rather leave that to him, but I'll give you a clue.'

He rose to his feet: back to business, obviously, and very much expecting me to do the same. 'Think Frank Pollard,' he said slyly. 'The man who nearly killed you. Reckless driving, you know.'

I do so hate it when the defence turns smug.

The security cabin was warm; a cosy defence against the night outside. Ex-PC Chamberlain had his own, strictly unofficial electric fire; two bars, full blast whenever he was on duty, and it must have added a fair old sum to the Daisy Dew overhead costs.

'Sod 'em,' he said cheerfully. 'Pay peanuts—'

'And you get monkeys, I know.' I could drink to that at one time, but familiarity was now beginning to breed a degree of contempt.

It was dark, was raining heavily outside, and a piercing March wind was busy doing its best to reduce the taxpayers' commitment to old age pensions along thirty or forty miles of exposed East Coast.

Outside, the immediate prospect was especially bleak. A strip of potholed concrete roadway beside the hut, a view of partially illuminated red-and-white barrier, and a shabby patch of wire fence fading away into the gloom beyond the reach of the security lights at the gate. And then there was the silence, apart from the distant, ominous rumble of the Daisy Dew production line: the twilight shift, busily chopping chickens, murdering innocent carrots and turning them into cash.

'Doesn't this job,' asked George, 'drive you completely round the twist?'

'Oh, I dunno; apart from the money, it's not too bad.'

'Oh yeah?'

'When you're on evenings you can make your own entertainment. Nobody else around; you're your own boss.'

Boss! Dyed second-hand police uniform, and stuck for eight hours at a time in an isolated brick-and-glass hutch. What sort of boss . . . Never mind; it takes, as George is so fond of saying, all sorts. Guests, on cold, rainy, windy nights, are simply asking for trouble, not to mention a long, exposed wait in the weather, if they go around insulting their hosts.

'What sort of entertainment?' asked George.

'Listen to the radio; make a cuppa. Not supposed to, of course, ever since they had a bit of an accident with a fire in here last year. But I keep a kettle in my locker, as well as the electric fire. What the eye doesn't see, y'know, eh?'

'And that's it?'

'You can always read.' Chamberlain, the almost perfect pastiche of the old sweat, indicated the cupboard under the counter and winked. 'The lads bring 'em in, mind you. Nothing to do with me.'

Idly, George rummaged; we both knew what to expect.

'Eight copies of *Penthouse*,' he said disgustedly. 'Five *Playboys*; *The Story of O*, and a new one called *Big Girls' Night Out*.'

'You can read 'em if you like.'

'No thanks; reminds me of the custody office in Aylfleet cell block.' Eddathorpe's was just as bad, and he knew it; chauvinistic George.

'Kettle on, then? Tea, coffee or instant soup?'

'Decisions, decisions!' George paused. 'Tea, I suppose.'

'Sybaritic,' I said. Not clever; nobody smiled; nobody even cared what it meant. Bored or not, there are times when I should learn to keep my big mouth shut.

I watched Chamberlain fill the kettle from a huge enamel jug; no running water in the hut. Entertaining it was not. The story of my police career; hurry up and wait.

'When is he likely to get back?'

'Pollard? Not yet; he always stretches the overtime as long as he can. He probably won't roll in with his wagon before half eight, maybe nine.'

Another hour, perhaps. Stick it out: wind, rain, night, factory rumble and that's your lot. We could bore for Europe in here.

I wandered over to the factory movements register, recently returned by the police. By this time I knew the format by heart: dates, times, vehicles, names; the occasional record of an employee search. Prior to the murder, it was little more than a record of lorry and van movements; loads in and out. Apart from ex-PC Chamberlain's records, that is. He was the model followed by everyone now: not a sparrow fell without an entry in the book. Talk about bolting the ruddy stable door . . .

I flipped the register back to the twenty-four hours covering the crime. Chamberlain, the morning man; neatly entered records, row after row. The day man; not too bad; encouraged, no doubt, by the ex-policeman until two o'clock. The afternoon man; two till ten. He'd recorded lorry movements in and out; he'd conducted a random search of two employees' cars at five o'clock. No management bookings; no office staff. He'd obviously regarded it as none of his affair.

As for the night security man, he might as well have been asleep. Probably was, although he'd livened up towards the end of the shift. Early vans out; one artic containing the body of the late chairman, on its way to what are laughingly known as the Aylfleet docks.

Back to Chamberlain; arrived at 5.47 a.m. Booking himself on to the minute; arrival of factory foreman; book out factory keys. Arrival of Weatherby; management member, own keys to the offices at the front. Police; more police; me. David Lang; Scenes of Crime; factory manager; the Special Operations Unit. Even Ronald Hacker, the day security man, then Uncle Tom Cobbley and all. Factory workers on time clocks and routine clerical staff with their own system had been ignored.

It was, I thought bitterly, an utterly useless listing of entrances and exits, and far too late to be of the slightest use. Pity that careful, conscientious Chamberlain hadn't been on nights; we might have found a record of something good.

But then I saw it: if he was as meticulous, as finicky as he said he was, we'd found our holy grail. Or rather we hadn't found what we should have, which probably meant that Weatherby, not Graham, was right.

28

'Frank won't have it,' said Paula, looking down at her overcrowded desktop with an air of considerable distaste. Point taken: she was overworked, and it was all my fault.

'Maybe there's nothing to have,' muttered George.

Eddathorpe nick in the cold light of morning. Frank Pollard was sitting in our cells, but gloom, combined with an almost indefinable atmosphere of mutual irritation, was the new name of the game. We now had a couple of refuseniks, instead of one.

Simon Weatherby was still stoutly denying the lot; shifting the blame. Frank was silent, apart from the occasional burst of the not-knowing-what-we're-talking-about stuff.

Weatherby was persistent, if nothing else. Frank was a likely party to the thefts: if anybody had ever stolen anything in the first place, that is. Not that he knew for sure, mind you. He knew *he* hadn't done anything wrong; he was just trying to help; therefore he had this other target in mind. And he'd based his newly formulated allegations on little more than how, against his better judgment, he'd been urgently persuaded to give our cowboy driver back his job.

Or, as George, unpleasantly cynical, totally unimpressed, had put it, 'He'll say anything, if he thinks we'll let him go home.'

'He must have needed Frank,' Weatherby had insisted, 'to help him do the scam.'

'What scam?' I kept to the bare essentials; I knew perfectly well who he meant.

'How the hell should I know? I only know he practically went down on his bended knees to get him back: *poor old Frank; worked here for years. And there he is now, unemployed through no fault of his own, with a wife and three kids.* That sort of guff. If there is a theft, Frank is obviously something to do with how it's done, and that was why the conniving bugger must have wanted him back.'

'And you fell for it, Mr Weatherby?'

'A driver's a driver; that's all I thought at the time. No skin off my nose.'

'But Sir Jeremy sacked him.'

'The old man's dead, and I've got a business to run.'

If Weatherby had fallen for a sob story, so had I: the tale of the frozen food director who hadn't done anything wrong. As a result, Frank the driver, equally innocent Frankie, was now festering downstairs, leaving Eddathorpe's finest with even more egg on their collective face.

Mind you, depressed or not, I didn't feel totally bad. Unknown to the troops, I still had a shot in my locker, an arrow in my quiver, and a card up my sleeve. In fact it was a miracle I could stand up straight and still carry all that metaphorical kit, but I was coming around to Weatherby's way of thinking. Some of the time.

Problem: the next stage depended largely on Frank Pollard, and Frank was not coming across. Hence the conference in Paula's office, but it did not entirely account for the irritability and gloom. Despite his claim to have cleared the air on a previous occasion, George still seemed to be promoting a return match; something along the lines of girls versus boys. Paula, I felt, was probably waiting to pounce.

'Cardboarding,' said George finally, making his bid for fame. 'What about that?'

'*Cardboarding?*' she moaned. 'Never mind the fancy slang, George; just spit it out.'

'Easy: you have a carbonated set of documents, right? When you complete 'em you introduce cardboard between the sheets, so the impression of the writing doesn't go right through. Then you fake up the bottom carbons, and bingo! You can falsify the deliveries.'

Paula, her professional competence challenged, turned snappish. 'Just one tiny problem, George. We recovered all the carbonated sets: general office, stores, signed delivery notes, the lot. I examined them; no fiddle, they're all the same.'

'Oh.' Short pause. 'Then how's about this? Genuine set of delivery notes. One given to the driver, one left in the stores. After delivery, driver obtains signature and returns the note. Stores clerk checks, and amends the stock records; he passes both notes to the office. Payment made, cheque fiddled, records destroyed, and villains share out loot.'

'You,' said Paula almost approvingly, 'have got a very twisted mind.'

'Years of practice.'

'And what about the document numbers?' I introduced a carping note, before this mutual admiration society got out of hand.

'What numbers?'

'The consecutive number on each carbonated set; they'd show up as a gap on the sales record, every time they did a computer run.'

Silence; we'd been batting this one backwards and forwards for hours. My detective inspector had piles of crumpled, numbered, multicoloured sales documents, including the latest batch of delivery notes we'd seized from Frank, and curling lengths of computer print-out, scattered all over her desk. My detective sergeant, never an enthusiast on a paper chase, looked annoyed.

'Those sheets you took off Frank last night,' Paula murmured, 'sometimes there's more than one addressed to the same firm.'

George shrugged. 'Probably nothing in it. Telephoned orders; more than one, on more than one occasion, huh?'

Paula spared him a single, ungrateful glance. She could do without critics for the moment, thanks.

'Numbers, numbers, numbers,' she muttered, concentrating on the sheaf of folded green delivery notes unwillingly donated by the latest occupant of our cells. 'Now why didn't I think of that before?'

I was more than willing to give the paper sift another chance. Not so George, the good practical copper; the man who hated crime conferences, paperwork and everything else which came under his personal heading of pussyfooting around.

He watched her working, comparing green delivery notes, shuffling pink store sheets into new relationships, different piles. I didn't know what she was doing; neither did he, but giving way to a malicious tendency to stroke cats backwards from time to time, he spoke.

'We could always try astrology,' he said.

Paula, provoked, replied.

Frank Pollard was something of an anticlimax after that.

She was still faintly glowing, still slightly pink about the ears, when we sat down to put the skids under poor, innocent Frank. Bollocking George had obviously been the highlight of her day. I wasn't exactly displeased myself; if Eddathorpe was going to retain the services of a senior detective sergeant, he now knew exactly where he stood. Moreover, we now had a properly established DI. No more ageing prima donnas; no more messing about.

A touch of ritual to start with: stiff backs and straight faces, and somehow Pollard began to sense that the game was up. Not entirely stupid; the tape was hardly rolling before he decided to get his blow in first.

'You two have got it in for me,' he said.

'Oh yes?' Paula was still paying out the verbal rope. One – nil already; no problems for her, slicing off and drying out another masculine scalp.

'You're such a lousy driver; that accident was all your fault.'

'You reckon?'

'That's why you've got me in the frame, 'cos you made a prat of yourself in front of your boss.'

Paula awarded him her slow, even smile. As a diversionary tactic, it wasn't even close.

'Come on, then, Frank,' I said genially. 'Just for the benefit of the tape: what about me?'

'You're covering up for her. Stick together like shit to a blanket, you cops.'

'Good.' Lady MacBeth widened the smile. 'I'm glad you've got it all off your chest, Frank. Can we get on?'

It certainly shook him, the refusal to rise to his bait, but he soon recovered. Head thrust forward, lips firmly clamped, he gave us a pretty good impression of a man determined to tough it out.

Frank Pollard; no previous convictions. He had either a natural talent for being bloody-minded, or he'd played a non-decisive game of musical cells before. One of those compact, stocky men with a bullet head and fair, close-cropped hair; busy promoting the dirty-overall image, combined with a touch of designer sweat. Not, on the whole, the kind of man you'd interview lightly on a hot summer's day.

'How long have you worked for the company, Frank?'

'Goin' over it again, are we?' he jeered. Deliberately, he thrust his head even further forward, staring at Paula's chest. 'Six, seven years; just the same as the last time you asked.'

'And you've always been a driver, right?' She stared evenly back, giving him the full benefit of a mild, not entirely concealed distaste. *You have to be joking, Frank; not in your wildest dreams!*

'Yeah.'

'So by this time you know all the routes, all the customers, pretty well?'

'That don't mean to say I'm flogging bent gear to 'em, does it?' Jumping ahead again; determined to outsmart the thick police. He stared fiercely at Paula, his face twisting into a sneer. 'I can see you lot coming a mile away, missy. You can't fix me.'

'Fix? What do you mean by that?'

'Turn everything against me with clever talk; that's what I mean.'

'Tell you what; you can do the talking, Frank. Explain the delivery system, for a start. That way nobody gets to twist anything against you, right?'

He treated her to a slow, suspicious glower. Another devious CID ploy. 'And I ain't falling for that, either.'

'All right; let's just agree about the paperwork, shall we? The stuff for orders and deliveries is based on four self-carbonating sheets, OK?'

'OK.' A monosyllable dragged out as if by main force.

'Each set bears the same order number, yes?'

'Yeah.'

'The original is an order sheet; it's white, and it stays in the office; the second is blue, and it goes to the customer to confirm the order. Right so far?'

A reluctant nod.

'The third and fourth sheets are delivery notes; pink and green. They both go to the stores; pink is the stores copy, green is the driver's delivery note.'

'You're bright, you know that? Wait till I tell the boss; he might give you a job – sweeping floors!'

'There might,' said Paula calmly, 'be vacancies for all sorts of jobs at your place, pretty soon.'

'Snotty cow.' All the same, it took some of the wind out of his sails.

'The stores staff use the pink sheets to make up the load. You collect the load and the green sheets. You make the drop; the customer signs your delivery note, and you return the signed receipt to the stores. Agreed?'

A silent, sullen nod.

'I've got two sheets here, both addressed to the same firm. Why?'

'Two separate orders; always happening, that.'

'And another three for Sykes' Supermarket.' She waved the documents in front of his face.

'Same thing.'

'All right; you make the deliveries, you get a signature, and at the end of the day you return to base. What happens then?'

'I draw me wages, and retire to the South of France.'

Paula sighed. 'You really are very funny, Frank. So funny that you're probably going to be awarded a prize; several in fact. Lunch here, followed by tea, perhaps an expensive gourmet dinner . . . you know?'

'You threatening me?'

'Threatening? I'm just explaining how time can fly, Frank, especially when you're having fun.'

'No skin off my nose.'

'OK.'

A long, uncomfortable silence; one or two sly, uneasy glances on the side.

'The notes go back to the office, all right?' The sound of Frank Pollard giving in.

'Sorry, I didn't quite get that.'

'The storeman checks, then he clips the pink and green sheets together, and sends 'em back to the fucking office; have you got it now?'

'Yes, thank you. I've got it now.' And spoken in a tone to make him feel even worse. 'So, eventually, apart from the customer copy, the general office ends up with all the carbonated sets?'

'Suppose so.'

'Three out of four copies of each individually numbered set?'

'I've already said so, haven't I?'

Paula pushed a bundle of green sheets across the desk.

'I am showing you a total of eighteen green delivery notes,' she said for the benefit of the tape. 'They were all recovered from your possession last night. Five are duplicated; a two and a three, addressed to the same two firms.'

He flipped casually through; I watched. He slumped in his seat and flicked them away dismissively with the back of his hand. Too nonchalant by half.

'So what?'

'Take another look, Frank. Ignore the two; look at the three copies addressed to Sykes and Co.'

'I told ya; additional orders. Always happening, that.'

'Three green notes; three orders, one delivery?'

'Yeah.'

'Three notes; two order numbers, Frank.'

Silence.

'Another funny thing; look at the notes again. One order for thirty cases of large chicken; another for two dozen cases of small, and a batch of assorted veg. Those OK?'

'Yeah.' Very, very reluctantly.

'Third order; same number as the second one, same quantity of vegetables, but ninety cases of small chickens. No signature whatsoever. Funny, isn't it?'

'Oh.' He looked sideways at the paperwork, hands flat on the desk. He might have been offered a tarantula, so reluctant was he to touch. 'Yeah, well. It's a mistake, obviously. Happens from time to time.'

'A duplicate number?'

'Yeah, well; I can't be held responsible, can I?'

Long pause.

'That's right, yeah. I remember now. Slip-up; it happens, that sort of thing. Taking the paperwork back, OK? No harm done.'

'Oh, good. I can expect to find some veg as well as ninety cases of chicken on board your lorry, then. I assume you were returning that to the depot last night, at the same time?'

Pollard looked across at her; rabbit fascinated by stoat.

'Yeah . . . No; you're confusing me,' he said.

Confused? Well, only slightly, I hope; me too.

29

'How long has it been going on?'

No reply; just a steady clenching and unclenching of hands on the table, eyes filling, and a white, twisted face.

'Four years; five?'

A tiny drooping of the head.

'For the tape, please.'

'Nearly four.'

'And you were in debt?'

Wearily, the head moved once from left to right; the voice was a dry, rustling whisper. 'You don't understand.'

'Why not try us?' said George.

It was horribly fascinating, watching a fifty-two-year-old man crumple up and cry. The lips trembled unwillingly, as if the muscles were being impelled by some external force; the eyes screwed up like a baby's, and finally overflowed, while the fingers spread before us knotted tightly into fists. John Marcus Causley began to grizzle; an ageing, balding kid.

I felt sorry for him; I almost always do. Sorrier still for the old man in the freezer truck at something like minus fifteen Celsius, of course. Bad bugger though he was.

'Here.' George removed his handkerchief from his top pocket. Causley used it noisily.

'No, I don't want it back.'

'What,' I said, 'don't we understand?'

'I'd flogged my heart out for him; twenty-three and a half years. Do this for me Jack – get on with that. And what did I get out of it? Nothing! Not even thanks.'

'You were an employee; you got your pay.'

He didn't seem to hear; he wallowed in self-pity for something like a minute, lost in a warm, damp, muddy world of his own. 'He – they – all relied on me for every little thing,' he said eventually. 'Every new procedure, every rotten detail; they unloaded everything on me! Good old Jack, the patsy who was always there.'

'I see.'

'No you don't; nobody knows. That business ran on my back, and what did I get in return? I'll tell you, I got their contempt. What else? Practically an errand boy's wage.'

'How much did you get?'

'As office manager? Fourteen thousand a year.'

'You were the company secretary too. What about director's fees?'

'Know . . .' A gulp. 'Know what I got? Another eighteen thousand for being the company sec.'

'That's not bad.'

'Bad!' His voice rose to a thin, unexpected scream. 'That little sh-shit got the same as me, and he'd only attended two or three board meetings in his life! Boy's pocket money, that's what I drew. The same pocket money as his boy!'

The voice wavered and he relapsed into silence. I waited for more. The silence lengthened, he snivelled, and the sense of embarrassment grew.

'Nobody was with him longer than me. Weatherby; eight or nine years. Fifty thousand, plus a bonus. That's how much Jeremy gave him for screwing his wife.'

'And Lang?'

'Less than four years, Mr Graham. He was only a manager, and he was getting almost the same.'

'And is that when you started taking money, Jack?'

He still wasn't wholly with us; he was taking in signals, but only on his own terms. 'Not a lot to ask for, is it? A bit of status, a touch of respect.'

'So you were getting your own back, eh? The money wasn't the most important thing.'

'I wasn't out to screw Jerry financially, if that's what you mean. He couldn't understand that, either. Bastards, Johnny-come-latelies, the smart bastards; that's who I was out to show. I did it right under their noses; I was better than them!'

'Of course,' said George soothingly, 'you'd been there a long time. I bet you even showed 'em all the ropes, didn't you?'

'Y-yes.'

'Then they laughed at you: all that ingratitude, huh?'

'Weatherby; Weatherby, mostly. Not even polite; he'd roll over anybody; just like a steamroller, that man.'

'So it was the frozen products side you went for; teach him a lesson, huh?'

Another nod.

'For the tape,' murmured George soothingly, 'Mr Causley just nodded affirmatively.' Incongruous Ameri-speak, but he didn't want to break the spell.

'Showing Lang wasn't quite so important, was it?'

No reply.

'So you left the egg side alone?'

It was truly grotesque; through the tears, a sly sideways grin.

'You didn't?'

'Not always, no.'

Lang too: significant, perhaps; he'd been around for four years.

'How did you manage it, Jack?'

'You know, the invoice and delivery sets.'

'How?'

'Because of the VAT.' Another damp, snivelly, sideways smile. 'VAT records have to be kept for at least six years. We had a system. Invoice documents were consecutively numbered on a yearly basis, and one figure showed the year of the VAT cycle.'

'One to six?'

'Yeah; one digit in the six-figure set; the last cycle started in 1993.'

'And what did you do?'

'Kept a couple of books from the previous cycle. Same numbers repeated.'

'Where are they now?'

'Locked in my safe.' Gotcha! And the keys with the rest of his property, secure in the custody suite downstairs.

'OK, and then?'

'Easy; don't you see? I'd get one of the girls to write up an excessive order; beef up something that had come through on my phone. She'd pass the green and the pink on to the stores. I'd hold back the customer copy and the office copy, then I'd write up the genuine order for the lesser amount, and send off the customer confirmation.

'I'd give Frank the genuine green, he'd collect his orders and notes from the stores, including the boosted order. He'd only deliver the proper amount, get a signature on the genuine copy, and, er, dispose of the excess.'

'Then he'd scrawl a signature on the bogus green copy, and take it back?'

'That's right.'

'What happened then?'

'Stores copies were checked, and came back to the general office, the girls entered them on the computer, and hey presto!'

'Hey presto what?'

'Frank returned the genuine delivery notes, complete with genuine signatures, to me; I stopped the computer run at the end of the month, erased the bogus entries and substituted the correct delivery values. Then I burnt the bogus notes. No trace.'

'What went wrong?'

'The total stock in the stores for one thing,' said Paula, chipping in for the first time. A three-handed interview; it looked excessive, but she was all we had in the way of expertise, so it couldn't be helped. 'Remaining stocks wouldn't reconcile with total sales?'

'Not in the long run, no.' Causley looked almost grateful. Somebody understood.

'I don't suppose it mattered too much,' offered Paula gently, 'so long as you were only taking a few cases at a time? Budgeted leakage, that sort of stuff?'

'That's right.'

'Frank Pollard got greedy, didn't he?'

'We-ll; he said that if we were doing it, it might as well be done in a businesslike way.'

Businesslike! So that's what he called it; I practically choked.

'And then,' said Paula self-critically, 'there was the audit trail on the computer, wasn't there? I'd never even thought of that.'

A strange man; the snivelling was over. He looked at Paula with shining eyes: appreciated at last. I began to feel slightly less sorry; slightly more sick. Twenty-odd years beavering away, the loyal employee playing buddy-buddy with his boss. And all the time the worm was growing, twisting inside his guts. Good old unappreciated, inadequately rewarded Jack; everybody used him, then they passed him by. Put upon by people he secretly despised, until . . .

'Whoa!' I said. 'Let's just go through this properly. Explanation for the tape!'

'The audit trail,' said Paula; she sounded miffed. 'Would you care to tell them, Jack, or shall I?'

'It's simple, really.' Jack Causley, unable to resist the idea of being in charge. 'The computer retains a record of the times it was switched on and off; the terminal used, stuff like that. You can get a print-out, if you know how.'

Thank you so very much, Ronald Hacker, computer expert, idiot and . . . Wait a minute, I was the idiot here: helpful Jack Causley. Poor old Silver, and poor old me, come to that. That was the point: I was looking at the man who'd taught our self-appointed security expert all he knew.

'The interruptions would show up; the times when you changed the sales records on the monthly run?' Time to ignore past failures; keep on plugging away.

Causley sighed patiently; his new apprentices were so dumb. 'That wouldn't have mattered a lot in itself,' he said. 'We do make changes from time to time. But Sir Jeremy picked it up in the end; times, dates, the stock discrepancies; he looked at the timing of the changes, and realised that I wasn't doing the amendments in office hours.'

'And that's why you killed him?'

'Oh dear God, you make it sound so calculated.' He looked from his hands on the desk in front of him to the ceiling, to the door, and back to his hands again. He didn't want to look at us; panic was setting in.

'But it wasn't?'

'I knew there was something wrong; he'd been rummaging through the sales records on and off for days. He started making life hell for people in the stores. I knew we'd gone too far . . .'

'And?'

'That night, I – I stayed behind to do some work.'

'What sort of work?'

A low, indistinct mutter in reply.

'I'm sorry, I couldn't hear that.'

'I was having a look at the monthly stocks.'

'To see if you could do anything to save the situation?'

'To put him off, you mean; yes.'

'And?'

'He came back just as I was going to pack up. He looked in on me for a minute, but he hardly said a word. Then he went into his own office and started working from his own screen. He knew, all right; I monitored what he was doing on my VDU.'

'And so you went in . . .'

'He called me into his office. He wasn't even angry; he was laughing. Said I could be proud of a nifty piece of work. Said I could boast about it; give me a bit of status in the nick . . .'

'Yes?'

'It wasn't pre . . . premeditated; it was spur of the moment. I must have been mad.'

'You hit him with an iron bar.'

'I didn't want to have to do it.'

'From the loading dock, downstairs? When did you get that?'

Silence.

'Unpremeditated, eh?'

'I'd got it . . . I'd got it just in case . . . Protecting myself.'

'Against what?'

'He could have been violent himself; he was a most unpredictable man.'

'After you hit him, what then?'

'I had a glass of water; I didn't feel all that well.'

Not in the spirit of the question I'd asked him, but I could well imagine that.

'You were well enough to load him on to the stationery trolley and take him downstairs.' No quarter, now.

'Load him into the freezer truck,' said Paula.

'Vandalise the premises and fake a burglary,' said George. 'Making it tie in with all the other incidents, the persecution of Sir Jeremy Blatt.'

He began to sway, head and shoulders moving from side to side; comforting himself. He'd picked up the rhythm of the words; if we didn't stop it he'd soon slip away from us again.

'It can't have been easy for you,' I murmured, cutting short the Greek chorus. 'Staying there all night.'

'Sorry.' He was very sorry; his eyes flickered, focused on me again.

He was back to the whisper, too. 'How did you find out?'

'Gatehouse records, for a start. Then Pollard and the thefts, of course.'

'But . . .'

'The gatehouse records were useless, eh? Lax security on the evening of the . . . murder?'

Use the word; back to reality. He winced.

'Not so, not with Alec Chamberlain on duty the next day. Being an ex-copper, he booked everybody in, with the exception of you and the office cat.

'Weatherby, Lang, all the office staff as they arrived. The foreman, the factory manager, even the uniforms who answered the three-nines. He did the CID call-out as well; then SOCO, me . . .'

The thin, pale lips twisted. 'And I wasn't on the morning records. Simple as that; I just wasn't there.'

'Clever, the way you handled it,,' I said. 'Staying in your locked office all night; changing into your cycling kit the next morning, as if you'd just arrived for work. Had us all fooled.'

Notoriety, if not fame, at last: John Marcus Causley, the long-suffering victim, the perennial dogsbody, looked an almost happy man.

30

'There have,' said Alec Chamberlain, 'been one or two changes around here.'

A visit to the Daisy Dew factory, accompanied by changes, surprises and a dose of downright shock. Just for starters, Kevin Cooke was grinning at us from the gatehouse door. Uniform, haircut and a slashed-peak cap. He looked something like a Grenadier guardsman gone very, very wrong.

'It's a wonder,' said George rudely through the car window, 'that you can even see, hidden away under that.'

'Smart, innit?' Kevin tilted back his head and peered down at George, eyes glinting beneath the flattened peak of his headgear. It was obviously his big moment; status, his very own niche.

'Jerry's gonna send me to the Tech,' he boasted. 'Certificate in Industrial Security; one day a week.'

'Jerry?' He noted a certain lack of enthusiasm in my voice.

'He's taking over; chairman of the firm.'

'Company,' I corrected automatically. 'Is this the same Jerry who had you beaten up?'

'Ah, er, yes, well – all a mistake wannit? Don't think we ought to go too far with that.'

Never mind what Kevin did or did not think; cousin Jerry had obviously bought him off. The Crown Prosecution Service would probably go spare; not to mention the judge. Case aborted; toe-rags triumphant. Not if I could help it; definitely no. It was not the place for an argument, however, not with a delivery lorry queuing impatiently at the barrier behind us. I argued anyway; there was no way I was going to pass this up.

'Cliff Housley's on remand for GBH, Kevin. I've got your statement, and cousin Jerry is on police bail.'

'No problem with Housley,' said Kevin dismissively. 'Don't worry, he'll plead guilty all right. But I ain't giving evidence against me own cousin, OK?'

'Kevin!' It was as far as I got; the barrier came up, George accelerated and I was pressed back into my seat.

'Sorry, boss, but that bloody big lorry was goin' to clip my back bumper if we hadn't moved.'

'I'm going to kill him,' I said. 'The conniving little crook.'

'Jerry?' George was being dispassionate. 'Or Kev?'

'Both.'

'Let's go and talk to Silver first,' suggested George. 'Then we can find out the score.' Humiliating, in times of crisis, when it's the subordinates who remain cool and calm.

'Mr Hacker,' said the girl on reception, the second employee in less than five minutes to look down her nose at the police, 'cleared his desk last night.'

'What?'

'Perhaps you ought to speak to Mr Lang.'

'I'd prefer to see Mr Blatt.'

'Our new chairman? He's out.'

'Mr Weatherby, then.'

'Mr Weatherby's suffered something of an ordeal.' She stared at us in a way that suggested there were no prizes for guessing its nature. 'He's taking the rest of the week off.'

We were not invited up to the executive offices; Lang came down. He was clutching a bundle of concertina'd computer paper. 'Are these what you want?'

'The print-out of the audit trail?'

'Yes.'

'OK.'

He thrust the bundle into my arms. That appeared to be all he wanted to say, but it was less than sufficient for me.

'What's been going on, David?'

He looked at us doubtfully. 'You aren't exactly popular around here. You seem to have done your best to bugger up the entire show.'

230

'And there we were,' said George, 'thinking we were going to get lots of grateful thanks.'

'From Simon Weatherby?' Iconoclast still; something like amusement flickered behind his eyes. He waved us into a couple of uncomfortable foyer chairs.

'Perhaps not.'

'The new lord and master doesn't care much for you either.'

'Jeremy Blatt Mark Two,' I said. 'I want a little chat with him; something about GBH charges, and police bail.'

'Devious, just like his dad. Much good may it do you,' said Lang.

'We'll see about that.'

'They've all ganged up. Christine, Simon and Jerry; the new board. They've got plans. They're out to dominate the trustees and run things all their own way. Once they've expanded the share capital, they're going to make me company secretary, too.'

'Congratulations.'

'I'm the new dogsbody,' he said sourly. 'Or so they think.'

'No?'

'No. And they've got rid of Hacker, of course. They didn't fancy him being so free with information to the rozzers, mate. They gave him three months' salary in lieu, and kicked him out.'

'A Silver handshake,' said George, and grinned.

'Anything else we should know?'

'Depends how you get on with that big fat woman down at Aylfleet nick.'

'We're beginning to understand one another,' I said.

'Make her happy, then,' suggested David Lang. 'Deliver the good news: Derek Rodway is just about to resign. In fact, from what I hear, his letter is already in the post.'

'Let me guess.' George's voice was heavily laced with irony. 'Christine's toy boy, the new security boss. Not to worry; it's sure to please Dorothea Spinks.'

'Not entirely.' Lang, in his role as the deliverer of bad tidings, was wearing an unconcealed beam. 'You know Derek; he's not exactly the soul of tact.'

Silently, we speculated on the likely contents of Derek Rodway's resignation letter; today I would pass the message. Tomorrow, in anticipation of the arrival of the Royal Mail at Dorothea's office,

I would not be journeying in the direction of Aylfleet nick.

'What are you really going to do about Jerry junior?' asked George, as we returned to the car.

'Leave it to the Crown Prosecutor, what else?'

He opened the CID car door, and half turned to contemplate the gaggle of low, grey, depressing buildings behind. A soldier's farewell, I suspected, to the low, grey, depressing people who slaughtered chickens, froze vegetables and fought their private battles inside.

'I hope Derek knows what he's doing among this lot.' Warily, he shook his head.

'You never know; a pretty woman, lots of money around. He might have landed on his feet.'

'The rich, especially that lot,' said George sententiously, 'aren't too keen on giving it away. They're a very exclusive club.'

'He might be joining the family, George.'

'Family; as in Cosa Nostra,' he said.

Potato Salad.

green salad

Rice.

Salmon
prawns (sauce on)
side

chicken, apple, sultana
+ walnut + celery salad
mandorins.
Ham (Baked with
marmalade)

potato Salad.
green salad
Rice.

---

strawberries + cream